D1642682

21:37

21:37

by Mariusz Czubaj

translated by Anna Hyde

STORK
PRESS

Published by
Stork Press Ltd
170 Lymington Avenue
London
N22 6JG

www.storkpress.co.uk

English edition first published 2013 by Stork Press
1

Translated from the original *21:37* © Wydawnictwo W.A.B., 2008
English translation © Anna Hyde, 2013

The publisher gratefully acknowledges assistance from the Polish Cultural
Institute in London for its support towards the publication of this book.

The moral right of the author has been asserted

These characters are fictional and any resemblance to any persons living
or dead is entirely coincidental

All rights reserved

No part of this publication may be reproduced, stored in or introduced into
a retrieval system, or transmitted, in any form or by any means (electronic,
mechanical, photocopying, recording or otherwise), without the prior written
permission of both the copyright owner and the publisher of this book

Paperback ISBN 978-0-9571326-8-9
ebook ISBN 978-0-9571326-9-6

Designed and typeset by Mark Stevens in 10.5 on 13 pt Athelas Regular

Printed in the UK by MPG Books Group Ltd

Pollution symbols are as necessary as the use of black in any depiction whatsoever. Therefore we find corruption enshrined in sacred places and times.

Mary Douglas,

Purity and Danger: An Analysis of Concepts of Pollution and Taboo

Some evils, indeed, are ministerial to higher forms of good; but it may be that there are forms of evil so extreme as to enter into no good system whatsoever, and that, in respect of such evil, dumb submission or neglect to notice is the only practical resource.

William James,

The Varieties of Religious Experience

prologue

IT WAS A DREAM. Just a dream. He would wake up from this nightmare in a moment.

He dreamt he was fifteen, spending holidays on the coast and learning how to swim under water. It was the last summer his father was alive. The last happy months of his life. The first twenty metres on the surface of the waves, then the same or even more under water, holding his breath. As long as he could take. Until the pain in the lungs became as sharp as if somebody was sticking needles into the flesh. Until the fear started paralysing his movements. Because it is fear, he was told during brutal training sessions, it is fear that always kills in the end. The more capable you are, the less afraid you are.

Though this time it was different. He overestimated his strength. He went down too deep and now had to resurface quickly. Blue dots in a greyish, metallic shade were becoming lighter and lighter and formed a uniform, monotonous picture. He was coming to the surface. In a moment everything will be back to normal. He will catch his breath. He will see cloudless sky. Perhaps he will see the outline of two boats with white sails in the distance.

The blue surface broke into a hundred pieces, like a shattered mirror. Multicoloured spots whirled in his eyes. He felt the skin on his cheek burning. He regained consciousness instantly.

He realised now that it was not a dream. He was not on the coast.

Something much worse than a nightmare was happening in the waking.

Pale sky turned into a shabbily painted wall with paint flaking here and there, exposing the texture of old wooden boards. Instead of the white sails he saw the whites of the eyes with threads of broken capillaries.

These were the eyes of a madman.

He took a breath, greedily, but felt no relief. He choked.

He was scared. But it was not because of the paralysing fear that his well-trained body was refusing to obey him. It was not fear that tied his hands to the back of the metal chair and it was not fear that bound his legs.

Bloodshot eyes were staring at him with the scrutiny of a referee looking at a knocked-down boxer, assessing his ability to keep on fighting. The man with distinctive dark stubble straightened up and moved away from the chair. The boy strained his muscles and pulled. Three metres away, on an identical, heavy chair, he saw his own doppelgänger. Also blond, with hands and legs tied, and – that detail was different – mouth covered with a piece of five-centimetre-wide, brown tape that they use for fastening parcels at post offices. The man ripped the tape off in one move. It sounded like a crack of a broken branch.

The doppelgänger screamed.

'Shhhh...' The man put a finger on his lips. 'I don't like screaming. I am used to silence. And so are you, I presume.' He patted the doppelgänger on his head. The boy flexed his neck and looked at the persecutor with loathing.

The madman laughed softly.

'OK, boys, the last round.' He traced his finger around the doppelgänger's mouth. There was a red mark there, a token of the tape ripped off so suddenly. 'I guess you know by now what it's like to lose your breath. However this slow, painful, terrible suffering is nothing. The worst is being aware of what's going on up until the very end. You stay aware of everything pretty much till the end.'

He was rhythmically clenching his fists and straightening his fingers. He was sauntering between the chairs as if giving a lecture.

'All of us here know that knowledge can bring pain. Biblical progenitors knew that already, so...' He broke off. 'So, who else?' he asked sharply. 'Who? I need to know!'

The boy looked between his doppelgänger and the back of the man leaning towards him. He moved his hands. He could feel that the ties were slightly loose and there was a little bit of space between his wrists and the metal back of the chair.

'I don't know anything ... I really don't ... I've already told you ... We both did ... I swear ... Please let us go. I won't tell anybody ... I will disappear ... Nobody will know ... I beg you ...'

The boy's voice was breaking.

The man shook his head in disgust. The floor was creaking with his every step.

'You are not leaving me any choice. And you,' he turned around. 'Look at your friend. Don't you feel sorry for him?'

He didn't wait for the answer. In one skilful move he put a plastic bag onto the doppelgänger's head and tightened it. Petrified eyes disappeared, obscured by the condensation. The head quivered as if from electroshocks. This looks like an installation, the boy thought. Like some nightmarish fucking installation, of which there are plenty in modern art galleries. This must be some kind of joke.

Not only was the head trembling now, the whole body started shaking. Trainers were tapping a nervous rhythm that no drummer in the world would be able to replicate. The boy started laughing.

The man did not expect such a reaction. He stiffened and let the doppelgänger go.

'What is it? What's so funny?'

Just a moment longer, the boy thought. A moment longer and my hands will be free. When he leans over me, I will grab his hair and headbutt him. If I can.

'You're a psycho, you know? Just a tacky psycho. Why are you doing this? You're not going to kill us anyway.' He laughed hysterically. He choked on his own saliva, which ran down his neck. He started coughing. Just a moment longer. 'You are mediocre even as a screwball. You've watched *Seven* and you've gone off your rocker. Yes, you are right, knowledge is painful. So, I wonder, when did you realise that you are an amateur? Tell me, when...'

Keep prattling away. Twenty seconds and I will be free. Then it's all in my hands.

A strong smack across the face stunned him. The plastic foil tightened on his head. His eyes darkened. His hands became heavy and limp. The wrists touched the cool metal.

A sudden jerk brought the light back. The pressure eased.

'Who? Who else?' he heard from above, but did not have the strength to answer.

A wheezing sound left his mouth.

Plastic foil tightened on his cheeks, forehead and nose again.

'A fox knows a lot of things. A hedgehog knows of just one, but it's the most important one.' The voice was drifting from somewhere far away. Or so it seemed to him.

The bag was cutting into his skin. His face was burning, there was a hum in his ears.

He was fifteen again, spending the holidays on the coast and learning how to swim under water.

***

Daniel Wedich took a deep breath. It was a sultry spring night and the starry sky was promising another hot day. Wedich looked up and thought with sadness that he was not born under a lucky star. He turned fifty-three two weeks ago. Nature had not blessed him with a tall stature. He was the shortest student in his class, and his classmates used their physical advantage every now and then. It went on until the school shrimp enrolled in the boxing division of Gwardia Warszawa club. That was when everything changed. From then on he was the one giving it to them; he ruled over the yard and the sports grounds. Nobody dared to call him 'weedy', 'wee dick' or 'weedjit' anymore. He fought in light flyweight. His strong-point was speed. That was how he won. He was progressing, the national team coaches noticed him.

And that was the end of the upbeat part of the story, which he so often told for a bottle of beer. Fate defeated the boxer. Fate sent him to the local shop where he got involved in an argument with two roughnecks lubricated with alcohol, who, as luck would have it, had two other helpful buddies. Wedich won the uneven fight, but he was left with a broken brow ridge. If not for fate, he would go to the GDR, to Halle, to take part in a prestigious tournament. And then, who knows?

From that moment on everything changed in Wedich's life, whom his colleagues started calling Halle.

Halle started on his night hunt along Podleśna Street. He passed Kępa Potocka Park, crossed Wisłostrada Street, deserted at that time of the night, and found himself close to the river. He was walking towards the Olympic Centre, which the sportsmen mockingly dubbed 'the Palace'. The proximity of the seat of the Polish Olympic Committee made Halle think again about what could have been, if ... If at least he was born a bit later. Towards the end of the 1970s, Polish boxing was still big in the world and Halle had to fight in the ring with real pros. In the next, lean decade there were no more young bruisers, and the old ones had dropped off. He would be without equal, of this Halle was sure. And what would happen if he became

a professional boxer? Nobody would say that he fought in a
laughable light flyweight. And he would change his name too,
because the unfortunate one given to him by his parents made
everybody think of one singer from the Military Song Festival
in Kołobrzeg. Sometimes, over a bottle of Tatra beer, Halle
would think up punchlines for interviews that he would give
to sports papers before important fights. 'What's your strategy
for this fight?' 'Oh, that's easy,' he answered in his thoughts.
'Hit, rip the head off and Bob's your uncle.'

Hit, rip the head off. That was his favourite bit.

Even though life laughed in his face, Halle was stoical and
knew how to enjoy what little he had. He did not start drinking,
like his friends from the boxing hall. He did not end up in prison
or at the cemetery, like many others. He was happy to live near
Kępa Potocka and not, like before, at Racławicka Street. He
would not be able to come out in the night, like now, and collect
rich people's leftovers. Racławicka and Żwirki i Wigury area
towards the airport was fenced off and christened 'Marina'.
Wedich quite liked the mysterious name, but he preferred the
anonymous spaces along the Vistula River, still untamed by
developers fighting for land in the capital like mad dogs.

Halle took a special liking to the area around the Olympic
Centre. He noticed good cars stopping there in the evenings.
Their owners would meet and then, after several minutes,
they would leave. Halle heard from somebody that it was
one of the favourite tryst places for those who – here his
interlocutors would always smile – 'do it differently'. Poofs left
behind not just used condoms, but also cans, unfinished bottles
of beer, cigarettes in crumpled packets and even clothes. Halle
could vouch for all of that: he himself found a t-shirt once,
admittedly way too big for him, as well as a pair of unworn
shoes. Somebody must have got really scared, he thought.
Otherwise who would leave their shoes behind? And a good
pair at that.

He recalled the shoe story now and felt better straight away. He had been in a good mood recently. The weather was nice, it had been warm for the last two weeks. There were more and more night rendezvous and plenty of leftovers to be scooped. Halle lit a cigarette. He was entering his hunt terrain.

A few cans and bottles were already clinking in his backpack when he noticed something strange. Somebody was staring at him from where the wall of trees started. Halle tossed the cigarette and put the backpack down. Years of experience had taught him that in this kind of situation it was best to have both hands free. Hands, which could still hit and rip heads off.

He looked at his watch, which he found in the bushes nearby last summer. It was 3.40 a.m. Nobody should be here at that time of night. He looked around. Strange. He could not see a car anywhere. He looked straight ahead again. The figure by the tree was sitting motionlessly and staring towards him. Wedich narrowed his nearsighted eyes and decided to come closer. Perhaps he would give the other one a fright? That would potentially mean an interesting loot. In such circumstances the most important thing is not to show any fear.

Halle made a step forward.

The other one still did not move. Strange. You are sitting somewhere in the middle of nowhere, at night, and somebody approaches you. Natural reaction would be to get up or even jump up, because you never knew what might happen and what the intruder's intentions towards you were. The person that Halle was approaching was still sitting with his legs stretched out in front of him. On his head – Wedich squinted again – he had some kind of a hat. Maybe he is drunk, thought the ex-boxer. He looked at the trainers, seemingly in good nick. He might be lucky tonight. The hunt was showing promise.

But something was wrong. The person was still sitting, but not leaning against the tree, as one could expect. There was somebody else there. The sitting man's back was resting against the other person. Halle noticed the second pair of stretched out legs. He slowed down. He could still only see the outline of those two, doing their strange gymnastics by the Palace at dawn.

'What are you staring at, faggots?' Halle said to the two sitting men. 'What are you doing here?'

Seize the initiative, that's the way.

They should jump up now. But there was no reaction. Halle heard something crunch under his foot. He thought with satisfaction that he had just crushed a snail's shell. Why do those bastards have to crawl under people's feet? Something was still not adding up here. He took one more step and finally understood.

The head. The sitting man had something on his head. Halle felt his stomach in his throat, as if he was taking a ride on a Ferris wheel. But it was not the head stuck in a bag that was the most terrifying. The ex-boxer saw something strange where the mouth should be. Something that scared him stiff.

He turned around abruptly and vomited onto his bag with the takings of the whole night. He wiped his mouth and beard with his hand.

'What the fuck... Holy shit!'

He could tell something really bad had happened. It would probably be wise of him to disappear. Pity about the trainers ...

He started walking towards the parking lot by the Olympic Centre. A drowsy song was oozing from the warden's box. Through the window Halle saw that the man in a uniform with the word 'Security' on it was asleep with his head resting on his hand.

Halle started banging on the plastic wall of the box.

'Hey, man, there, by the main footpath ... A bit further down ... Somebody is lying there ... Or rather sitting ... I think there are two of them ...'

The drowsy man considered pressing the alarm button which would summon the patrol. But the security company did not like sending cars here, so he should expect trouble. Two young musclemen with shaved heads, wearing black uniforms, would surely laugh at his inability to deal with the situation. At the fact that he was not able to take care of one pint-sized hobo collecting tin cans.

'Yeah? And what? I go there and you mug my box, right?' He looked at the battered radio, still on. 'I'm not an idiot.'

'No, that's not it... There...'

Halle pointed towards the trees.

There was something in his face that made the security guard change his mind. He pressed the alarm button on the remote. If the worst comes to the worst, he will have to explain himself.

The patrol arrived twelve minutes later.

It was 12ᵗʰ April 2007, the beginning of spring.

At 4.45 the birds' morning song by the Vistula river was interlaced with the howling of the police sirens.

1

HE CAME HERE every four weeks. Always mid-month. Always on the fifteenth. Routine and repeatability stop you from going crazy – that's what he used to say on courses for young students of forensics. Routine and repeatability, he would add, looking at their nodding heads, is also the calling card of psychopaths and madmen.

He brought roses, as usual. He also brought a new jar, which previously contained Krakus pickles. A month ago, when the ground could still get frosty, he noticed that the old jar broke. He never owned a vase. He did not buy one now either, not to tempt the thieves. He was certain that sooner or later somebody would take it, even from here. And then he would have to admit that his sacred place had been violated, defiled.

The cross was simple, metal, speckled with rust here and there, especially on the endings of the arms. The man leant down to light the candle. It was not easy. His Dirty Harry-style crumpled corduroy jacket with patches on the elbows got oddly tight over the winter. He was about five feet six inches tall and weighed fourteen stone. With his right hand he patted the hair on his temples, mostly grey. He touched his hair again.

At the base of the cross there was a pine plank with carved initials and the dates 1966–1991. He got up and looked towards the road. Two cars passed by, significantly exceeding the speed limit, he thought. Signs were recently placed between Bogusławice and Grabowa informing the drivers that they were in a danger zone. When it happened, nobody put 'black spots' (yellow signs with a black 'x' within a circle) on the roads and nobody thanked drivers for their careful driving. It was a warm, sunny day, just like today. For unexplained reasons a car with three people inside drove off the road onto the shoulder and into a tree. That was what the official statement said. There was nothing to pick up – that was what he heard unofficially from the traffic police officer.

He looked at the candle. The flame was dancing to the left and to the right, as if it was a skier during a slalom. The man rubbed his few days' greyish stubble, which never disappeared from his face. Yes, he definitely preferred this place and the cross by the road to a family tomb at Sienkiewicza Street in Katowice.

He was not a fan of cemeteries. He did not like crowds at all. Even when it was a crowd of the dead. This aversion was getting stronger every time he passed the cemetery alley with his favourite actor's grave. You could always sense the constant presence of the pretentious fans of the 'Polish James Dean', gathering by the Cybulski family tomb. Once, while passing by, he thought that the train must have been crowded too, when Zbyszek Cybulski was trying to jump onto it for the last time in his life.

He took his mobile out of his pocket and looked at the screen. It was almost 4 p.m. In two hours he will meet his three colleagues and they will play rock standards for two hours. He got into his car, put sunglasses on and did what was also part of the monthly ritual. He put a CD into the player, chose a track number and waited for Jimmy Page's guitar to start the intro, gently, quietly at first, as if absentmindedly. *Since I've Been Lovin' You*. Good question, since when? How many years has it been? When was it? Empty road filled with images from the past.

The blues in a minor scale, showcasing Led Zeppelin's genius, was approaching its end, when he looked at the mobile on the passenger seat. There were two missed calls.

He swore under his breath. He should have switched the phone off. He had a feeling that if he called back, the band's rehearsal would be as viable as him running a 400 metre race. He would sooner die of a heart attack.

He made a phone call.

'This is Rudolf Heinz.' If the person at the switchboard did not know his voice, they might think it was Al Pacino calling or some charismatic female volleyball team coach. It was the effect of five beers drunk the night before with Lambros Kastoriadis, a Greek karate master. 'Somebody has just called me.'

The officer on duty quickly connected his call.

'You have to come,' he heard the familiar voice. 'I know it's the fifteenth today... but you have to come. Today. There is a case. A big one. As you always say – enough of it.'

Epic, stylistically profuse phrases were never the speciality of the Chief of the Homicide Department. Ample lunches on the other hand... That was a different story. It was Sunday afternoon, so the Chief should be sitting at the table at home and inhaling the aroma of the second course served by his anorexic and ghastly talkative wife. Something must have happened that made Heinz's boss come to work and, at best, drink disgusting coffee.

A big case. He would not make it to the rehearsal today and that was big for him.

Heinz sighed and found the number of the man he has known for thirty years. The man whose fingers moved equally fast on the computer keyboard and on the bass guitar fretboard.

2

THE BUILDING of the Voivodeship Police Station disproved the common misconception that the architects of the late 1970s lacked imagination. Yes, the massive structure tallied with the common concept, however, the undulated façade introduced some tension and had little to do with monotonous seats of the authorities from the time of the People's Republic of Poland. Heinz liked buildings from that era. He remembered the times when Zenit and Skarbek department stores were rising, perhaps because he himself was growing up then.

He was nine years old in 1972, when the main railway station was opened to the accompaniment of the solemn sounds of the orchestra. It was, as was said, one of the most modern stations in Poland. Three years later he ran away for the first time, with his mother's wages in his pocket, and took a train from this very station to the coast. He was brought back home by the Militia. It was from here that he travelled to rock gigs in Jarocin, the best ones, those in the first years of the festival, with unending, mad processions of punks, Rastamen and heavy metal fans.

The first beats of Zeppelin's blues came back and Heinz thought there was nobody he could talk to about all those things. There hadn't been for years.

He was a profiler, the best in the country, a specialist marking out unknown criminal offenders. A lonely hunter

tracking savage, unique types such as serial killers, rapists
or pyromaniacs. And he was a hunter barely tolerated by the
police regulars.

He finally understood it would never change when he
turned forty. He would never find his place. At work they
saw him as a weirdo and an outsider, a specialist in out-
of-this world, imagined theories, which, by sheer luck, could
be useful in capturing murderers of different sorts. He did
not like the city he spent most of his life in, but at the same
time he could not bring himself to leave Katowice and part
with the railway station, which was getting more and more
shabby as time went by. In the flat, which he shared with
his son, he did not feel at home either. Perhaps because
he never managed to create a family atmosphere on those
several dozens of square metres. There was a time when he
felt guilty about it and tried to make some changes. When his
son turned sixteen, he started spending more and more
time out and coming back home later and later. Heinz
understood that he had failed. And it was the most painful
of all his failures.

'Don't be offended, Hippie,' Lambros Kastoriadis once
said, 'but I would get more empathy ordering a Big Mac in
McDonald's than from you.'

He felt good at Sensei Kastoriadis's training room but, as the
years went by, he went there less and less often. He preferred
meetings over a beer. There was only one place left where
Hippie came back to life.

Hippie. It was the colleagues from the band who gave him
this nickname. In foul-smelling pads turned into rehearsal
rooms, cellars cluttered with music gear, warehouses without
any ventilation and lit by a single bulb, Heinz felt quite
all right. They played and he felt free. *Freedom's just another
word for nothing left to lose*, sang divine Janis, one of the idols
of his youth.

But then the brutal truth caught up with him. Police Commissioner Superintendent Rudolf Heinz, a profiler, a guitar player and a holder of the karate brown belt, was forty-four and had nothing to lose and less and less to gain.

The Homicide Department was silent on Sunday afternoon. Permanent reorganisation meant that Heinz and other policemen from the Criminal Unit were constantly moved from room to room. Strangely, the size of the room would always get smaller, however the number of its residents – as they were called – tended to grow. Heinz shared a claustrophobic little room with Chief Inspector Krzysztof Kobuz and Aspirant Antonina Trzcińska, whose job it was to enter the classified data into the computer database.

'She's got everything in the right place, but there is no place,' Kobuz dished out one of his numerous proverbs when the new resident arrived.

More and more rooms in the building at Lompy Street were taken over by the officers of the Internal Security Agency and the Central Anti-Corruption Bureau. And it did not look like it was about to change. Quite the opposite, it was getting worse with every passing month, Heinz thought, and knocked at his boss's office door.

He came in and gagged on the smoke. He himself had smoked since he was ten years old, but he still could not get used to cigarettes the Head of the Criminal Unit, Henryk Krygier, was smoking. If he was to describe the smell permeating the room, he would say that it was a stench of burned, used wellington boots mixed with bonemeal. The Head was more overweight than Heinz. His face was the shape and size of a Wiener schnitzel and he had a bushy moustache that made him look like a walrus.

'If there was a smoke detector here, it would have a coughing fit,' Heinz rasped.

Krygier laughed.

'Good one, Hippie. You could be a stand-up comedian. The audience would die of laughter.'

'I'll think about it when I retire...'

The Head's face became serious.

'Not now, Heinz. Don't talk to me about your retirement now. There is a case.'

'A big one,' Heinz repeated the words he heard on the phone.

'Exactly. Here's what it looks like: early morning on April the 12th, by the Olympic Centre, two dead bodies were found. Young boys, about twenty. They were students at a theological college, which does not make the case any easier.'

'Two seminarists,' Heinz whistled.

'Indeed. The case, as you may imagine, was taken over by the Central Bureau of Investigation. But you know how it goes with them...'

Heinz did know. Success has many fathers, but failure is an orphan. When the officers of the Central Bureau of Investigation thought that the case might be difficult – unsolved or dragging on for months – they preferred to pass it on to the police. It will probably be the case this time as well. That did not bode well at all.

'They created a special team at the Metropolitan Police Headquarters,' Krygier went on. 'This is where your role begins...'

'Wait a second,' Heinz interrupted him, 'I understand that we have a double murder and it is seminarists we are talking about, so it is a sensitive case, but why did they need to create a special group straight away?'

'You don't know everything yet. Seminarists, two of them. That's the first complication. There is another one. They did not look good. They had plastic bags over their heads...' Krygier waited for reaction. 'According to initial findings, somebody smothered them with those bags,' he added softly and grabbed another cigarette. 'This guy found them, a bottles and cans picker. He almost died of a heart attack.'

'Sensitive guy,' Heinz commented. 'Unless...' he looked at Krygier. 'Unless there is more.'

He felt sick. Must be the cigarettes.

'Complication number three is...' The Head inhaled deeply. 'That somebody drew triangles on those bags, where the mouths were.'

'Triangles?'

'In pink lipstick.'

'Wow, real no-holds-barred fun...'

'Wait... It seems there might also be a complication number four. But I don't know what it is. I'm just following my nose. I asked, but the guys from Warsaw do not want to say what it's about. They obviously think that the fewer people know...'

'The smaller the shame afterwards...' Heinz interrupted. 'Now I understand why CBI was so quick to pass this case on to us.'

'They passed it on, but not entirely. As you know, Katowice rules again. As in the good old times.' Krygier smiled, which made him look even more like a walrus. 'Yes, prosecutor on the top level, but Internal Security Agency people are from here,' he indicated with his hand. 'They think that the Warsaw killing, with those bags and lipstick, is some kind of a staging. And somebody in CBI remembered a certain Mr Rudolf Heinz from Katowice, a staging specialist.'

'But I can't go,' Heinz stood up from the armchair. 'We have the killing in the Aniołów Woods. And my son is doing his A-levels. Boss, I don't need to tell you that he and I... We do not really get along. They have their own people there, they created the special group, what else do they want?'

'You will go, have a look, give Warsaw a bit of fresh air and come back. You will not be a member of the special group, rather a coordinator. Something like...' Krygier was looking for the right expression. 'A free electron, working in its own way. I know we have some shit to deal with on our own home ground, in the Aniołów Woods, but the Headquarters insist. And anyway people here remember that you were good in cases of that kind.'

'What kind?'

'Cases with religious subtext. You know how to navigate it. You graduated from a Catholic boarding high school...'

'So what? It was a long time ago. I'm a policeman and the existence of the police is the ultimate proof of the non-existence of God. And anyway I haven't even finished that high school. I was given the boot after I organised a match on the corridor. We played with the waste basket. And then I used a foam extinguisher by accident.'

'Good one. But you'll go anyway,' Krygier added. 'Somebody from the Bureau remembers the Inquisitor case. They suspect it might be another religious freak.'

Heinz flinched. In his imagination he saw the male face with a network of small wrinkles by his eyes, which were the colour of steel. The face like so many others, which could easily disappear in the crowd of similar ones. Perhaps it was only the strange, absent gaze that made it stand out. Calm and ruthless. In the last few years Heinz recalled that face less and less often. He almost forgot it.

The smoke of Ukrainian cigarettes had become unbearable. Heinz choked again. Krygier went to the window and opened it widely.

'I didn't want to remind you about it,' he said softly. 'You will go, have a look around and come back. You know the city, you lived there for years and CBI will give you what you like so much – a free hand. And don't forget, I sense there is something else, something they didn't tell me. You are to be there tomorrow.'

Krygier looked at his watch. 'Well, it will be cold chicken soup for me now. But before you disappear, tell me what you think about the shit in the woods.'

'Middle-aged woman punctured with a knife. Literally punctured. The offender stabbed her almost forty times. The area is turned upside down, as if a herd of wild boars went through it. Lots of unreadable traces. He was stabbing her at random; she, when she still could, was trying to run away... Perhaps she was running away... That's the first impression anyway. And finally the highlight – a bird's feather in the victim's hand...'

'You already said that at the meeting. I don't understand why you find it so surprising. She was dying and she clenched her fingers. The feather happened to be there. I still don't get what's so strange about it.'

'I am sure that the feather wasn't just there. I can't prove it,' Heinz went to the window, 'but I am sure the feather was brought by the killer. You mentioned a staging, boss. It is true in this case. The fucker staged a show for us.'

The sun entered the Head's room and Heinz squinted.

'He undoubtedly knew her, but it's not like he took his chosen one for a walk and then things got out of hand, there was a fight and it happened. He planned it. He went there thinking that he was going to kill her. The feather is the key. Do you remember John Joubert?'

'I only remember those I captured myself,' Krygier answered. 'And I don't remember that name.'

'This was about a pencil. Whatever... doesn't matter... Let me put it this way: the guy will be back. I'm afraid he will kill again. And the stink of the shit will be even worse. Enough of it.'

Heinz patted his hair.

Krygier looked at his watch again and sighed. He grabbed his jacket and started towards the door. They left the building and entered the empty parking lot. The Head stretched like a huge animal woken from the winter sleep.

'You know what? Fuck it all. It's Sunday, after all. Opole beef roulade is waiting for me.'

'I don't have good associations with Opole, boss.'

Heinz imagined green shreds of pickles and pink pieces of bacon twitching on Krygier's lips and moustache.

'Ah, yeah, Opole...' The Head stopped stretching. 'You are...' he was looking for the right term. 'You are a defeatist, Heinz. Because you choose to be. And your programmed sadness means that you can't move forward. You are stuck.'

Heinz did not respond. He lifted his hand as if to say goodbye and turned away.

Krygier looked as Heinz's car moved towards the barrier.

'Enough of it,' he murmured, watching the Commissioner disappear.

3

HE DID HIS GROCERY SHOPPING not far from the police station, even though there was a cheap Lidl supermarket round the corner from his place, known as the Trough or Helmut's Revenge. He mostly bought frozen goods. Heinz did not like Sunday shopping, unpredictable holiday drivers in the parking lot in front of the supermarket, the clatter of shopping trolleys against other shopping trolleys, customers looking reproachfully when their bolide of consumption brushed against another trolley. He could not stand the ever-present queues to pay, which got even longer since they introduced new services allowing you to pay your gas, water, telephone bills and whatever else you could imagine.

This time, unusually for him, Heinz put more products into his basket. He needed to leave something for his son and he was not sure how long he would be away.

Give Warsaw a bit of fresh air. He expected trouble in the capital. As if a double homicide was not bad enough, there were also special circumstances. Two seminarists with bags on their heads, pink triangles and – as the Head said – probably something else, known only to the people running the investigation. The Central Bureau of Investigation's involvement. He has not had a case like that for years. He was back at the Estate of the 1,000-Years Anniversary, the pride and glory of post-war Silesia, when he felt that his shirt was soaking wet.

In contrast to what you read in novels, murders are the most banal crimes, the easiest to detect. Three-quarters of dramas with the dead body in the picture are family stories. Heinz remembered the title of a certain book, *Murder as a Fine Art*. Not at all. He could still remember the surprise on the faces of FBI agents when he presented the statistics of homicide in Poland during his internship in Quantico. Americans shook their heads in disbelief, when he told them about the number of murders committed with an axe, shovel or pitchfork. Evil is banal and primitive, he used to say to students. You will probably never meet a serial killer.

He knew he was disappointing them by saying that. And so be it.

Somebody honked at him. You could tell that proper spring had arrived, Heinz thought. A line of cars was coming from the direction of the Silesian Central Park, those green lungs that Silesians owed to General Ziętek. For the first time this year the visitors took the parking spaces of the residents of the Tauzen, as the estate was often called. Heinz was by the stop at the Giraffe, created by an architect who definitely spent too much time looking at Salvador Dali's surrealist paintings, when he heard a spark jumping on the overhead tram wires. This sound always made him think of crackling of the melting fat. Of sizzling of the burning flesh. He saw the cruel eyes the colour of steel for the second time today. He stepped on the brakes suddenly. He heard screeching tyres behind him and a furious blare of the hooter.

Heinz was breathing heavily.

'Look what you are doing, moron!' A ruddy 40-year-old stuck his head out of the lowered window of his car. He was screaming, as if he was a rock singer. Some lame, makeshift Axl Rose.

Heinz felt he was coming back to reality. He looked into the rear-view mirror. There was a Mercedes with German plates behind him. A blonde on the passenger seat was busy fixing her make-up.

'The green lungs don't do you good...' he said through clenched teeth, staring through the windscreen.

The Mercedes driver was out of his car and walking towards Heinz. He stuck his head in Heinz's car window.

'You wanna talk? Park on the side, man, and let's talk. Or call the police,' Ruddy's face was red-hot.

He wanted to say something else, but two hands locked his head in a steely grip. He yanked his head away, trying to free it and pull it out, but he felt a sharp pain in his nape. Heinz's thumbs were rammed into two soft points below his earlobes. Ruddy singer groaned and pulled his head. It did not help. Heinz pressed his thumbs even more.

'I am the police. And now get lost, jerk, or there will be trouble.' Heinz let him go. He quickly looked into the rear-view mirror. Cars were stopping behind the Mercedes and intrigued people were jumping out. 'This is called aggravated assault upon a police officer, understand?' Heinz rasped. 'You and that doll in your car, get the fuck out of here. Enough of it.'

Ruddy jumped away, as if stung by hornets. He ran back to his Mercedes. The girl in the passenger seat stopped filing her nails.

'What took you so long, darling?' she asked. 'You look strange,' she looked closely at the man. 'You have something red under your ears.'

Heinz's car was gone.

I met a psycho, the driver of the Mercedes thought. And he promised himself that it was his first and last visit to the Silesian Park.

4

NERVES. I don't control myself. The day will come when it ends badly. It always happens when the Inquisitor reappears on the stage. Why did the killing of two seminarists make somebody think of that case from long ago? The case which ruined his career and his health. He couldn't stop himself and reached for his mobile. He found the number, which he used to know by heart in the past. He heard the voicemail message and the signal indicating the start of the recording. He hesitated. It took him a few seconds before he left a message.

'This is Heinz speaking. I haven't been in touch for a long while. I need to ask you a favour. Could you check how our charge is doing? Just asking. Pure curiosity. Let me know.'

He parked the car by the 'corn-on-the-cob', one of the three big ones on the Tauzen estate. The residents of the twenty-four-storey towers were of the opinion that two other 'corn-on-the-cobs', merely eighteen stories tall, were simply not in the same league. It was like comparing the Silesian Stadium to a nice but provincial football pitch. Heinz was never sure if he should share the pride of the residents of the big 'corn-on-the-cobs'. He lived on the second floor, which seemed as appropriate in the case of a tower block as listening to Stevie Ray Vaughan's blues in a helicopter. Or Anna Jantar's songs while circling above Okęcie.

Heinz had felt really proud of his flat only once, when they first moved in here, with their little one-year-old son. The tower block rose amongst the fields, the People's Republic of Poland was dying and everybody, according to the slogan used in the elections for the new parliament, was supposed to feel at home at last. Years later, the shabby, dirty corn-on-the-cob – never renovated because the housing co-operative didn't have money for it – was for Heinz a symbol of unfulfilled dreams about 'the Polish Manhattan in Silesia'. The symbol of incompetent capitalism, like some bad driver on a highway, speeding and dangerous. Recently he started hating his flat, which only for a short period had been a home for the three of them, and then, for years, the two of them. Nowadays, more and more often, he was on his own in those three rooms.

The lift came to the ground floor and the Commissioner saw a familiar face in the little window. He wanted to move back, but it was too late. A moment later, the bony fingers of the old lady living on the second floor, just like Heinz, tightened on his jacket. The other hand held a dog on a leash. He looked at his crumpled sleeve and imagined the old hag getting lockjaw.

'Have you heard, Inspector? Horrible things are happening.'

The old woman always referred to Heinz as Inspector. She moved into the corn-on-the-cob around the same time they did and was quickly dubbed 'Rubber Ear'. The woman knew everything about everybody and, worse than that, was ready to share that knowledge as happily as she was to talk about planting trees in the Silesian Park in the times of General Ziętek.

'As you know, I'm not really interested...'

'The police need to do something about it,' Rubber Ear interrupted him.

Heinz froze. For the old woman he was the police. Once, when some hoodlums destroyed benches in Krzywoustego Avenue, she kept pestering him for two weeks.

'I really can't right now...'

He heard a quiet snarl. He looked at the dog and thought that he would happily crush it into the ground.

'You know Mr Karolak? Sure you do,' she answered her own question. 'He lives right below you. He has a doggie like my Kubuś. And recently his dog was attacked by rats by our rubbish bins. And then Mr Karolak saw the rats ripping a pigeon to pieces. He saw it with his very own eyes...'

'You see, I'm going away now, but when I come back, I will make some phone calls.'

'Call today! Things like that can't wait.'

The Commissioner squinted and imagined Kubuś's remains being wrenched by the rats. And then he heard his mobile ringing.

'Oh, there you are,' he freed his hand from her grip. 'What a coincidence, that will give me a chance to tell them about it right away.'

He disappeared into the lift. Being overweight, he should walk up those two floors, really.

The phone kept ringing. Heinz reached into the inside pocket of his jacket. He heard a familiar voice.

'Our charge is on a secure ward in a loony bin. So no changes.'

There was a slight hesitation in Doctor Kornak's voice.

'Thanks. Anything else?'

'I'm not sure if it matters... But... It's a bit strange that you leave a message asking about him, while he recently asked about you...'

They talked a while longer. Finally Heinz disconnected the call. He rang the doorbell to his flat. There was silence on the other side of the door. The key grated in the lock. His hands were sticky with sweat.

He forgot about his telephone conversation. So this was what life in the land of ever-present coldness was like.

He opened the door to his son's room and saw the crumpled bed sheets. Nobody had been here since yesterday. He reached for his mobile, but then changed his mind. They were not getting along too well recently. Heinz felt that their relationship was dwindling, if there ever was any to speak of. Perhaps there was, six years ago, when he was in the hospital after the Inquisitor case. When he saw the frightened eyes of his son who came to visit and when he heard the whispering of the aunt from Warsaw who came to take care of the boy.

He was tired. He had two beers while taking a bath, packed his things and grabbed his guitar. The ash Epiphone Les Paul produced warm, low sounds. He played a few notes and turned the amplifier up. When he stopped, he heard Mr Karolak, the owner of the dog bitten by rats, banging the ceiling with something. Heinz decided to do what he usually did. He went to the wardrobe to take out his baseball bat, which he brought from the States. He wanted to whack it against the radiator, which would surely make Karolak cower, just like his dog, and stop making the racket. He opened the squeaky door, put his hand in, but could not find the cold handle. He opened the wardrobe wider and started fumbling in the pile of crumpled clothes thrown in carelessly. The bat was not there. He thought of his son and grabbed the phone. No, that was not possible. He must have got too drunk after the last clash with Karolak and forgotten where he left the dreary bat.

Dreariness. Dreary life has become the norm.

It was almost ten and his son still wasn't home. He dialled the number. After ten rings he disconnected the call and redialled. With the same result. Not that he was surprised. That was exactly why he delayed the call as long as he could. Now he could only do what he usually did in similar situations. He took a yellow post-it note and wrote down that he was going away for a few days. They got to the point when they communicated via post-its on the fridge. On the other hand it was not so bad when compared with his relationship with his own father, Heinz thought bitterly. Perhaps that's how evolution manifests itself.

Since the Inquisitor case, he needed music to fall asleep. He was now listening to John Lee Hooker singing about Tupelo, a little flooded town in the state of Mississippi, which could not be saved. He was tossing and turning.

In his head the blues bars were jumbled with the voice of the Head of the Criminal Unit. Two dead seminarists, plastic bags, pink triangles in lipstick. And probably something else. A bonus. Like the ones you get on CDs and DVDs. After all there must be a reason for that strange nervousness in CBI. They asked for his help even though the bodies were found less than a week ago. April the 12th early in the morning and today was the 15th. Only four days. The first forty-eight hours are the most important in any investigation. That's when the case needs to get closed or at least the perpetrator singled out. Every hour beyond that is a failure. After a week, you start running on the spot. Somebody must have decided that in this case trotting in place started even earlier, it seemed.

Heinz was restless. He couldn't go to sleep. He went to his desk, took a cardboard folder out of a drawer and put it in his bag. The woman punctured in the Aniołów Woods. He would have a browse through it on his way to Warsaw.

The CD was on a loop and the tracks started playing again from the beginning. John Lee Hooker was again singing about Tupelo and Heinz was again going through in his head through what he heard from Kornak.

'I'm not sure if it matters... But the charge recently asked about you...'

'He asked?'

'The doctor I talked to said that the charge asked him yesterday if, by any chance, he knew what Rudolf Heinz was doing nowadays. When he said that he didn't, the charge said something like, "If you meet him, ask him if he remembers the poem".'

'The poem? What poem?'

Kornak hesitated for a long while before he answered. Heinz knew that there was something else.

'Perhaps I shouldn't be telling you this, but what the hell... He then said: "I wander around looking for my gallows".'

'That's all?'

'No. He also added, "And where are your gallows, Heinz?".'

5

THE INTERCITY TRAIN to Warsaw was to leave at 6.40. Heinz passed three empty compartments and went into his. Of course, he thought. He always got a seat in a compartment with somebody else already there. His seat was by the window. A 30-year-old with a tonne of make-up on her cheeks was sitting opposite. With blonde roots showing through the black dye she looked like a tigress. Facing her crossways by the door was a boy in cowboy boots and a tight, white polo shirt.

Heinz knew what was going to happen now. And he was not mistaken. Tigress took her make-up bag out, checked in the mirror that her make-up remained perfect, took out two mobile phones and a bi-weekly about the stars of soap operas and stage, as well as the flocks of their apprentices slowly making their way from behind the scenes on to the first pages. The boy stretched. He put his mobile on the seat next to Heinz, as well as the latest issue of *Runner's World* magazine. *Improve your fitness. More running — better sex*, the headline on the cover glared. And then Tigress and Runner put their laptops on their laps.

As soon as the train started moving, Heinz got up and went to the restaurant carriage. He ordered two coffees with cream. He always felt like an intruder in InterCity trains. Amongst the uniforms of the new system, suits and business jackets, managers and directors of different levels, he felt like a tramp. Walking along the corridor, he saw fear in other travellers' eyes. They clearly expected this man with shabby facial hair, in a crumpled corduroy jacket with patches on the elbows that must remember the 1970s, to approach them and ask for money. Only foreign tourists were dressed worse than him, with their shapeless t-shirts challenging the business chic.

But this time he wasn't the one most shabbily dressed. A young guy in a hoodie was sitting at a table furthest from the bar. He did not order anything for half an hour. He kept staring at the lamps with matt glass shades.

'Mister, this is no waiting room,' Heinz heard the irritated voice of a waiter. 'This is a restaurant. You need to order something or leave.'

'But I'm allowed to think about it, aren't I?' The boy did not give in.

'Hurry up then.'

Heinz sighed, finished his second coffee and went back to his compartment.

Opening the door he realised that Tigress and Runner were having a lively conversation.

'Oh, no,' the woman chirped. 'We don't just produce the weak-current appliances. We also keep an eye on our resellers... They sometimes need to be brought into line...'

The boy nodded with respect. He was fanning himself with the *Runner's World*.

'It's the same with us,' he said. 'Even though controlling central management systems in intelligent buildings is a more complex process.' He got into the rhythm of a presentation. 'Our products need to be standardised and scalable in a certain way. We need to take care of customisation and integrators.'

Now it was her turn to nod with respect.

'Our company is constantly faced with problems at the supporting level.'

Heinz looked at the trees in blossom outside the window. The enthusiastic female manager's face was reflected in the window pane. This was not just a conversation between two professionals. This was a song of songs. They stopped talking only when one of them had to answer the phone. There was no chance of them being quiet. He might as well try smacking a Barbie doll with a baseball bat and expect her to become an alterglobalist.

Turn on, tune in, drop out, hippies' guru Timothy Leary used to say. Heinz decided to turn off. He took out the grubby, yellowed folder tied with a black, dirty string. A muscle in Tigress' face twitched and a fracture appeared in her flawlessly powdered façade.

He knew the Aniołów Woods well. A few years ago several skinheads attacked some homeless people there. They beat an old man to death and injured two women severely. Now the woods will be avoided again. The crime scene was on the territory of the City Police Station in Częstochowa, so that was where it was investigated, however – as was often the case – Heinz was asked to consult.

The victim was a forty-five-year-old woman, widowed four years ago, resident of Interior, as the city towered by the Jasna Góra Monastery was often called. She was single and quiet. How could such a quiet woman have been stabbed forty times? Heinz was shuffling the pictures as if they were playing cards. The terrain was turned upside down. But did that happen during the fight? It was highly likely that there would be evidence allowing for identification of the victim. But under the victim's nails there was no – as the police technician described it – 'interesting material'. Analysis of microtraces on the clothing did not reveal anything either. The murderer – almost certainly a man – was thorough. Methodical. Heinz looked at the picture again. He smoothed the hair on his temple. No, that didn't add up. The area had been disturbed after the killing. Perhaps to give the impression that the crime was committed after a violent argument.

Heinz took out another photograph. It showed a female hand covered with clustered lumps of soil and dried spots of blood. Between the thumb and the index finger, there was a bird's feather. A pigeon's feather. No way that was an accident. Heinz thought about the conversation with Krygier yesterday. He asked him about John Joubert.

His past caught up with him again. His first internship in Quantico, in the Behavioral Science Unit of the FBI. That was when, amongst many other cases analysed during the sessions, he heard about the man who was stabbed to death with a pencil. The murder weapon indicated an ex-prisoner, as delivering justice with a pencil is a prison classic. However, the then guru of American profilers decided that this was not the case: the pencil indicated a greenhorn, somebody who kills for the first time with whatever he has at hand. One way or another, the pencil was the key to the whole case.

The feather was of no less importance than the pencil. The efficiency of the crime in the Aniołów Woods ruled out any chance of coincidence. The feather in the woman's hand was the killer's calling card. It was a signature, though still illegible to Heinz. The trampled ground was just a part of the staging. The most horrifying though was the number of thrusts. Forty stabs, of which half were probably lethal. Why did he stab the woman without restraint? Because her death was not enough. The death did not satisfy his needs. He wanted something more. Somebody more.

And this fucker is now at work. Or eating big breakfast at home and watching telly. He goes through a cooling-off period now. A masking phase, as colleagues from America call it. But the normality stage will end at some point. He will strike again. It can happen in a week or in six months. But it will happen. He closed his eyes. He put the folder in his lap. He was tired; he hadn't slept much last night. He might have got a few minutes' sleep.

'And in my opinion I could be a PR account manager,' Tigress babbled with the speed of a Kalashnikov. 'But that's a dead end. There is no higher position above a PR account manager. So I couldn't get a promotion. Unless I became a president...'

She realised that the man sitting opposite was looking at her.

'Oh, we're not sleeping anymore, are we?' she almost sang, clearly bored with the conversation with Runner. 'And you, if you don't mind me asking, what do you do for a living?'

'There was a time when they would call me an alienist,' he recalled the title of one of the many crime novels he read a long time ago.

'Excuse me?' She didn't understand.

'Doesn't matter. I'm a consultant.'

The boy, still fanning himself with the magazine for the runners, nodded with respect.

'A consultant?' he asked.

'In English they call me a profiler. I assess if other people are right for something or not. If they are capable of doing what others can't do.'

He felt the two coffees drunk in the restaurant carriage car pressing mercilessly on his bladder.

'Excuse me, please,' he stood up.

A few pictures slipped out of the folder.

The boy picked them up from the red carpet and went pale. They were photographs of the woman's dead body. There was so much blood that it looked like it could start dripping from the picture any moment.

'I'm sorry,' Heinz mumbled. 'Those pictures are not, so to speak, standardised. This woman,' he flicked the photo with his fingers, 'doesn't need supporting any more.'

He looked at Tigress, who suddenly went very quiet. The colourful magazine was on the little table by the window. Heinz saw a famous singer on the cover and a dazzling title: *Why did she cancel the wedding?!*

'What's your opinion?' he asked the silent Tigress. 'Why did she cancel the wedding?' he pointed to the cover.

'She probably had a change of heart...' he barely heard her.

'Some change of heart... They agreed with her fiancé to move the wedding date a month, so that the papers can write about them again. Enough of it.'

He put the dirty, yellow folder away and went out into the corridor.

He reached the toilet, but somebody was faster than him. There were two plastic holders fixed to the door. Both stuffed with the same leaflets. Heinz opened one at random and read: *Team building is directly linked with coaching. And once you build a team, you cannot leave it without support.* Coaching. Just like customisation and supporting. At the bottom he read that the leaflet contained *'Summer Musings on Management'*.

It sounds like some fucking spiritual retreat for managers.

The toilet was empty now and Heinz went in with some hesitation. You never know what awaits you in a train bog, even on an InterCity train. No coaching would help here. Last time he was going for a lecture to Poznań, he saw a trail of white powder on the olive green toilet seat cover, which for any half-smart police officer meant one thing. Heinz took a piss and flushed. Retreat for managers, resisting the water, disappeared in the cesspit.

The train was approaching Warsaw Central Station. Heinz left his compartment without saying goodbye. There were two old ladies holding magazines on the platform by the escalators. The magazine cover was filled with lightning in different shades and a fierce, bearded face coming through the clouds. *When will Armageddon come?*, it said in red letters.

'Will you buy?' one of the women asked. 'A very interesting read.'

6

THE COMPANY CAR was taking him towards the Mostowski
Palace. Heinz could barely recognise the city where he went
to university. Studying in Warsaw was his second attempt to
break away from Silesia and the childhood memories, which
restrained his freedom like a straitjacket. The first attempt –
when he agreed to be shut away in a boarding school – ended
in the disaster, shame and disgrace the insubordinate student
brought to the family. It seemed the second attempt would end
up differently. Heinz studied sociology in Warsaw, worked in a
student co-operative, earned extra money as a night watchman
and specialised in window cleaning in high buildings. And
then a coincidence called love brought him back to Katowice.

The car stopped at the traffic lights on the corner of
Marszałkowska and Królewska Street. A Romanian woman
holding a child approached them. She extended her hand
towards the driver, and when he ignored her, she looked at
Heinz who was sitting in the back seat. She stretched her hand
out again, then pointed to her mouth and to the sleeping child.
Finally she started making a sign of the cross in a sweeping
move. A three-, maybe four-year-old child twitched, woken
up. Through the tightly shut window Heinz heard crying. The
Romanian woman crossed herself again and the child started
shaking its fist towards the drivers in a threatening gesture. The

woman showed her middle finger for everybody to see. The car started sharply towards Bankowy Square.

Some things never change, Heinz thought when the company car was passing the entrance gate by the Mostowski Palace.

Every time he came here, there was a renovation going on in the Factory, as the Metropolitan Police Headquarters was called. This time too the sound of drills effectively drowned out conversations in the corridors.

The meeting of the special group was taking place in a small conference room, which, despite the fact that it was a sunny day, was plunged in depressing semi-darkness. You could see rusty scaffolding behind the window. The rest of the light was obscured by legs, which suddenly filled the window frame. The drill's racket resounded and everything disappeared in a haze of plaster.

'This is madness,' a forty-year-old man with a long face said glumly.

One could think that he spoke without opening his mouth, which formed a thin line. Another, parallel line went across his forehead, as if somebody had cut it with a scalpel.

Deputy Inspector Osuch indeed had reasons to be in a foul mood. The case of the double murder was not moving forward. It's not every day that seminarists get killed, so no wonder the case aroused interest in the Ministry itself. Even more worrying was his telephone conversation yesterday, which spoilt his weekend good humour. The message was clear: the special group was to be supported by an outsider. A profiler from Katowice. Rudolf Heinz. The Deputy Inspector had heard about him in the past and what he knew did not bode well. The message was clear: the star profiler of unknown perpetrators liked working on his own, while Osuch liked order and discipline in his team. Lonely hunters often become role models for others who might want to follow suit. And then, Osuch's experience was telling him, everything goes tits up.

But it wasn't the profiler's discretion that was the Deputy Inspector's biggest worry. Osuch simply didn't like strangers on his territory.

'A policeman really is a dog,' he used to say to his people. 'Do you know why? Because he knows his territory and is capable of mauling anybody who enters it.'

He unsuccessfully tried to persuade his interlocutor over the phone that his people would do all right on their own. He needed Heinz like an asshole on an elbow.

Heinz felt he was an intruder; he felt that all six people in the room were registering his every move, even the slightest one.

'Commissioner Heinz is here to help us,' Osuch swallowed, 'solve the case. He has some...' he stressed that word, 'experience in cases like ours. As I told you earlier, he is a profiler...'

'Meaning he reads tea leaves,' mumbled a ginger-haired officer sitting opposite Heinz.

The man sitting next to the ginger one smiled, exposing nicotine-stained teeth. He then whispered something back, but his words were deafened by the noise of the drill.

'I think it would be best,' Osuch went on, 'if we went through everything one more time and had a close look at that mess. Rudi,' he nodded to the ginger-haired one, 'please summarise all we know.'

Heinz flinched, hearing his own name. Red-haired Rudi. A made-up nickname, how original. He looked at the cigarettes lying on the table. It seemed that nobody here smoked Ukrainian smokes without excise duty stamp. Thank goodness. He took out his packet of Chesterfields.

'The mess,' Rudi started, 'consists of two men, most likely smothered. Most likely, as the circumstances we found the bodies in might indicate that somebody is trying to put us on the wrong track. The bodies were spotted around four in

the morning on the 12th of April in the bushes by the Olympic
Centre at 4 Wybrzeże Gdańskie. They were found by a bottle
picker...'

'The guy almost vomited his own heart and liver,' the one
with yellow teeth said. 'Hours later he was still shaking like a
leaf.'

'No wonder,' Rudi went on. 'The victims had plastic bags
on their heads. It seems likely that they were smothered with
those bags tightened on their heads, unless it is some kind of
a show for our sake. Anyway we are almost sure that the men
were dead when they were brought to the Palace...'

'Palace?'

'That's what they call the Olympic Centre,' a woman
explained. 'I presume you've never been there. It's rather...'
She paused, looking for the right term. 'Lavishly decorated.'

Heinz looked at her closely. Short black hair, black jumper,
finger nails painted purple. As if she was going to the Gothic
rock festival in the Bolków castle.

'So somebody killed them and then brought them there,'
Rudi continued. 'Of course nobody has seen or heard anything.
On top of that we also don't have any interesting evidence,
at least so far. And when it comes to those bags...' He took a
cigarette out. 'These are standard white plastic bags, nothing
printed on them. The type used in thousands of shops.'

So that's no trail.

He took photos out of his briefcase and passed them to
Heinz.

'And here the mess turns into a lil' theatre show.'

Two policemen, who were so far silent, giggled softly in
unison.

'The offender painted triangles at the height of the mouth.
Pink triangles,' Rudi added. 'He drew them with lipstick. Before
I say more about that, a few words about the victims. Karol
Rakowiecki and Grzegorz Leski, the first one from Warsaw, the

other one from the outskirts of Warsaw. Both were seminarists in the diocese theological college in Żoliborz district.'

'How did you manage to find out who they were?' Heinz asked.

'Neither had any ID on them. But one of them had a little pocket on the sleeve of his jacket where we found a folded piece of paper with a mobile number. We called and there you have it – we got through to Father Jan Rutger, Professor of Biblical studies. We followed the lead and, bit by bit... In the end Professor Rutger identified the bodies. And then slumped to the floor. Believe you me, it was very impressive. He is some strange priest anyway...'

Rudi scratched his head.

'Why?' Osuch asked.

'He came dressed, so to speak, like a civilian. Not like a priest. Those two did not look like seminarists either. Perhaps that's how they dress nowadays, who the fuck knows. Anyway we know who they were...'

'Seek and ye shall find,' the police officer with yellow teeth added.

'We started the investigation in three directions.' Rudi lit another cigarette. 'They,' he nodded towards two officers, 'questioned families, seminarists and professors from the theological college...'

'So far with no results,' one of those pointed at by Rudi interrupted. 'The boys were innocent like lambs, no enemies, no trouble at all. Nobody knows anything in the seminary. They are too frightened to breathe, not to mention talking. But we do ask.'

'Secondly,' Rudi went on, 'we let slip to the papers that the killings were the result of gangsters getting even. Admittedly these were only seminarists, not mafia, but you never know. If there was some truth in it, we would hear something from our people out on the town. There would be some commotion, but there is nothing.'

The room went silent. You could hear hollow blows of the hammer from the distance.

'There is one more track. The one linked with plastic bags and pink triangles. This was how the Nazis marked homosexuals: with pink triangles. The area around the Olympic Centre is well known in Warsaw as a rendezvous place of those,' he smiled, 'who like to do it differently. And our boys were into that kind of sport...'

'Two-man bobsleigh on natural tracks.' Yellow teeth appeared again.

'Exactly,' Rudi took over. 'In case of one of the victims we can talk of regular penetration... Jesus, it sounds so...' he shook his head. 'We are not sure about the other one. Anyway, there are no traces of intercourse shortly before death. This direction,' Rudi was clearly approaching the end, 'seems to be the most promising so far. We are checking the circles of fierce nationalists and skinheads who could have something to do with our case. Our colleague,' he looked at the policewoman, 'asked questions in gay clubs. That's more or less it. More or less.'

'Supposedly I get along with the regulars, boss,' the Goth fan looked at Osuch.

'So what does our master think about it all?' Osuch asked.

Heinz was silent. Cigarette smoke hovered above the heads of the policemen gathered in the room.

'I still don't know,' Heinz said, 'why I am here. Double murder, plastic bags on the heads, pink triangles painted with lipstick... That does not explain me being here.'

'Should I tell him?' the police officer with yellow teeth looked at Osuch.

Heinz stood up abruptly. One of the plastic cups fell and coffee spilled onto the officer sitting next to him. He jumped up.

'Enough, for fuck's sake!' Heinz rasped. 'Nobody in our line of work likes strangers entering their territory. But from now on,' he looked at them all, 'no more games. I am supposed to co-ordinate this investigation. One phone call to CBI and your arses will be on fire. So what is it that I don't know yet, eh? What did you leave for dessert, to test me?'

'Easy, Heinz!' Osuch did not budge. 'Nobody here is trying to test you.'

As if. What bullshit.

'Pink triangles were painted by the offender where the mouths were. But that's not all. At the back of the heads he wrote numbers in the same lipstick.'

'What numbers?' Heinz screwed his eyes.

'One seminarist had twenty-one, the other: thirty-seven. Do you know what that means?'

Heinz didn't know.

'These are not lottery numbers. Or the two poofs' shoe sizes. You can tell you didn't cry with the nation when...'

Heinz still had no idea.

'When the Holy Father was dying. It's the time the Pope died. Our...' he stressed, 'Pope. At twenty-one thirty-seven. Every idiot knows that. And every idiot understands that it's no joke. That's why this murder caused panic in the Ministry, you see? That's why they created a special group. Only a handful of people know about those details.'

'Yes, now I get it,' Heinz said.

He finally understood why somebody wanted him to work on this case.

7

IT WAS EIGHT in the evening when Rudolf Heinz went into a bar in the police hotel at Sierakowskiego Street. The man he was supposed to meet was running late. The Commissioner ordered a beer. The radio was playing more aggressive ads and competitions than songs, but tonight Heinz didn't care. Some two metres away, at the next table, two men were talking, every now and then reaching for glasses lined evenly as if they were members of the ceremonial unit at the Tomb of the Unknown Soldier.

He ordered a beer. Nowadays he had three, four beers a day, not like in the past. He remembered times of his alcoholic *Sturm und Drang* when he often came to Warsaw as a consultant. He would get off at the Warsaw East Station on purpose and go to the Golden Fish, a station bar taken over by ticket inspectors and train conductors who came there to sit over aromatic dishes of chicken liver with fried onions and count the dough earned from passengers travelling without tickets. Heinz would always get an enormous mug with 'Cappuccino' written on its side, full of warm beer with a thick head. Only after two, three mugs he would feel that the day had started well and go to the Mostowski Palace. The ritual would be repeated while he waited for the train back to Katowice. Often the journey itself was like a black hole. A meaningless episode between arrival and departure.

He recalled the morning journey on the train and the book he was thinking about. Caleb Carr's *The Alienist*. To his colleagues' surprise, Heinz liked reading crime fiction, especially those books that featured serial killers. In his opinion the analysis of the fictional *modus operandi* was a good exercise of the mind. However, Carr's novel got him hooked for different reasons. 'Alienist' was a term used to describe police psychologists who dealt in deviants and degenerates of different shapes and forms. In those who didn't fit into the social norms. Very often an alienist would become no less of an oddball than the person he was tracking. Heinz often thought that he was just like that. An alienist.

I change when I sense blood. First the victim's blood. And then the offender's blood. When I lay the motherfucker open to be shot down.

The men at the next table were speaking louder and louder. After all, here, in the police bar, they were all in their own company. Heinz looked in their direction. They were more or less the same age, around forty, wearing identical black t-shirts, as if they both bought them from some 'bamboos' – a snide name given to Asians trading nearby, at the biggest bazaar in Europe. The man sitting closer to Heinz had thick, black hair, the other one was a blond with thinning hair sticky with pomade. He made Heinz think of a seabird, which survived an ecological disaster and was now desperately beating its wings, caked with grease and oil.

'It used to be different.' The dark-haired man put two filled glasses on the table. 'You know what, Limahl? I will tell you something.' He hiccupped. 'I liked working with the Belarusian boys best. Even in the 90s. They understood what our job was about. I remember once we were tipped off that they got a guy suspected of two jobs on our territory.'

'But you had no proof of anything,' the blond one interrupted. The dark one nodded.

'They didn't have anything either. So here is what we did:

they put the guy in a private car. Into *popiełuszka*. Into the trunk, you know...'

Limahl hiccupped signalling that he knew that in police slang a car trunk was called '*popiełuszka*' in memory of the Solidarity chaplain, Father Jerzy Popiełuszko, who was kidnapped by the Militia and put in the car trunk before being killed.

'So,' the dark-haired one went on, 'I drove to the border, also in a private car. They pull the guy out and say: "Go, cross the border" but the fucker is refusing. So they shoot a series from a Kalash at his feet. The guy jumps onto our side and there we are, waiting for him with a tender welcome. He wants to know what he is arrested for. So I tell him, "For illegal border crossing".'

They both laughed and took a drink.

'I will tell you something too, Gypsy,' the blond-haired guy named after the 1980s pop star said. 'I told you about the guy called Hocus Pocus...'

'I don't remember,' Gypsy shook his head.

'The guy's real name was Józek Kaleta. He was called Hocus Pocus because he could rip a man in half as if it was nothing, and the client, before he conked out, had a chance to listen to Józek going through what was being cut and which organs bled the most and so on, and so on. A concise course in anatomy. Imagine that? He would just make a small cut and you were looking at your own guts surfacing.'

'A professional,' Gypsy expressed his esteem.

'Indeed. Hocus Pocus didn't overly exploit his skill. He got rid of the competition and he was happy to share his knowledge, so he was useful to us. But in the end his time came as well.'

Limahl filled the glasses in silence.

'Józek got quartered and burned in a coke oven. Including the head. The boys from the police station couldn't believe it. They say that a head won't burn in a coke oven. And here was a surprise... Even after death he did a little hocus pocus.'

'Let's drink to Józek then,' Gypsy lifted his glass.

'And to the boys from the town,' Limahl added. 'I'm going to retire in a few months' time. I will only invite the town guys, they are the only ones who still deserve it. The only ones you can still hit it off with.'

'Nothing lasts forever,' Gypsy said and wiped his mouth with the back of his hand. 'OK, another round.'

They had a point. Nothing lasts forever. The police had changed, too. When Heinz first started his job, he learnt from old, experienced Militia officers. And then suddenly, in two, three years, all those people disappeared, as if swiped by a tsunami. Washed away by the waves. Young wolves entered the police forces, bringing new habits with them. Now Heinz himself was like a dinosaur from *Jurassic Park*. He was an old-timer, he crossed the police shadow line.

He was again reminded about it today, a few hours ago, during the late morning meeting at the police headquarters.

There were three of them left. Osuch nodded to the police officer with yellow teeth to stay.

'This is Commissioner Paweł Chlaściak,' he introduced him. 'One of my best men. And I don't want,' he squinted at Heinz, 'any disturbance in my team, understood?'

Heinz spread his hands in a conciliatory gesture.

'I don't want that either. That's why I suggest the following: the team works at their own pace and I have a look at the case from the sidelines. I will be a free electron. I only want support from someone who can give me a fuller picture.'

'Anything else?' Osuch growled.

'A company car. I am a co-ordinator, after all...'

'Agreed. Just stay out of my team's work. Ah, and, Heinz...' the inspector paused. 'One more thing...'

'Yes?'

'This case needs to be concluded, get it? Even if there is no offender.'

'The truth is one thing, the statistics another,' Chlaściak quickly added.

'It is exactly like he says.' Osuch wiped his sweaty forehead. 'There must be order in the paperwork. CBI will insist on it too. And no unnecessary publicity. If you want to be a star, go to television. There are *Crime Detectives* or *W-11*.'

'Is that all?' Heinz asked.

'I have a question...' Chlaściak smiled. 'I have been thinking about it all through the meeting. That jacket... Don't you ever sweat in that jacket?'

Heinz didn't answer right away. He went closer to Chlaściak. He didn't look him in the eye. He looked at his yellow teeth exposed in a wide, toothy grin.

'Never. And you?' he added a moment later. 'Don't you ever brush your teeth?'

***

He looked at his watch. Eight thirty. They were supposed to meet forty-five minutes ago. The bar was getting more and more crowded. He decided to pay for his beer. He turned towards the counter and then felt somebody's hand on his shoulder.

The man in front of him was taller by a head, had an oval face and spiky hair. Even in the dim light you could see the scar going from the top of his nose all the way to the right corner of the mouth.

'Commissioner Heinz?' The voice was surprisingly high.

'Heinz. Just like ketchup. Ends with a "z".'

'My name is Piotr Karewicz. Still a Deputy Commissioner. At work they call me Karloff. You can probably figure out why.'

Indeed.

Karloff smiled and the scar on his face stretched to double its length. Now the association with a famous horror actor seemed almost banal to Heinz.

They heard the sound of broken glass. They looked towards

the nearest table. Gypsy was sleeping in the chair tilted backwards. Limahl's head dropped onto the table. A trickle of vodka was seeping from a fallen glass. There was broken glass from two other shot glasses on the floor, crunching under Limahl's shoe. He was grinding it as if it was a cigarette butt he wanted to put out.

'Perhaps we could go somewhere else?' Karloff suggested. 'There are more interesting places in this part of town. We would be able to talk in peace there.'

If he was on his own, he would probably miss the entrance to this establishment. Karloff explained that Ząbkowska Street had lost its reputation of a dangerous place located in the Bermuda Triangle. Heinz remembered from his university days that solitary roaming around the Triangle, under the watchful eyes of thugs of different ages standing in squalid courtyards, was like tempting fate. Now he was surprised to see that one of those courtyards still sported the signboard for a music store selling t-shirts with names of deathmetal bands. He recalled being here many years ago and buying several pirated tapes. They passed by the Virgin Mary shrine and crossed the street. Karloff opened the door and Heinz bumped into a white plastic head of a bull terrier.

The only available table was close to a little stage where some boy was singing a Frank Sinatra standard.

Swing is in fashion again, Heinz thought. Neo-swing and old, run-down furniture. He was like that too, completely out of tune with the times. Karloff brought two beers.

'OK. So what do you think?' Karloff asked when they both settled down.

'I don't know much. I need to talk to the medical examiner.'

'I thought so. That's why I made us an appointment with Shaggy for tomorrow,' Karloff smiled.

'With whom?'

'You will see for yourself.' The scar by the mouth stretched again. 'So what does the first snort of a seasoned cocaine addict tell you?' He sniffed theatrically.

Heinz didn't answer. Years of work in the police had taught him that in this job you had no friends. You rarely even had colleagues. Every dog pees on its own little tree and defends its territory. Karloff's questions seemed way too obtrusive for his liking. Perhaps that was why Osuch assigned him a helper without a murmur of complaint.

Karloff stopped smiling.

'You don't trust me, eh? You think I'm Osuch's ear? That I will give him reports on your brilliant theories and if, by chance, one of them happens to be true, we will take the spotlight?'

They heard clapping and girls screaming. Clearly the boy on the stage had some faithful following.

Heinz looked at Karloff who was clenching the glass in his hand as if he wanted to hurl it.

'Everybody is suspicious,' he mumbled. 'I read recently about this tribe. Dobu or something like that... So those Dobu people value suspiciousness and consider laughter to be unbecoming. They located the cemetery in the centre of their village...'

'Nice guys. They would create a sensation on YouTube...'

'We are like Dobu, with our obsessive distrust and secrets. You, me, her...' he nodded towards the table in the corner.

Karloff looked at the couple pointed out by Heinz.

'When this man is not looking, she constantly checks her watch,' Heinz went on. 'And reacts nervously every time the door opens...' He leant over the table. 'How am I supposed to know if you are not switching a dictaphone on in your pocket when you raise your beer glass to me? It has become our national sport.'

Karloff's face now resembled a monster.

'If we are to work together,' Heinz continued, 'I need to know that you are OK. You were forty minutes late. Why?'

Karloff put his beer down. Heinz thought that it looked as if the huge hand had left an imprint on the glass.

'I had some errands to run. Up until yesterday,' he lowered his voice, 'I was suspended.'

'What for?'

'I supposedly took this guy to the woods and told him to dig a hole in the ground to force him to give evidence.'

'And, surely, it's not true?'

Karloff smiled. He must have been practising that smile while watching old horror movies.

'You can't possibly think I would be capable of doing something like that, can you?'

He raised his glass and drank to Heinz.

'I have one more question. There, in the hotel, how did you know who to approach? How did you know it was me?'

'I was given a detailed description. You want to know it?'

Heinz nodded.

'They told me to look for a guy with a face so wrecked he must have been around when they caught Marchwicki the vampire. A guy in a crumpled jacket. A Mr Cords... Well, you asked for it.'

The boy on the stage said that he was going to sing one more Frank Sinatra hit and then he would take a half hour break. His female fans groaned in disappointment.

'So, Karloff, frankness in exchange for frankness. I will tell you what I said to the people from your team. To my knowledge in Poland there are...' he hesitated, 'seven, at most ten, active serial killers. That's an estimate, but I won't go into explaining how I got that number. Judging by – as you phrased it – the first snort of the cocaine addict, I don't think those seminarists were victims of one of the serials. Those cases usually involve a sexual element, sometimes there is a robbery motive added to it. And here we have a show like in an opera house. Plastic bags, triangles, numbers to do with the Pope's time of death… It's some kind of…' he was looking for the right term, '… a joke.'

'A joke?'

'Perhaps they were having a party in a bigger company, they were using the bags for choking and got carried away. We'll know more after the meeting with the medical examiner. Enough of it.'

'A joke…' Karloff said again. 'The person who did it had a very unique sense of humour.'

'Just like you when you took that guy to the woods…'

This time Karloff didn't reply. He just tightened his hand on the glass again. The woman at the corner table stole a furtive glance at her watch.

8

I STILL DIDN'T TELL HIM everything, Heinz thought in his hotel room. He took the worn leather string off his neck, the one that caused so much bewilderment. Funny. Nobody blinks an eye at a medallion with the Virgin Mary or a cross, or a locket bought by your beloved during holidays. Why do people raise their eyebrows and respond with laughter when they see a guitar pick around his neck, like some kind of an amulet? The purple plectrum with a hole drilled in it, visibly more worn off on one side, was more than a relic for Heinz. It was an object, which merged the element of life with the death. The plectrum came from the Alpine Valley Music Theatre in Wisconsin, where Stevie Ray Vaughan played his blues for the very last time. Several dozens of hours later the guitarist crashed into the ground together with the crew and other passengers of the helicopter. Heinz bought that pick for shitloads of money on an Internet auction, making sure first that the guitar relic's authenticity was confirmed by two certificates. Good, old, sentimental Rudolf Heinz.

But it wasn't the death of his idol that he was thinking about late in the evening. He was thinking about the murderer.

What he saw and heard in the Mostowski Palace made it clear to him that they were dealing with either a complete amateur or a highly sophisticated psychopath. Whoever the killer was, he didn't bother with removing the evidence. Removing the evidence meant first and foremost removing the bodies. He could have buried them somewhere in the woods, which would change everything. The families or the college would report the boys missing and a whole different chain of events would unfold. After all, nobody calls a special group to investigate a disappearance case, even when it is a disappearance of two seminarists. Cases like that are not treated like priorities, even if nowadays it is difficult to say what takes absolute precedence in police work. CBI would not get interested in the case and he wouldn't be working on it either. What's more, the perpetrator didn't check the victims' pockets. Thanks to the slip of paper with a telephone number they could identify the victims fast. Totally unprofessional. Therefore this couldn't have been any of the boys from the town, because they were all pros in their line of work.

Unless the situation was entirely different. All the time he couldn't stop thinking about the horrifying, weird ostentatiousness of it. The theatricality of it. As if the murderer wanted us to see the bodies of the two boys. As if the murderer put the bodies of the two boys on display on purpose, he rephrased the thought. And not just the bodies. What's more the motherfucker has nerves of steel. He leant the dead bodies back to back and tied with a string. What does that mean? He had to know that the place would be deserted. Conclusion? He must have watched the area beforehand. Perhaps somebody spotted him, perhaps somebody remembered the car?

Heinz took out his notebook and started writing. He knew that nobody but him would be able to decipher his scribbling.

Now, about the triangles. Pink triangles painted with lipstick. He recalled an article he had read recently. It was about homosexuality in the Third Reich. One of Himmler's brilliant ideas was the national Central Office for the Combating of Homosexuality and Abortion as well as pink lists, consisting of the names of all those who were suspected of degenerated disposition. Pink triangles were used in concentration camps to mark homosexuals. A pink triangle was at the very bottom of the camp hierarchy. Murdered seminarists were gay and that gave the case a specific flavour. The murderer must have known that. By marking the victims with pink triangles, he has challenged us.

He has challenged me.

Is it possible that it was the revenge of a rejected lover? Not very likely. Who would take such a big risk? Perhaps it really was some ultra-rightist who fished the boys out of a club and then played with them a bit too hard? That was not a bad trail to follow. Anyway, by leaving the triangles, the murderer said, 'I know who they were. And you will find out now that I knew that.'

Heinz heard buzzing. A fly swooped towards the lightbulb, alternately hitting the hot glass and the cheap lampshade with its wings.

One more thing, he thought. The Pope's time of death written on the plastic bag. Which alarmed the CBI so much. As if the pink triangles were not ostentatious enough, on top of that there were the numbers. Twenty-one thirty-seven. The Pope's death and the seminarists' death. What if that double murder was indeed an act of another unfulfilled visionary? Not everybody thinks death is the end. It can also be the beginning. Death as rebirth and salvation, he scribbled. Isn't death the best salvation for two sinful seminarists? Is there a better way to start fixing the world? There isn't. In the end the two homosexuals got converted, they crossed over to the side of light.

The fly's wings were hitting the bulb. He recalled the sound of an electrical spark jumping the wires. For a split second he saw the face of the Inquisitor. He blinked.

That would be the worst. If they are dealing with a vindictive psychopath, he will strike again. In this case the killing of those two boys is just the beginning. Especially as it went so smoothly. A piece of cake.

He grabbed the mobile and dialled his son's number. After several rings the voicemail kicked in. There was a new message: 'This is Krzysiek. I'm studying for my A-levels. I will call you back when I've learnt everything.' He hesitated for a moment, not sure if he should leave a message. In the end he disconnected the call.

He was about to put the phone away when it started ringing.

The display read: 'Korn'.

'The charge got very active,' Kornak said.

Heinz's heart started pounding.

'How so?'

'First he wanted to send you a text, then an e-mail and finally a regular letter.'

'I also use Skype and other forms of communication,' Heinz added snidely.

'When they refused, he said to pass on to you that he was catching up on reading.'

'I'm impressed. Shall I send him some books?' Heinz was slowly losing patience.

'No. He wants you to flick through Beckett. He said, "Beckett's *Last Tape*. The ending gives a normal person the creeps. But what about an abnormal person? That's something right up Heinz's streak".'

'And? Have you perhaps checked what he was on about? I'm not a walking library of quotations.'

'No. But I don't like the fact that he is suddenly talking about you so much.'

There are many psychos around me, Heinz thought half an hour later, lying in the darkness with earphones in his ears.

He was listening to John Lee Hooker singing about the flood in Tupelo. Yet again it took a long time to fall asleep.

WHEN HE WOKE UP, his fingers were ice cold. He tried bending and flexing them alternately, but every move brought pain. He looked at his pale fingers. He knew what was going to happen: they would soon go blue and then red. The feeling of coldness will recede and the swelling appear. The fingers will resemble cooked sausages.

Raynaud's phenomenon. Heinz experienced the first symptoms of the mysterious disorder three years ago. He was gigging with his band in a small club in Sosnowiec. He remembered they were playing their own version of *Black Magic Woman* and he was about to start his guitar solo when he felt he couldn't move the fingers of his left hand. As if they were glued to the guitar's fretboard. Later, during the treatment, he found out that Raynaud's phenomenon is sometimes brought about by extreme stress. The medical examiner from Katowice helped him get a prompt appointment for a consultation in the Institute of Rheumatology in Warsaw and for a few months Heinz was a regular visitor in the grey building at Spartańska Street. He got used to seeing people twisted in pain in ways so sophisticated that even the most talented sculptor's imagination would not embrace it. He also got used to people taking water from the artesian aquifer by the Institute and offering their own services in treating all possible diseases. He got used to the view of clothes hanging on the Institute's fence, sold cheap as chips. To shorten the waiting time for his doctor's appointment, he learnt the timetable of the buses terminating at Spartańska Street. Sometimes he went to watch the plants through rusty skeletons of greenhouses with roofs ridden with holes.

There was just one thing he could not get used to. The diagnosis.

'You must have been through a lot,' he was once told by Piotr Poraj, his doctor at the Institute. 'Raynaud's phenomenon can get worse during stressful periods, and in your line of work... Besides, Raynaud's phenomenon may be a symptom of something much more serious... Something that might manifest itself in a few years' time, maybe a dozen or so. What I'm thinking of is rheumatoid arthritis.'

Heinz preferred not to know what it was. He couldn't stand his own weakness. He started hating it after having a dream. It was two years ago. He dreamt that he was to shoot a murderer, he reached for his gun, pointed... And felt his fingers going stiff. He wasn't able to pull the trigger. The murderer escaped.

The following day he stopped carrying his police issued Glock with him.

And now, too, something must be out of order. Something that Heinz couldn't name, but felt instinctively.

He was still thinking about it when the tight-lipped driver sent by the Metropolitan Police was taking him to Oczki Street for the autopsy. As a student, Heinz used to rent a studio flat in the remote district of Targówek and in his opinion downtown Warsaw was psychos' abode. He actually had quite fond memories of three of them. He remembered a mad old lady who used to stand at the crossing in Jerozolimskie Avenue by the American Embassy and usurp the role of a person directing traffic, kitted with a Militia lollipop and white helmet of the type you could find on many construction sites at the time.

Two boys wanted to wash their car windows and the silent police officer at the driving wheel opened his mouth for the first time.

'Fuck off!' he yelled. 'Or I'll call the city wardens.'

Heinz saw another man approaching them. His legs ended at his knees. The stumps were resting on a white board with wheels. The man had gloves on his hands, the type used by builders. The cripple pushed hard against the ground and passed a Land Cruiser standing in front of them. He was by the driver's door when the light changed to green. The driver burst out laughing.

'Let me tell you something. You know what they remind me of?'

Heinz was quiet. He could see the eyes looking at him in the rear-view mirror. He shook his head.

'Of dolls. Dolls in prams. Did you see his hands?'

Heinz repeated his gesture.

'Thick builder's gloves. Supposedly so he doesn't graze his knuckles. With cut-off fingers though, so he can grab money fast. These are professionals, you understand?'

Heinz nodded for the third time to indicate that he indeed understood. They were supposed to give him a company car. He was sick and tired of the driver. He wanted to be by the post-mortem table as soon as possible.

A proper welcoming committee was waiting for him in the dissection room at Oczki Street, named after the court doctor of two Polish kings. Karloff was accompanied by a well-groomed, dark-haired man in his twenties wearing a beige leather jacket. He looked as if he had come straight from a beauty salon. Heinz looked again at his jacket and shook his head in exasperation. The model was standing between Karloff and a short, bald man. His smooth head was gleaming, although the same could not be said about his coat. The man had pale cheeks with no facial hair and Heinz now understood why they called him Shaggy.

The welcoming committee also included two motionless bodies lying on the tables.

'Doctor Jan Talar, our own genius of forensic medicine.' Karloff pointed to Shaggy. 'And this is Deputy Commissioner Leszek Baryka, freshly graduated from the Police Academy.' Noticing that Heinz was staring at Baryka, he added: 'It's his debut at Oczki Street and that explains why he is wearing his Sunday best.'

'If you need to lose your virginity, do it in good company,' Shaggy laughed. 'And here,' he made a theatrical gesture towards the tables, 'we have something rather special...'

'Then let's have a whiff of stiffs,' the Deputy Commissioner who had just been called a virgin was trying to be funny.

'For the record, my name is Heinz. Spelt just like the ketchup. Is the Prosecutor going to join us?'

'I called him,' Baryka explained quickly. 'He said he would be late and not to wait for him.'

Karloff sent Heinz a lingering look.

'That's of no consequence,' Shaggy said. 'The bodies are already opened. See for yourselves...'

He swiftly removed white covers.

'They were found,' the medical examiner checked his paperwork, 'at four in the morning. Considering where the bodies were and what the weather was, we can assume that they died on the 11th of April between 4 p.m. and 8 p.m., eight to twelve hours before they were found.'

'What was the cause of death? Does it have anything to do with the plastic bags on their heads?' Heinz was staring into the dead face nearer to him.

'Look here. The neck.' The medical examiner turned around. 'Same with the other one. You can see traces of sticky tape or some other adhesive, which tightened the bottom part of the bag. This was how they were asphyxiated. Of that I am certain. But there are also other traces, like abrasions to the epidermis on the neck and face, ecchymosis in the mucous membrane of the lips, some extravasations in conjunctiva...'

'And the red marks by the mouth? In both cases...' Heinz interrupted.

'That indeed is very interesting,' Talar agreed. 'It seems their mouths were taped.'

'That doesn't make any sense,' the model in beige leather decided to tip in. 'If they were smothered with the bags, why did they have their mouths taped?'

'And we also have those abrasions to the skin on wrists and legs, by the ankles.' The medical examiner ignored Baryka's question. 'They were tied to something... Tried to free themselves... Ah, and in case of one of them, Leski, there are traces of defecation on his body and underwear. Most likely the result of being asphyxiated or of stress.'

'Does being smothered with a bag...' Baryka swallowed. 'Does being smothered... hurt?'

'Does it hurt?' Shaggy gazed away from the bodies and looked at Virgin. 'My professor used to quote Franz Kafka who said that death is just an apparent end that causes a real sorrow. I'll tell you something, young friend: there is no greater torture than being smothered. There is simply not enough oxygen in the bag over your head, so you start suffocating quite quickly. But that's not the worst. Seemingly, you are not in a physical pain, but you know that you are dying and that brings fear that cannot be compared with anything else. It's this fear that really hurts, so to speak. Of course we know many variations of that method – from the primitive dunking when the victim is submerged in water, to more sophisticated ones. Have you seen *The Battle of Algiers*?'

All three of them shook their heads.

'I shouldn't have even bothered asking.' Shaggy was clearly disgusted. 'It seems I'm the only person who remembers such old films. There was a scene there when the Frenchmen tie a guy to a wooden plank and submerge him in water. They keep him under water long enough so that he starts suffocating for real. Then they pull him out and repeat the whole procedure. *The Killing Fields*? Maybe you've seen that?'

'I have,' Karloff and Heinz said almost simultaneously.

'I don't believe you,' the medical examiner smiled. 'It's worth knowing that thousands of people were killed using plastic bags by Pol Pot's people in Cambodia. It was a spectacular – and cheap – way of killing... That's more or less it. Uh-oh, you're feeling unwell, are you?' he looked at Baryka.

The Deputy Commissioner went pale.

'No... I'm all right,' he stuttered.

'How were those two overpowered, in your opinion?' Karloff asked. 'Two young, fit boys... That couldn't have been easy. Even if you had a weapon... He didn't knock them down, after all...'

'Theoretically he could have. I don't need to tell you... A sock filled with sand or a baton wrapped in fabric would be enough... It's possible that there would be no traces on the body after such a blow. But there were two boys. And there are no signs of any fight. Anyway, what's the point of going to such lengths when there is pharmacology...'

The medical examiner was cut short by an unexpected sound. They all looked towards the old cast iron sink. The Deputy Commissioner was clutching its edges with his head leant down. A spasm shook him.

'Barf, little boy, barf away. Best on the floor, so you don't clog up the sink,' Karloff said and then turned back to the medical examiner. 'So you think that the victims were given gamma-hydroxybutyric acid or something similar?'

The medical examiner nodded.

'Yes, some date-rape drug, I suppose. Something more subtle than, for example, the popular Clonazepam.'

'Why?' Karloff was exceptionally inquisitive.

'Because Clonazepam can be easily detected during the autopsy, as well as in a living organism. Toxicology tests of the blood and urine are enough. In our case the offender... or the offenders,' the medical examiner corrected himself, 'could have used something like Rohypnol, which quickly incapacitates the victim. You take a dose and a moment later you have no idea what is happening to you, you let friendly acquaintances lead you out of a restaurant without any protests et cetera... On top of that Rohypnol and similar drugs cause retrograde amnesia, they are metabolised fast and quickly removed from the body, which makes the later diagnosis difficult. Those beauties are best served with alcohol, but they can also come in a sandwich of some strong, distinct flavour.'

From the vicinity of the sink came a sound adding more splendour to Deputy Commissioner Baryka's debut at Oczki Street.

Heinz was silent. He examined the dead men's hands thoroughly and checked the signs on their wrists. Signs of a fight for life.

'Where are the victims' clothes?' he asked Karloff.

'They should be in the deposit storage, but you know how things are...'

Heinz knew. Even the clothing secured as evidence was usually kept in police rooms packed in black plastic bags.

'I will want to have a look at them. And we'd better take him out of here,' he pointed towards Baryka, who was a tad wobbly on his feet. 'Or he will splash the doctor's place top to bottom.'

'I would be very much obliged,' the medical examiner smiled. 'And I recommend *The Battle of Algiers* when you have a spare moment.'

The three of them loitered outside. Baryka was clearly enjoying inhaling car fumes. It was as if he was suddenly transported into an oxygen bar.

'Let me tell you something, Karloff,' he said, clearly feeling better. 'Don't you ever call me a little boy again.'

'Oh, let me tell you something,' Karloff squinted. 'So far you are only good for fetching me hamburgers from McDonald's. At best...'

Heinz pushed Karloff to the side and looked at Baryka's green face.

'There is something I'd like to share with you,' he rasped, shouting over a blaring siren of a passing ambulance. 'But first let me add something to what the croaker had said. There is another variation of smothering people with a plastic bag, used by our special forces... Actually, various special forces around the world use it. Imagine a modern, well-equipped operating theatre. You are lying down, tied to a table, as you would during an operation. You are intubated, just like before surgery. A guy in white scrubs and a surgical mask gives you an injection. It's a drug that relaxes your muscles of respiration. For example infamous Pavulon. Remember the case of "Skin Hunters" from Łódź?'

He didn't wait for Baryka's answer.

'You start suffocating,' Heinz rasped on. 'What you feel is an animal-like fear of dying. You are fully aware that you are about to die. Then they give you an antidote and you start breathing. And the cycle repeats. Pavulon. Antidote.' Heinz's fingers pushed hard like knives into the Deputy Commissioner's shoulders. Atemi points. Weak points on the human body. Compared to Atemi points the Achilles heel – as Sensei Kastoriadis used to say – was child's play. By the way, I wonder where Lambros had learnt that term, thought Heinz. 'Pavulon. Antidote. Pavulon. Antidote...' Heinz repeated as if in a trance, poking at Baryka's armpits. 'How many times could you die like that?'

'Are you saying...' The officer, who had only just lost his virginity, got his voice back. 'Are you saying that special forces have something to do with this killing?'

'You don't understand.' Heinz took a step back away from his victim. 'But perhaps you will get there eventually... Perhaps...

That was a lesson. Now, it's time to sum up. Firstly, never call the Prosecutor to ask if he is coming to the autopsy. Nine times out of ten they don't come anyway. They try to avoid unpleasant experiences. But he will remember your name now and next time you call him with a really important issue, he will use some excuse to get rid of you.'

'The guy knows what he is talking about,' Karloff laughed.

'And another lesson. Those two on the table looked rather inconspicuous, didn't they? You couldn't tell what they went through before they died. But you can be sure that they suffered. They suffered like hell. Your puking is like an innocent caress in comparison. So never speak of the victims with disrespect. Even when you are trying to disguise your own lack of confidence or just your retching. Don't make fun of them. They are not just some "stiffs", understood? And finally...' Heinz paused. 'The third lesson. You will have to dish out for dry cleaning or eco laundrette. You've barfed all over your jacket.'

Baryka looked down. There were contrasting stains on the beige leather by the pocket on the right-hand side and on the sleeve.

'Fuck... Oh, fuck, fuck, fuck...' The Deputy Commissioner was rubbing the stains with vehemence. 'What will Jolka say? She really likes this jacket...'

'I will tell you something else,' Heinz interrupted. 'When you pick your jacket up from the dry cleaners, you will sense that something is still wrong. You know why? Because a dead body's smell clings to leather like there is no tomorrow. Never come here,' he nodded towards the entrance to the forensic medicine laboratory, 'dressed like that. Or to a crime scene if there is a chance you could find a decomposing body there. That's your lesson number four. Enough of it.'

He combed the grey hair on his temples with his fingers.

He travelled to the Mostowski Palace with Karloff while Baryka went to look for dry cleaners. They didn't talk on the way.

'Why did you treat him like that?' Karloff finally asked when they were entering the courtyard. 'Why all the preaching on respect for the victims? They are dead, and the little boy needs to do whatever he can to stop being a little boy as soon as possible...'

'You should also add,' Heinz said with bitterness, 'that the future belongs to the likes of him. Young and ambitious... You will still be a deputy commissioner while he will be climbing up the ladder. And he might want to take it out on you...'

'You didn't answer my question. And anyway, Heinz, why are you so aggressive?'

'Why I treated him like that?' Heinz was staring vacantly into the front windscreen. 'One day I will tell you.'

'Tell me now!' Karloff lost control.

Heinz looked him straight in the eyes.

'OK. Let's see if my story thrills you.'

Karloff did a U-turn with screeching tyres. Heinz noticed that the officer standing in front of the police station looked at their car with curiosity. Five minutes later they were sitting in a pub at Bankowy Square.

10

IT ALL STARTED on a cloudy September day in 2011 in Mysłowice when the police entered a burnt house. In the garden at the back they found the charred body of a young woman. It was obvious how she had died. The murderer had made her sit in a chair and tied her hands to the back of it. Then he poured petrol all over her and lit the fire. Nobody in this peaceful neighbourhood heard screams of the victim being burnt alive.

That was when Rudolf Heinz joined the investigation. *Voodoo Child*. A proper witch doctor's child. A profiler trained in Quantico and Liverpool, a police officer who – as they used to say – could conjure up the criminal when the others were forever analysing secured evidence and reading through the interrogation transcripts for the hundredth time. But every witch doctor's child has a dark side too. And Heinz was no exception. The time spent in rehab after the family tragedy and the deep depression that came afterwards stopped his climb up the ladder of the police career. His colleagues were getting promoted while he remained the eternal deputy commissioner. In the end he wanted to leave the police and had this crazy idea of fulfilling his life dream – playing rock hits in pubs. He was ready to give notice when this happened.

There was evidence left on the plot in Mysłowice. Four small dents in the ground. Heinz actually suggested looking for them. He spent hours thinking about what the murderer did. He didn't just kill, oh no. This was an execution. He burnt at the stake. Like an inquisitor. Heinz's suspicions were confirmed when the victim's background was checked. The woman, officially registered as unemployed, was in reality a member of the oldest profession in the world. And she was doing quite well amongst the numerous competitors. But burning her alive was not enough for the murderer. It was just a morning bath. Cleansing the body. He had to serve the punishment in another way too. What was he doing when he lit the rag, which he used as a fuse? Heinz figured it out. The murderer was talking. He was talking to the woman. He was telling her why he was going to kill her and how he was going to do it. How she would suffer. He took another chair out to the garden and sat opposite her. Not too close, because close proximity might result in compassion unexpectedly taking over at the last minute. And not too far away either, so as to maintain the contact. He sat there to feast on her fear, to watch her burn. Four indentations in the ground made by the legs of the chair were found three metres from the burnt body. Heinz knew how it had been done, but he still didn't know where to look for the perpetrator.

The sexual context of the crime didn't make it any easier to single out the murderer. The Inquisitor struck again two weeks later in Tarnowskie Góry. The scenario was similar. A plot of land on the edge of a street, no witnesses, middle of the day. The victim was tied to a chair with an electric cable. Four indentations in the ground not far from the body. There were two differences though. This time the Inquisitor killed a man. And the man well-known to the police. The guy was a 'guardian' of Katowice prostitutes.

'One pimp less. Good riddance,' Tarnowskie Góry police officers said. 'But to do something like that?'

Two cables were hanging from the victim's ears. At some point the murderer closed the electrical circuit. The victim's t-shirt was drenched in blood. When the man was dying from electrocution, he bit his tongue off and that resulted in heavy bleeding. First time round it was death at the stake and now the electric chair. And, invariably, the executioner's speech before the execution. The speech of the executioner who then became the witness of the execution and absolved himself.

Then Heinz came up with an idea, which shook the Voivodeship Police Station in Katowice. Krygier, the Head of the Criminal Unit, must remember that meeting very well.

'Of course I might be wrong,' Heinz suggested to his colleagues. 'But somehow I don't think he is a sexual maniac. He's an avenger. Somebody, who kills for ideals. Somebody who burns the evil out. And he uses the only fully destructive force – fire. I don't need to tell you,' he was reporting expertly, 'that every professional will choose fire if they want to avoid trouble and leaving any evidence. Blood may be everywhere. Sometimes its presence seems to defy the rules of physics. And yet it is there. Basically you can't hide it with one hundred per cent certainty. With one exception...'

'You can kill and then burn the building,' one of the colleagues said, Heinz couldn't remember who that was. 'Is that what you are talking about?'

'Yes. Fire devours everything. It's an absolute recipe. Antibiotic of antibiotics in the crime world. Fire devours flesh. There are stories about fire – and our perpetrator likes telling stories – devouring the soul. In Mysłowice the body was burnt, because the victim used her body for work and sinned. In Tarnowskie Góry the murderer focused on the head itself, because the "guardian" of the girls was the brain, the organiser. So he was given a "mercy seat".'

'A what?'

'A mercy seat. There is this song about a guy who is about to be executed on an electric chair...'

'Are you saying that this Inquisitor of yours listens to rock?'

'No. But he chooses his method of punishment carefully. And with precision. Planning turns him on, you know? It's often the case with serial killers.'

'Wait a minute,' Heinz remembered the remark made by the Prosecutor working on the case, who was also present at the meeting. 'In the second case it is not burning but electrocution that we are talking about.'

'But the offender knows very well how the electric chair works,' Heinz answered. 'I'm sure that he knows descriptions of convicts's heads burning, their hair burning, of the stench of burning flesh permeating the whole prison...' He took a deep breath. 'Therefore I have an idea...' They were all listening to him intently. 'What I'm trying to say is... The perpetrator thinks of the punishment in literal terms. The body committed the offence, so let's burn the body. You were a pimp and you organised whores' work, so let's burn your brain. In my opinion we should also think in literal terms about the name the Inquisitor that we have given him. Because he is an inquisitor.'

'Meaning?' Krygier bit his lip.

'Meaning it could be a priest... A former priest. Or a monk... Enough of it.'

On many ocassions Heinz wondered what the sound of silence was like. The one from the old Simon and Garfunkel song. Once in his lifetime, at that very meeting, he experienced its real sound.

Finally Krygier said softly:

'Oi, Hippie, this time you really got carried away.'

And then everybody started shouting over each other. The Prosecutor went very red in the face. There were fists banging on the table and papers thrown around. Eventually somebody went to fetch a bottle of vodka.

'The Commandant will never buy this,' Krygier tried persuading more calmly after two rounds of vodka. 'The authorities have a good relationship with our bishop and diplomacy is of utmost importance.'

In the end they agreed that Heinz would contact priests from the Silesian diocese. He managed to compile a list of priests who left the priesthood. He was especially interested in those who were diagnosed with mental issues. Perhaps it wasn't a coincidence that the Inquisitor was the prosecutor at times, the executioner at times and always the witness of the execution. The woman from Mysłowice and the man from Tarnowskie Góry were both tied to the chairs with the same electrical cable of 3 mm diameter. In the case of the second killing there were traces of hazelnut cream on the victim's wrists.

Heinz made another phone call. He heard laughter at first and then an echo of his own hoarse voice.

'An old trick. A little professional secret.' Heinz's interlocutor was an electrician with thirty years' experience and qualifications in installing electrical wiring. 'Greasy cream. Hazelnut or not.' Again he heard laughter that made him think of a bad horror film. 'Doesn't matter. You smear it all over the cables so they go easily into aluminium pipes. Into the casing. Especially when it is an old installation. And, by the way, when in trouble you know who to call, eh?'

He found him in the end. Jerzy Urbaniak, a priest from Katowice. Even when he was still a priest, he was considered weird. Supposedly he got worse when he left the priesthood. That's what his sister said. Urbaniak lived with her. He always had a knack for technical things. He worked for years as an electrician in Katowice and Sosnowiec.

That was when Heinz started making mistakes. He was too confident and that was his undoing. That's the way it goes. One mistake provokes another mistake. Heinz did something that even police officers with much less experience wouldn't do. He decided to talk to Urbaniak on his own, without witnesses. To make sure that he was right before the final confrontation.

Luckily he left a note at work explaining what his plans were. He was sure that Urbaniak's sister wouldn't let slip that she had been asked questions by a police officer. He didn't foresee that she would see him by chance during a banal activity of watering her plants and that she would recognise him. And tell her brother. Later, when he was climbing the stairs to the second floor of a sleepy *familok* building in Nikiszowiec, which looked like it was transported straight from one of Kazimierz Kutz's films, he forgot the lesson of the master of all karate fighters, Gichin Funakoshi: 'When you enter a household you face thousands of enemies.' Heinz didn't anticipate being attacked by the former priest. Somehow... Somehow this was unthinkable. Later the Inquisitor kicked his sister out of the flat. She ran to the neighbours and called the ambulance and the police. When Heinz regained consciousness, he was sitting tied to a chair, intoxicated with the smell of petrol.

He was praying then, for the first time in years. And – of that he was certain – for the last time in his life. As if the flames engulfing his body were burning out the faith in him once and for all. The cobblestones in Nikiszowiec filled with the police, ambulances and fire brigade. Brick *familok* buildings, a rust-coloured flame in the window on the second floor and the sunset at the end of a Polish Indian summer created a harmony of colours.

Never, even years later, did Heinz understand two things: he didn't know why the police came so fast and why – seeing that they were there – they didn't use a 'dynamic detainment' procedure. Why didn't they simply kill the motherfucker?

The specialist hospital in Siemianowice Śląskie fought for the life of one more burns patient who didn't want to live. Heinz went through several skin grafts. He was unconscious and delirious for days. When he regained consciousness, he couldn't stop thinking that it would have been better if they hadn't saved him.

And the Inquisitor managed to avoid a life sentence. The court ordered a psychiatric observation and then decided that Jerzy Urbaniak, a former priest, was not sane at the time of the offence. Heinz couldn't be present at court due to his rehabilitation. He did, however, give evidence in writing, but the court turned a blind eye to it, even though Heinz proved that the Inquisitor's actions were as sane and methodical as if he was Garry Kasparov playing a round of chess. Urbaniak ended up in the psychiatric institution on a maximum security ward.

Enough of it.

**

It was the middle of the day and the heat was unbearable. Heinz took off his jacket. The waitress twitched at the sight of scars on the forearm of a man with shabby facial hair.

'Fuck it all,' Heinz pointed to his arm. 'The thing is... The thing is, Karloff...'

He didn't finish. He wanted to say that when he was burning in that chair and looking into the Inquisitor's eyes, eyes shining with excitement, his life was being burnt out of him together with his flesh. What was best in Heinz was being burnt out.

He had it all at the tip of his tongue, but he decided that there was no reason to confide in Karloff. Why should he trust him? After all everybody here played for themselves.

Karloff was silent. He got up, went to the bar and only then got his voice back. He placed an order and drank three glasses of vodka at the speed of a sprinter running for 100 metres. When he came back, he leant on the tabletop and rocked the table as if he was dancing salsa.

'Your story didn't thrill me, Heinz... It didn't thrill me one little bit. But,' he goggled at Heinz, 'you can count on me. And there might be two more people who will help you. Of course...' he paused. 'All within reason.'

11

AT THE POLICE STATION Heinz flicked through the victims' belongings. He was surprised to see designer trousers, Diesel and Levi's, polo shirts and trainers. This was not a seminarist's wardrobe as he had imagined it. You didn't even have to be a worldly stylist or a reader of fashion magazines to understand that the clothes the seminarists were wearing when they were found would be more fitting on club regulars going through a selection process each time they wanted to enter an establishment than on students of an ascetic theological college. True, times have changed, nowadays priests drive Maybachs and Jaguars, their faces appear on wine labels and they themselves become kind of church managers, but for it all to start so early...? Karloff was watching with astonishment as Heinz wrote down the clothes' brand names in silence. In the pocket of one of the garments there was a piece of paper with a college professor's telephone number. Did the murderer leave it there on purpose or did he miss it? Perhaps he wanted to point at something or somebody?

'Which one had the note with the telephone number?' Heinz opened his mouth for the first time in a long while.

'Rakowiecki.' Karloff pointed to clothes scattered around. 'He was wearing the pale, leather jacket.'

Light-coloured, leather jacket. Almost beige. Has Virgin

taken his leather to the dry cleaners yet, Heinz wondered? And what did Jolka say?

He checked the pockets of the other, thicker jacket of grey, fleece-like fabric.

'It doesn't hurt to check again,' he mumbled, seeing Karloff's aggrieved look.

He also checked the soles of the shoes. He put one pair to the side and had a good look at the other. He squinted his eyes, put one hand into the red-and-white Puma and stepped closer to the window. He beckoned Karloff to follow.

'Can you see that?' he pointed to the almost unblemished tread. 'What's that?'

The light-coloured sole was in a practically ideal state. The boy has either only just bought those Pumas or hasn't worn them much. The sole, with tens of small protrusions and linear grooves, made Heinz think of the surface of the Moon. He thought of TV commercials. Technology from outer space. *Comfort in life, convenience in the time of death* – he composed his own advertising line spontaneously. There was something stuck to the instep, between two protruding points. It looked like a pebble. Heinz took a pen out of his jacket's pocket and tinkered with the shoe. No. That was not a pebble.

'What's that?' he repeated.

Karloff shrugged.

'No idea.'

'Where did it come from? Does it match the ground where you found the victims? Is that a thorn or an insect?' Heinz showered Karloff with questions.

The scar on the police officer's face lengthened. But this time the Deputy Commissioner was not smiling.

'Listen to me carefully... We have two dead bodies, heads in plastic bags, painted triangles and the Pope's time of death... And you...' he pointed to the shoe. 'And you come with some shit on the shoe. What the fuck are you thinking?' Karloff lost control.

'That you are some Jodie Foster and the game we are playing is called *The Silence of the Lambs*? Yeah...' he spread his hands in a dramatic gesture and drawled, demonstrating his acting skills. 'I reckon this is a cocoon of *Erebus odora*, also known as the Black Witch moth. I remembered that name because that's what I used to call my girlfriend...' Oh, you are so lovely, Karloff. 'Give us a moment and we will probably find a moth that lives on tears too. In a butthole of one of those faggots!'

Karloff hadn't seen *The Battle of Algiers*, but the plot of *The Silence of the Lambs* he knew inside out. Minus the moth in the butthole, of course.

'I'm not thinking anything.' Heinz was trying to stay calm. 'Let's just check what it is. It's probably not important, but let's do it, just in case. OK?' He put his hand on Karloff's shoulder.

'As you wish. I will give it to the boys from the criminal lab. They should be able to sort it out.'

'I wouldn't want to rush them...' Heinz was trying to sound as conciliatory as possible. 'However please tell them to do it ASAP.'

They packed the clothes back into black plastic bags and left. Heinz was told that he wouldn't get the company car before tomorrow, so he had to ask again to be given a lift to the Olympic Centre.

On his way to the escalators he saw the policewoman he met yesterday at the team meeting. She had just come out of one of the rooms. Black, army boots, short hair the colour of tar, the rest in the same funerary style. Black Witch, he thought. A sullen singer from a Gothic rock festival. He approached her.

'Excuse me, I have one question... We met yesterday...' His embarrassment was growing.

'Yes, I remember. Commissioner Heinz, in some circles known as the "nice dude"...'

'Glad to hear that,' he said dismissively. It didn't take them long to develop quite an opinion about him. 'I'd like to ask you something, as a woman...'

The Black Witch froze.

'It's to do with nails. How do you call it when nails have a rectangular shape and a white, two- to three-millimetre-wide strip?'

The female police officer stayed silent for a bit longer than she should have.

'It's called a French Manicure. Apart from being a woman I am also a Commissioner. Jolanta Biedrzycka. You can call me Jolka. Are you thinking of getting French nails?'

Jolka. *What will Jolka say?* Heinz remembered. Could it be the same Jolka? Words of Deputy Commissioner Baryka, deflowered today at Oczki Street, kept coming back like an echo.

'Hey! You didn't answer my question, sir...' *Erebus odora* was staring at the profiler. Dark rings made her eyes seem even bigger.

'I'm sorry... Could you please, ma'am... Jolka, could you...'

'I could,' she interrupted. 'I asked if you were planning to get French nails. Men quite like it nowadays. Remember the first and second series of *Big Brother*? There was a bloke who shagged this bird in a jacuzzi for everybody to see on the telly. Bubbles flew into the camera... He used to sport French nails...'

They talked for a while longer. The lift stopped a few times on their floor and then went downstairs. Finally Commissioner Biedrzycka looked at her big watch, which would look more in place on a man's wrist. They said their goodbyes.

Heinz heard her heavy boots striking an even, firm rhythm on the stairs.

He was relieved to see that they assigned him a different driver. As soon as he got to Wybrzeże Gdyńskie, he understood why the building of the Polish Olympic Committee was ironically called the Palace. The overwhelming opulence of the building remained in stark contrast with the meagre achievements of Polish sportsmen, usually only winning medals in some peculiar sports. Precision flying, duplicate bridge, strength athletics. That's what we are good at. As well as

– he remembered the questionable joke – two-man bobsleigh on natural tracks.

They went past the VIP parking lot with several cars, mostly SUVs.

'I'll have a look. Won't be long,' he told the driver, who reached into his glove compartment without a word of comment and took out *Our Legia Team*.

Heinz carried a folder with photographic evidence and plans of the terrain. He looked towards green scrubs and several massive trees. He noticed that somebody was watching him from the warden's box. The doors opened and a short man in his sixties appeared. Heinz approached him.

'It was there, sir,' the warden pointed. 'At the end of the main path, where the bushes start. Under that tree over there. You are here because of those two, aren't you? I can't go with you, because somebody might want to leave the parking lot. You go to take a leak in the bushes, you are gone for some thirty seconds and here...' he nodded towards cross-country vehicles, 'whole hell breaks loose. As if those few seconds could really make a difference.'

Heinz didn't say anything. The silence stretched and the man, who was holding the door to the warden's box with his hand, lost his confidence.

'Unless you have some other business...'

'No. How did you know I was here because of those two?'

The man straightened up.

'I can read people, sir.'

He can read people. Well, let's see.

'So how exactly did you figure it out?'

Heinz approached the warden closer. His black shirt was adorned with a nametag that said 'Zubrzycki'.

'A man with a driver. Alone. With a folder in his hand. You are not a journalist. You are too old, nowadays they only send kids. Who could you be then? Must be the forces. Simple...

Hey, so what do you have there? Their pictures?' He looked at the grey folder.

'I understand you were not here when they were found...'

'And thank God for that! There are nicer ways to spend a night,' the warden cackled.

'But I guess you have shifts at different times of day,' Heinz wasn't giving up. 'Perhaps you noticed something unusual recently... Some unexpected guests... Perhaps somebody was having a look around?'

'And what could be so unusual about it? We have a beautiful April, it's warm. In the evening cars drive up here every few moments and, you know...'

'I don't know,' Heinz interrupted quickly.

'Sodomites, sir,' the man whispered. 'Where is this country heading? Either poofs or Jews or Germans,' he pointed to a building in the background of the Olympic Centre. 'See the signboard? Deutsche something something... And you want this country to thrive? Apart from that,' the warden wouldn't stop talking, 'it was midweek. The place is at its busiest at weekends. You can see for yourself,' he pointed towards Wisłostrada Street, 'dog training here and,' he turned to the right, 'horse-riding there. Madness. That's what weekends are like. But during the week it's just poofs...'

Heinz rummaged through his pockets, always stuffed with useless pieces of paper. His wallet, his mobile phone. As usual, he couldn't find anything. Finally he took out a blank scrap of paper and a pen.

'You really do have a knack for reading people,' he said. 'I will give you my telephone number. If you remember anything else, please give me a call at any time of the day...'

'And who should I ask for?

The man's eyes were alert now.

'Commissioner...' he hesitated. 'Commissioner Krakowiak,' he wrote below the number.

When putting his pen back into the pocket, he felt a stack of business cards.

Control. Self-control. You give your business card instinctively. You never know when people might remember something seemingly unimportant. But this time he behaved differently. *Either poofs or Jews or Germans.* He imagined the warden's face upon reading a German sounding name on the business card: Heinz. Or the first name: Rudolf.

He started towards the place where the bodies were found.

He opened the folder and looked at the pictures. Yes, it must have been here. That was the place. His mouth went dry. He closed his eyes.

The victims were left by the main pathway. Bang in the middle of the stage. If it was a stage indeed... All you needed was to park the car across the road, then take the bodies out and lay them down by the tree. Heinz walked further to the right, where the less used path went down, all the way to a fallen birch tree. Behind the tree the track towards the Vistula was even more overgrown. He turned around and a few metres away he saw the corner of the wire fence surrounding the Olympic Centre. He suddenly remembered Igor Mitoraj's statue of Icarus with a wing broken off, which was standing in front of the Palace. Icarus – a symbol of noble naivety and failure – fitted in with the seminarists' bodies in a strange way. Who knows? Better remember that association for later, just in case.

The ground was getting more and more boggy. He decided to go back. He returned to the spot where the seminarists' bodies were found. He closed his eyes again.

He imagined it was night-time and a car was approaching. He was 90 per cent sure it was a lone perpetrator. Why? Because murderers, if they work in groups, usually avoid stagings like this one. What turns them on is working together, co-operation with others. Whenever there are two or more killers, they always hide the body. The risk of one of the accomplices spilling the guts or the police finding it by accident is statistically higher. On top of that there were several less obvious details attesting that the murderer worked alone. For example the fact that he drove all the way to the spot, where one person could easily lay down two heavy, limp bodies.

No, not lay down. Arrange.

But why did he take the risk of leaving them by the main footpath? Why didn't he go where it would be safer, towards the fallen birch?

Heinz's mind was working at full speed.

A lonely murderer wouldn't be able to carry the bodies there. It was too much effort for one man. A man too weak and unfit or simply too old for such stunts. Or perhaps he was afraid that his car would conk out on the rough terrain by the Vistula? Perhaps he owns a shoddy car? That's not impossible. Nevertheless, not everybody has the guts to move the body from the crime scene and transport it to a different, carefully selected place.

Transporting a dead body. In this case – two dead bodies. Most likely in a trunk. In *popiełuszka* – he recalled the conversation in the hotel bar. Whoever transports two dead bodies must have nerves of steel. After all he might be stopped by the traffic police. Some bored, moustachioed sergeant stops you. Or you get a flat tyre. Somebody decides to help you. And all your plans suddenly go pear-shaped.

Heinz looked around once more. There was a petrol station several hundred metres to the left. He was certain the police carefully checked the CCTV footage from the 11th and 12th of April. He turned around. A wide thread of Wisłostrada Street cut across enormous, green stretches of land. There was a pub on the other side of the road, a relic of once numerous bars lined along the river. The guys from the Metropolitan Police probably paid there a visit too.

He heard birds singing by the Vistula.

We are dealing either with a mentally ill individual who is unaware of the risk or with a total desperado. With a desperado, who thought everything through in the smallest detail. The murderer knew what he was doing. He left no space for improvisation. The murderer reserved time to paint triangles and the Pope's time of death in lipstick. Unless he did it beforehand, in the place where he killed the boys. This way or the other, it was premeditated. He knew the seminarists were gay. Hence the triangles. Hence the homosexuals' rendezvous place.

Read the traces, even the faint ones, Heinz said to himself. It all matters. Sexual orientation is key. As well as the fact that the victims studied in the same theological college. That has to be important.

He focused on the victims now. The murderer staged a show, but the victims also played their parts before they died. New designer clothing. Shoes. They were wearing clothes worth at least a thousand złoty each. Boys who go to beauty salons and sport French nails. This was not a grey world of the monks shut away in their cells. They went out to perform. To pull. For a set-up rendezvous. Like male whores, Heinz thought frantically. They expected to be back late at night, hence warm jackets. He checked in the papers that the 11th of April in Warsaw was a warm day. Real summer weather. But nights in April can still be cool. The boys were well prepared. But then something unexpected happened. Somebody, the person who smothered them, knew of their plans. Or managed to find out enough to be able to act with a clockwork precision.

The images in Heinz's head were similar to a Prodigy music video. Now he could see the two dead bodies on the cold autopsy tables. Abrasions on wrists and ankles. Similar marks on the lips. They strained and screamed. Why? Because the murderer probably tied them to the chairs and taped their mouths. He was worried that somebody might hear their screams.

Why didn't he kill them right away? Why did he tear the tape off their mouths? How did it all go?

There was a slight breeze and Heinz felt the damp shirt clinging to his body. He shivered.

He imagined the scene again. The murderer keeps them somewhere shut away. Perhaps in a cellar. Perhaps in a summer house. He chokes them a bit and then, when there is no oxygen left, gives them hope. He rips the tape off their mouths. He wants to listen.

You motherfucker, what did you want to hear? Begging for mercy? No, that's not what it was about. That's not what turned you on.

Heinz shivered again, but this time it wasn't caused by the breeze coming from the direction of the river. He remembered himself sitting with his arms and legs tied to a chair, he remembered the smiling Inquisitor leaning towards him.

'Confess your sins,' he heard then, in that old Silesian flat.

The seminarists were supposed to confess as well, he thought. The murderer wanted them to confess. Whatever that meant. He was smothering them and then letting go. He was waiting. And they were dying and rising from the dead.

Heinz buttoned his corduroy jacket. No, there was no element of improvisation here. Self-control. Full control. He remembered what he was thinking when he gave the warden a piece of paper with his telephone number. The same could be said about the murderer.

For a long while he stared into the spot where the bodies were, as if he wanted to conjure the ghost of the perpetrator. Or, even better, not just his ghost.

Sex for money. Seminarists. Confession. The last confession. Unburdening of your sins as an element of a crusade. He recalled the statistics. Few murderers killed for religious reasons, except for insane ones thinking they were tools in the hands of God. Even in such a fucked-up country like the United

States, not to mention Poland. Although, admittedly, famous serial killers such as Henry Lee Lucas and Ottis Toole declared that they belonged to the Satanic sect 'Hand of Death' and Richard Ramirez showed a pentagram tattooed on his hand during his trial. But that does not change the fact that serial killings for religious reasons remain a rarity. And here we have the Pope's fucking time of death. The numbers, painted in pink lipstick, which alarmed the police all over Poland.

Richard Ramirez. He remembered the man who looked just like the Doors' Jim Morrison in his mirrored glasses. The motherfucker had a nickname, 'Night Stalker'. I wonder, Heinz thought, what are they going to call our seminarists' connoisseur? If he ever reappears... the 'Bag Preacher'? 'Karol's Son'? Or perhaps the 'Bloody Olympian', considering where the bodies were found?

He sank into the passenger seat. He was tired. He had a bad night. He decided to go back to the hotel and get some sleep.

He smelt it when they started moving.

'You were walking and walking and you must have stepped in something, Commissioner,' he heard the driver's voice. 'It's springtime: dogs' poo resurfaces.'

They stopped, so that Heinz could wipe the sole of his shoe. When he was examining the now clean sole, he remembered the trainers of one of the victims and the strange trace on its sole.

No element of improvisation. No mistakes. Was it really?

12

SHE LAUGHED. She was doomed.

Her eyes widened, her lips parted suddenly, revealing wrinkles hidden under the thick layer of make-up. He heard loud, guttural laughter and noticed her abundant breasts billowing heavily. No, he didn't find her beautiful anymore. Or loving, or delicate. Suddenly, as if an invisible partition was removed, he saw her for who she really was. He realised that her ageing body was just heaps of fat. He noticed her boorishness and uncouthness. He finally understood that she was just like all the others.

The woman was still laughing. More, she pointed a finger with chipped pink nail varnish at him. When he saw that finger aiming at him, he took a step back and shuddered. His sisters, then female classmates and teachers used to point at him in the same way. Pointed fingers and laughter. The first stage of torture and humiliation.

'Hey, little boy, look at you, you are blushing! You went all red, you know? Your cheeks are as red as boiled lobster. Look, like this!' She puffed out her cheeks and pinched them. She let the air out with a whoosh and started laughing again. 'Lobster, lobster!' Suddenly she went serious. 'You are terribly shy. I just wanted you to kiss me...' She narrowed her eyes and started beckoning him closer. 'Come on...'

You are just like all of them, he thought. They all want the same. To make a fool out of me.

He took a step backwards towards the door.

'I wi-i-ill go make so-o-me tea.'

She laughed. He noticed that one of her central incisors was pink, the shade of her lipstick and nail varnish.

'And you have a stammer too,' she sighed.

He went to the kitchen. He opened the tap and was staring into permanent dark stains on the sink. Just like spots on the hands of a sick old person. Just like spots on the hands of his aunt who raised him and his two elder sisters. The aunt, who started visiting his bedroom when he turned ten. He lived on his own now, in a derelict house. His age was a mystery to everybody. Some people look the same at the age of fifteen and in their forties. They look equally awful. He rolled up his sleeves. There were dandruff flakes on his black shirt. He has been struggling with dandruff for the last twenty years. He felt a wave of warmth on his cheeks again. Thank goodness he was here, in the kitchen, on his own.

He stared into the sink plughole, at water going down, drowning out the woman's laughter. He was sure that this fat, laughing whore was now sitting comfortably on the sofa, waiting for his return. He recalled the image from a moment ago, when her eyes opened wide in surprise. Her irises were not hazel but green. Just like the other woman's, the one he punished in the Aniołów Woods.

'She is just like all of them,' he murmured.

'Did you say something?' she yelled.

'N-no. No-o-othing.'

He cut the lemon with too much strength and nicked his thumb. He looked at his blood mixing with the sour juice. He gritted his teeth. It hurt. Soon she will be the one hurting. A lot.

When he came back to the room with a plaster on his left thumb and tea in his right hand, he saw that she tilted her head and was busy rummaging through her handbag. All you needed was to hit her hard. Perhaps just once.

You are dead. To me you are already dead.

'How about,' he put the tea on the table, 'we go for a walk the day a-a-after tomorrow? The weather is supposed to be good this week...'

'How about tomorrow? I'm doing the morning shift again... I finish at three.'

'Tomorrow is not good for me. I have a me-e-eting at the club.'

She sighed.

'Oh, yeah, I forgot. That club of yours. And that president geezer that I saw once. The one with a little Hitler moustache...'

'Don't make fun of Jurek. He is a grrre-ea-at guy. So, day after tomorrow?'

'Why not?' she said. 'Perhaps you will be more daring then.'

She got up and switched the TV on.

Don't you worry, I will be more daring, he thought. I'm always daring in the woods.

You have no idea.

13

PERSISTENT KNOCKING woke him up. Confused, he looked around the room, which was steeped in darkness. It was dark outside, he must have slept for a good few hours. He went to the door and opened it. Karloff held onto the doorframe, as if he wanted to pull it out and take it somewhere with him. He tilted his head forward. Even in the dim light Heinz could see the beginnings of a bald patch. He also smelt undigested alcohol. For some reason Heinz thought that the police officer standing in his doorway was sobbing.

'You did not answer the phone,' Karloff smiled uncertainly and his head jerked up again. 'There is this... There is this company party going on in Mokotów. I thought perhaps you would like to join us. That would give you a chance to get to know the boys better... And tomorrow... ' He hiccupped. 'Tomorrow we will get busy.'

Get to know the boys better. He didn't feel like it at all, but he knew he was dependent on their help. At least if he didn't want them to hinder, make his life miserable and backstab him. On top of that he didn't know the city, didn't have any contacts or connections to the right people. And the dead seminarists' case – in this respect he was in agreement with Osuch – needed to be run in many directions simultaneously. He could see a tiny light in the tunnel and felt that he was slowly beginning to understand what had happened to those two impeccably dressed, well-groomed boys from the theological college, but he knew he needed to tread carefully. Perhaps he should really go with Karloff? If nothing else, to get him off his back.

'I can see that you've made up your mind,' Karloff laughed. 'I'll wait in the car. What?' he added when Heinz sent him a surprised look. 'After all I'm a police officer, so I'm allowed, aren't I? Fuck breathalysers.'

And he breathed vodka straight into Heinz's face.

They went to Regeneration in Puławska Street. On their way there Heinz was told that it was a fashionable place with more artists per square metre than anywhere else in the city. The car kept jumping up and down on Puławska Street ridden with holes. Heinz had to listen to a good mouthful addressed at the Warsaw authorities.

'My uncle came to visit recently.' Karloff kept manoeuvring to avoid the biggest craters in the road. 'He ordered a cab and asked to be taken to Puławska. The cabbie drove for a bit and then said that he would not go down Puławska because he didn't want to wreck his car. Thankfully Uncle made a note of the registration plate...'

Suddenly Karloff swerved into the middle lane, trying to avoid another obstacle. They heard furious tooting from the car behind them.

'What you honking for, prick?' Karloff looked into his rear-view mirror. 'So Uncle wrote down the number and I paid the cabbie a visit and taught him a lesson... As a result he gave back the money my Uncle paid for the ride. Justice triumphed yet again, no?'

They parked the car and crossed the street. They went by Matejko's statue accompanied by Stańczyk who looked just like Matejko himself, only – as Karloff in the role of a city guide explained – in the last stages of anorexia. They passed the Moor House dotted with graffiti stencils and finally they were there.

The first people Heinz saw were two thirty-year-olds. The taller one was wearing something that made Heinz think of ancient chitons. But he couldn't remember if Greeks used to combine it with silk pink shawls encrusted with imitations of gemstones. The other man had a black jumper on, surely inherited from some dissenter of the 1980s. The strangest of all was the dissenter's highlighted hair. It was clear proof that the guy had already been transported from the ancient times to the metrosexual era, when the world is not ruled by sportsmen and film stars anymore, but by hairdressers, make-up artists and dancers. The Greek in the chiton made a rectangle from his thumbs and index fingers. He was staring through it at the aluminium pipes running under the ceiling.

'Yes,' he said to himself. 'We will frame it like that. And then cut, different angle and back to the main music theme.' He stretched his hands, as if he was conducting an orchestra or saying a mass.

'Brilliant,' the one in the dissenter's jumper whispered. 'I would never have thought of it myself.'

Give them a moment and they will have an orgasm, Heinz thought and started towards a round table where several hands were waving to them. He saw two familiar faces. One was Chlaściak, the officer with yellow teeth, the other was Baryka. The Deputy Commissioner was wearing a faded denim jacket.

So, getting rid of vomit stains from leather was not that easy after all.

'We made a bet that you wouldn't be able to drag him here.' Chlaściak looked at Karloff, trying to outshout the noise.

'Welcome, Dirty Harry!' laughed a man Heinz didn't know. 'I always wanted to have a jacket like yours. Those patches on the elbows...'

'Come to Katowice.' Heinz tried sounding as natural as possible. 'We have a few more jackets of that kind. You won't find them in Warsaw. It seems here a jacket like mine is synonymous with embarrassment.'

Baryka burst out laughing. The rest of them either didn't hear or didn't know what the word 'synonym' meant, Heinz thought.

'We have just been talking about the seminarists,' Baryka said.

'And?' Heinz, like a seasoned boxer, was waiting for the blow.

'In my opinion,' Heinz didn't know the blond guy in glasses, 'it was done by one of the associates of our Papa, may he rest in peace. Perhaps the new cardinal?'

He laughed. His aquiline nose almost touched his chin.

Freddie Kruger. A spitting image of Freddie Kruger, Heinz thought. All he needed was an old hat and knives instead of fingers. But he was no less revolting.

'Joking apart,' Freddie continued, 'it must be coke. One hundred per cent. Plastic bags, erotic stimulation... Do you remember this writer whom they found in a bathtub with a plastic bag on his head? Quite a cemetery could be filled with guys who just tried restricting the oxygen to get a hard-on. And coke gives you a nice rush too, so it is all linked. I'm sure those two owed money for drugs.'

'I didn't think about it...' Heinz looked at the blond guy with exasperation. Light reflected in his glasses.

'But seriously...' Heinz looked at the police officers gathered around. 'Let's talk about something else.'

'He's got a point,' Karloff nodded. 'What do you think? Will the Eyeties outsmart us tomorrow and get the Euros?'

'The Mafia's canniness is one thing, but our shrewdness is another,' a previously silent man joined the conversation. 'It's gonna be us and the Ukrainians who get the championships. Wanna bet? Fifty each.'

Five men automatically reached for their wallets. Just like gunslingers in the Wild West. They looked at Heinz.

'And you?' Karloff asked.

Five pairs of eyes bored into him.

'Football is not my thing,' he mumbled. 'I stopped following...' He pretended that he needed to count. 'Exactly in 1966.'

He got up and went to get a beer. The wall was adorned with the emblem of the People's Republic of Poland, an eagle without a crown. Another retro bar. While waiting for his beer he found out that the dish of the day was vegetable curry with basmati rice. The thirty-year-old in a black jumper – the shorter one – was standing by the bar, still staring at the aluminium pipes.

Somebody whacked him on the kidney. He hissed in pain and turned around.

'Get your beer and come with me,' Karloff said. 'I want you to meet somebody.'

They approached a table where the thirty-year-old in chiton was sitting. His hand was adorned with a ring with a pale green stone. The ring sparkled when the man brought an orange drink to his lips.

'Let me make the introductions,' Karloff panted, as if the distance between the two tables tired him out. 'Jacek Latoszek is a film director. You've probably heard of him.'

He introduced Heinz, who nodded to confirm that he knew the name of the guy.

The director smiled, exposing two rows of unnaturally white teeth.

The pink shawl, the green ring, the orange drink, the white teeth. All those colours could make you dizzy.

'I'm working on a new project.' The director spoke with the speed of a machine gun. 'It's about a boy who wants to start a sports radio station. It's to be a retro station, where old broadcasts get replayed, for instance from the match at Wembley or the Polish boxers fights at the Tokyo Olympics.

The guy has this longing for the past, for something that is no more. You get it?'

Karloff tried to say something, but Latoszek was faster.

'And the boy succeeds, but he is never satisfied. What he really wants is to be a full-blooded journalist. And he finds his topic. He discovers an emerging star of female sprint. He falls in love with her, but then finds out that the sprinter is actually a transvestite. So now our hero doesn't know what to do. Should he reveal the secret and make a reportage of his life or...' He took a sip of the orange drink. 'It's supposed to be something à la Almodóvar. A story about seeking identity. Good, isn't it?'

Heinz nodded again. And it was a second lie in a very short space of time. He had never heard of Latoszek, a directorial dunce who had light years to go to catch up with Almodóvar.

'Not bad.' Karloff was impressed. 'We have a little secret for you too.' He reached into the inside pocket of his jacket and took out two photographs. 'Have you ever seen these two gentlemen? Perhaps...' he paused. 'Perhaps you invited them to a casting session?'

Almodóvar's successor went quiet. He narrowed his eyes and his face was now devoid of the smile, which only a minute ago was plastered, seemingly for good.

He fixed his eyes on the pictures.

'No. I don't know them.' He looked at Karloff and again exposed the row of even teeth. 'I would surely remember such nice bodies.' He licked his lips involuntarily.

'The thing is the bodies are not fresh. Very unfresh.' Karloff shuffled the pictures on the table with the skill of a fortune-teller from the ITV channel, home of astrologers, oracles and palm-readers.

Latoszek became alert again, like an animal roused out of its lair.

'Wait a minute... Aren't these the two...?' He looked at Karloff cunningly.

'The two?' Heinz decided to join in the conversation.

'The two seminarists, right?'

The police officers looked at each other.

'I am a well-connected man, aren't I?' The regular smile was back on Latoszek's face. 'A director needs access to information. There is talk around town about some madman and his crusade against gays... Is that true?'

He looked at the policeman whom he had never met before.

'Do you know them?' Heinz ignored the question and pointed to the photos again.

'I already told you that I don't. But...' Latoszek leant towards his interlocutors and looked around warily. 'I would suggest you go talk to this guy...' He took his business card from the pocket and wrote two words quickly on its back.

Karloff and Heinz looked at the card and then at each other. Karloff whistled softly.

'Why?' Karloff looked piercingly at the director. 'Why,' he repeated, 'should we talk about it with one of the richest people in Poland? A guy who, as they say, might be the number one in the country in a few years' time, and not just in business?'

Latoszek winced.

'There is talk that he likes... so to speak... That he likes to borrow seminarists... But you haven't heard that from me...'

Suddenly it became crowded around the table. The thirty-year-old in a black jumper was back with two giggling blondes.

'Jacek, these ladies would like to talk to you. I told them about your new film. Unless...' He looked at the two silent men. 'Are we interrupting something?'

'You are not interrupting anything.' Latoszek quickly regained his composure and presented the newcomers with one of his well-rehearsed smiles of an African ruler from the post-colonial era. 'We were just talking about the two boys who became an object of an extra Love Parade.' He laughed. 'By the way, that's a good idea for another film.'

Some Love Parade, you motherfucker.

Heinz stared long and hard into the director's face, as if he wanted to remember it really well. This pretentious little stinker already had a place on his list. A list of people to get rid of.

He was sick and tired of the conversation with this fucker. And of the company of other police officers. He went to the toilet and took a leak. On his way back to the table he heard snippets of conversation. He had no doubt who they were talking about.

'What a loser... Some oaf... I simply can't stand him,' he heard Freddie Kruger saying to Baryka.

Heinz sat down and took a sip of beer. They were all talking about football now. He was transported to a place far away, to a flat in Opole painted in bright, happy colours. He remembered the admiration of his mates when his father, Józef Heinz, scored goals for Odra Opole team. And then that moment when the kids suddenly stopped playing with him. When he became the object of mockery. And when his tearful mother told him that they would have to move out of the apartment with big windows and live in a place that made the boy think of a mouse hole. Around the same time little Rudolf noticed that his father, the main striker in the Polish league, who was always a rare visitor at home, stopped showing up altogether. He disappeared. Just like that. A few years later Rudolf understood that his father chose life in the Federal Republic of Germany and scoring goals for his new team as Joseph Heinz. It was 1966. Gomułka and the party would not forgive the Polish bishops for their letter to the German bishops in which the hierarchs *forgave and asked for forgiveness*. German revengists, Werewolf and its inheritors, spies and subversives, as well as Silesian footballers choosing hard German cash and a new life were not even worth the candle.

One way or another, Heinz had more than enough reasons to hate football.

Freddie Kruger got up from the table and wobbled towards the bathrooms. At exactly the same moment Heinz reached for his mobile phone.

'Hello,' he said.

He excused himself from the table and got up to continue the conversation.

Freddie was standing by the sink when he heard talking, the clinking of glasses and bits of music coming through the open door to the toilet. Somebody had just walked in. He couldn't be bothered to look at the newcomer. He was drunk and he could feel it. He knocked the soap to the floor, took his glasses off and put them on a shelf by the sink. He put his head under the tap. The last few months had been like a nightmare from which he still couldn't free himself. Today was a tough day again. He hadn't eaten anything, but kept drinking for a good few hours now. He could feel a bad knot in his stomach. He always felt like that when he was annoyed. And few people annoyed him like that profiler from Katowice, a bighead looking down on football fans, which he considered entertainment for idiots. Some oaf from Silesia. Cold water ran through his hair and around his ears.

I will stick my head under the hand dryer, he thought. I will be all right. Once I regain my balance, I can keep drinking.

He wanted to lift his head, but something was in his way. It felt like tongs tightening on his neck. He jerked his head instinctively, but was not able to lift it up and free himself from the merciless grip. He realised with dread that his face was speeding fast towards the white ceramics. He whacked the top of his nose on the edge of the sink. Before his knees gave in he saw that the water going down the drain turned red. The logo of the sink producer faded in front of his eyes.

14

HEINZ WANTED to get a taxi, but Karloff insisted on giving him a lift. Police officers sitting around the table were quickly dropping off. The party ended when the blond guy came back to the table, supported by Chlaściak. Freddie's shirt was soaked with blood. His eyes were almost invisible in the swollen face.

'I found him in the john,' the police officer with yellow teeth said. 'I think he slipped on a bar of soap. I spotted it on the tiled floor. I don't know if he is OK. He might have a concussion... He keeps going on about some tongs...'

Freddie sank down onto a chair.

'My nose,' he whispered. 'My nose. My nose is broken. Tongs... I was held down by tongs,' he kept mumbling.

Fifteen minutes later Baryka took him to the hospital.

Heinz and Karloff travelled in silence. Suddenly Heinz realised that they were not going in the right direction. It was not a route to his hotel in Praga.

'Where are we going?'

'Take it easy,' Karloff drawled. 'I will take you where you want to go, eventually. I just want to show you something.'

They drove along Żwirki i Wigury Street. By the Soviet Military Cemetery the car turned right into a small alley.

'Let me show you something,' Karloff repeated and jumped out of the car. He quickly reached the nearest car, a Toyota Camra.

Only now did Heinz notice that there were several cars parked in a line behind the Toyota not far from each other. They all switched their lights on and started the engines, as if given an order. He got out of the car and saw Karloff taking his police ID out of the pocket and then dragging a moustachioed man out of the car. The Toyota driver's trousers were down to his knees. Karloff pushed him onto the bonnet and reached inside his pocket.

'Do you know them?' he barked, pointing to the picture. 'Spill the news, and hurry up! I'm sure you know them.'

The man shook like jelly. Other cars were leaving one after another.

'I've never seen them... I swear... I don't know them...'

'Nice car you have here. Is it yours, you motherfucker, or is it a company car?' Karloff jerked the fat man by the lapels of his jacket. 'Company car, eh? Let's see where you work,' he whispered dramatically. 'I wonder what your colleagues will say when they find out that you are... well, you know what... A faggot. I bet their fucking white collars will go yellow with sweat.'

'What's going on? Sir, I have nothing to do with anything, I've never seen those guys.'

An amateur jogger ran past them. When passing the Toyota, he looked nervously at the two men and sped up.

'Then let's ask your friend. Somehow I don't think it's your company's driver.' Karloff went to the passenger door. 'Get out.'

A massive guy in his twenties scrambled out of the car.

'What is it, sucker?' He looked defiantly at Karloff. 'I've already called my father. You are fucked. He is... Well, soon enough you will find out for yourselves... And this one here,' he pointed at the fatty with a moustache. 'He works for me.'

'Sucker?'

In one swift move Karloff pressed the big mouth's face into the windscreen. Give him a moment longer and he would dent the glass with it. The boy's distorted features and his muffled moan reminded Heinz of faces of the two ill-treated seminarists. But the vision of the two dead bodies quickly dissipated and the profiler was again looking at the scared twenty-year-old.

'Hey, chubby, get into the car and switch the windscreen sprinkler on. Chop-chop!' Karloff ordered as if in a trance.

He knows what he is doing, Heinz thought. He's played this game before.

The driver pulled his trousers up and stepped towards the car. A moment later Heinz smelt the familiar smell of detergent.

'Lick it off!' Karloff said to the boy when the foamy liquid covered the windscreen. 'Call me a sucker one more time and I will pour battery acid straight into your mouth.'

The boy tried to break free. In the end Karloff pushed him towards the fence separating the street from allotments.

'Let's go,' he nodded to Heinz.

They jumped into the car like some gangsters fleeing the crime scene. When they pulled out, Karloff turned the radio on. Tina Turner was singing her old hit.

'*Private dancer*...' Karloff hummed, out of tune now and then. 'There, by the cemetery... Plenty of private dancers go there. It's a gay tryst place as popular as the one by the Olympic Centre. One of the regulars might have known our two boys.'

'Aren't you afraid that the big mouth had enough time to write down the numbers?'

'It's a company car,' Karloff shrugged. 'And anyway, do you think that his old man, whoever he is, will really kick up a fuss when he finds out that his son was caught in an embarrassing situation?'

They drove in silence, to the accompaniment of the 1980s hits on the radio.

'But what was this circus about?' Heinz asked when they were passing the Legia stadium. 'Why this ostentatiousness? Why drag them out of the car to show pictures...'

Karloff quickly changed into a bus lane and stopped abruptly at a bus stop. Heinz got the impression that the Commissioner was not looking at him, but into some spot in a faraway distance. As if he was absent.

Karloff turned the radio off.

'That's the only way to get anywhere,' he whispered. 'You want to find the truth and I promised to help you. Within reason. Your subtle methods might perhaps work in a crime fiction novel, but not in the modern world. The truth needs to be extorted! Wrenched!' He clenched his fist on the driving wheel. 'Do you understand?'

Heinz didn't answer.

Later, in his hotel room, he went through Karloff's behaviour one more time. What was the source of all that aggression? What was this scene supposed to mean? That we are different? Or perhaps the opposite, that we are very much alike? That he could see through me?

He took off his necklace with the plectrum. He looked out of the window. It was a hot, spring night.

A night like the one when the murderer dragged the two dead bodies to the banks of the Vistula. But what happened before? Both seminarists had grazed wrists and ankles. One of them had more visible marks. The boy had fought, struggled to break free. He was the one with a small cut on his cheek. As if he was hit there. Why did the murderer hit him if he had chosen a different, more cruel way of torture? Something threw him off balance. But what was it?

The boy must have said something that the murderer could not take. Did he call him impotent? Start making fun of him? Perhaps to demonstrate that he was not afraid? There was a stark contrast between his behaviour and the other boy's. The other boy was compliant and submissive. And the actions of the hardy boy spoilt the murderer's show. Took away the satisfaction.

Heinz grabbed his notebook and started writing.

What could have been the other reasons for Rakowiecki to make fun of the murderer? He knew him. He knew him well enough to dismiss his threats.

No. That did not make sense.

He crossed out the note abruptly.

Of course it was possible that the murder happened by accident. The guy got carried away, killed one boy and then didn't have a choice but to kill the other one as well. Let's say he only wanted to scare the victims. But he needed to be sure that he scared them properly. He wanted to scare them so much that they would both, for example, disappear. Go away. The attacker needed to make sure that he was untouchable. That nobody would get him even if his crime – as serious as kidnapping, blackmail and torture – was revealed. He thought of the name written down by Latoszek the director in Regeneration. It would have to be somebody of that stance.

Somebody untouchable.

That might have been the case, but then again, might not. Heinz lit a cigarette and inhaled deeply.

After all he couldn't be sure, not sure at all, that the marks on the boy's cheek were the murderer's doing; he could have got them in thousands of ways. But it might be an important piece of information, if indeed they were that psycho's doing.

He started recreating the note he had just crossed out.

Perhaps it wasn't just the murderer who knew the victims. Perhaps the victims knew the murderer as well, which was not exactly the same. They could have known his weak points. And the murderer figured out that Rakowiecki and Leski knew something that could put him in big trouble. Trouble? What does it have to be, how big a hidden secret, to make somebody torture two twenty-year-olds and smother them in cold blood? And finally – Heinz wrote down another question – has the murderer got what he wanted by torturing and killing? Did they tell him what he wanted to hear? Extort, wrench. He recalled Karloff's words from earlier on.

No. There was no light at the end of the tunnel. I'm still lost.

I have instinctively focused on Rakowiecki, because the telephone number to the Professor was found on him. And he was the one not giving in until the end. But there was this other boy too. The submissive one, who was so scared that his sphincter let go in the end. He remembered the autopsy. Leski was the weakest link in the game where the executioner stays in touch with the victim. The executioner cut the inflow of air the way the supply of energy or gas is cut when you haven't paid the bills. And then he brought the boys back to life. Gave them hope.

Many times did Heinz hear that story from people who went through the hell of torture in the Stalinist times. At some point the victim starts feeling grateful and fond of the executioner. Starts appreciating his humane attitude. And the executioner waits for that very moment. That's exactly when people break and start talking. Or even singing. And get rewarded. More time and more air. More hope. And then, suddenly, unexpectedly, the perpetrator becomes almost your friend. The one who understands that nobody could take that much pain, that everybody would break. He is full of sympathy. If they were to swap places, the executioner would have surrendered a long time ago. And surely the torturer feels grateful too. Grateful to the victim whom he doesn't need to torture anymore.

These are the thoughts that come to mind when the pain takes over. That's how it works.

Heinz knew that the more sensitive the person is, the more intelligent, the sooner he rationalises his situation. He sees a shadow of a chance even in a totally hopeless situation. As a young police officer he was told that it is the roughest villain who is the most difficult to break. Or a woman in love. You detain one for forty-eight hours. You think that's long enough, but a minute passes after another minute, an hour after an hour, and you are still left with nothing. The chance is lost irrevocably. Forty-eight hours, and not a second longer. You have to convince a wife or a lover that the bloke she is protecting does not deserve her.

He sat straight in the chair. He got sidetracked. After all he was not dealing with a case of a woman in love or a primitive murderer. Not at all.

The letters were less and less legible. He could feel his fingers going stiff again. He dropped the pen. His pulse rate increased. Stress.

Mr Raynaud awaited him with the whole welcoming committee of symptoms.

After fifteen minutes of stubborn bending of fingers into a fist and flexing them, he could write again. Raynaud's symptoms have been reappearing a bit too often recently. Heinz promised himself that in the morning he would call the Institute of Rheumatology at Spartańska and make an appointment. He was in Warsaw, he might as well take advantage of it.

He lit a cigarette and went back to his notes.

A person committing a premeditated murder does not take unnecessary risks. And with hours-long torture it is easy for things to get out of control. An outsider might notice or hear something. So the perpetrator must be absolutely determined to keep torturing his victims. He must be sure that they could point to something or somebody.

Heinz shook his head. Apart from the killer and the two victims, that puzzle must include somebody else. The murderer wanted to find out who that person was.

Now he understood why he felt so uneasy. If there was somebody else, somebody Rakowiecki and Leski knew, then the killer will reappear. He will stage another hunt.

He heard a woman's scream outside the window. He didn't even budge. He carefully went through his notes one more time. Unless... Unless he was totally wrong. He shouldn't ignore the fact that in his line of work nine times out of ten the easiest hypotheses turn out to be true. A murderer is usually a relative or a close acquaintance of a victim.

He put the pen down. Yes. Let's stick to the facts. And the facts were simple – he had two dead seminarists. Students of a theological college, especially in pairs, do not get killed every day. The boys were members of the same family. Of the family living behind the walls of the institution educating priests...

The theological college. He browsed through the folder, then opened a map of Warsaw on his laptop and typed the name of the street.

It was time to pay them a visit.

There was something else that didn't let him go to sleep easily.

He switched the lamp on and grabbed a piece of paper. He wrote down two names. Jacek Latoszek and Jan Kunicki. Almodóvar's bastard and the businessman, who, supposedly, liked playing games with seminarists.

There was something that bothered him.

Why did Latoszek tell them about the influential entrepreneur and stock market player? He didn't have to. Was he protecting himself? Was he indebted to Karloff? Or perhaps he wanted to direct their attention elsewhere? Away from himself?

Somebody untouchable.

He surely wouldn't have thought about it, if not for the over-zealousness of a certain director.

15

PAIN WOKE HIM UP. He felt as if he were lying in a dark passageway somewhere in the Bermuda Triangle in Praga, with several teenagers kicking his head, already bored with this monotonous entertainment. The latest generation medicine – supposedly addressing pain locally – didn't help either.

Advertising bullshit.

Heinz stuck his head in the sink and felt some relief, when the cascade of ice-cold water ran down his brows, ears and cheeks.

He made several phone calls. He rang the Institute of Rheumatology. Then he asked the police officer from the Headquarters to make him an appointment at the theological college. When he was done with everything work-related, he dialled one more number.

'Answer, you son of a bitch.'

He waited for the voicemail to kick in and then pressed the red button. His son never called back and didn't reply to any of his text messages. So it didn't make sense to leave another message.

He came to the Mostowski Palace before noon. When he got to the first floor, he heard shouts and loud clapping. Exuberant policemen were running out into the corridor and hugging each other.

'We won! Jesus Christ, we won! You hear me?' Chlaściak shook Baryka by his shoulders.

'What's up?' Heinz asked sourly. 'Is today the Day of the Smiling Police Officer?'

'Better!' Chlaściak yelled. 'We were appointed the organisers of Euro 2012. Get it?'

Chlaściak looked at Baryka dazedly. He didn't seem to have sobered up after last night's drinking yet.

'Hey, junior, go get a bottle, we need a drink. There is a reason to celebrate. Will you join us, Heinz?'

'No. But I might have a chance to pray for you today. Ah...' he added, when Chlaściak sent him a startled look. The guy had no idea that Heinz was planning a visit to the seminary. 'No matter...'

He sensed it rather than heard it. There was somebody behind his back.

'Happy day, isn't it, Heinz?' He thought he heard a hidden caustic tone in Inspector Osuch's voice. 'Come with me for a second.'

They went into a small room the size of a large lift in the old block of flats. You could hear excited voices behind the doors and sense intensified activity in the corridor. The only source of light was a table lamp in the corner.

'We call this place the Claustrophobe's Den.' Osuch made a gesture of a tour guide showing tourists around. 'My office is undergoing renovation and the conference room has been booked for a meeting. They are having a discussion on how to improve the image of the police.'

'I would simply catch that motherfucker who killed the two boys. Then we wouldn't need to worry about the image of the police.'

Osuch's face was devoid of any emotion. Looking at the two of them somebody might think that they were listening intently to the animated voices outside. As if these were the most beautiful sounds in a philharmonic.

Chlaściak wasn't the only one. Clearly there were others

who were ready for some booze, Heinz thought.

'It's a happy day today,' the Inspector said at last.

'Did you ask me to come to this claustrophobe's den of yours to share your happiness with me?' Heinz could feel his irritation growing. 'Forgive me, sir, but...'

'A happy day, Heinz, because we finally have a breakthrough. A strong trail to follow.'

This time it was Heinz who made sure not to give anything away.

'We tracked down a neo-fascist group,' Osuch went on, 'who threaten on their website to get rid of all the blacks, Jews and... surprise, surprise!' the Inspector raised a finger, 'Gays! We took it seriously and linked it with the information about – would you believe it – a priest beaten up three weeks ago in front of a gay club!'

'Did he report the beating himself?' Heinz was sceptical.

'He couldn't do it himself. He got beaten so badly that they had to wire his jaw. He would probably not report it himself anyway. He's a priest, after all. But there are people who make sure that the club's vicinity stays safe, you know? So as not to scare the rich clients. This way or the other,' Osuch looked at Heinz, 'it seems that our man of the cloth was hammered by fans of the master race and all that shit. So,' the Inspector patted the lamp, 'it's a good trail. And what makes it even better,' he looked around triumphantly, 'is the fact that it is free from any profiling trickery.'

The light swayed, making the shadow around the inspector's head alternately bigger and smaller.

'And now,' Osuch raised his index finger, 'for the best part.'

He waited for some reaction. To no avail.

'Three years ago our assaulted priest was a teacher at a certain theological college. Guess which one?'

The corduroy jacket suddenly started bothering Heinz.

'Congratulations, Inspector,' he said. 'It really is something. What's this priest's name?'

'Kowalski.'

Heinz spread his hands.

'Nobody in the police database can be called Kowalski.'

'Apart from a Kowalski.' Heinz thought he detected a sneer. 'I think if we push those neo-fascists, they will sing, and sing chirpily,' the Inspector went on. 'But I also have some good news for you. You have that company car that you asked for. One of my boys,' he looked at Heinz studiously, 'had the misfortune of smashing his nose quite badly, so he won't need a car for a while.'

Later, standing in the corridor, he went through the conversation with Osuch once more. He heard the clinking of car keys and turned around. Freddie Kruger was standing in front of him. With a plaster covering pretty much all of his face, he looked like Michael Jackson after another operation.

'You look like Michael Jackson after another operation. Shit, man, what happened to you?'

Freddie gave him the keys.

'Just be hygienic.' Heinz heard mumbling muffled by the dressing. 'Keep the seat clean, don't forget to wash every day and change clothes. If the car gets dirty, I will make you scrub it.'

They glared at each other in silence.

'Cheer up, man. Relax. It's the Day of the Smiling Police Officer,' Heinz said. 'Brighten up. If you can,' he whispered and fixed his icy stare on Freddie.

16

A SHARP SMELL of detergents, floor polish and something sickening, almond-like mixed with stearin.

It never changes. During the short period of time Heinz spent in the Catholic boarding school, this smell permeated his clothing. He knew it before too, when he was an altar boy.

Some smells are like a blues chorus. They never change despite the passage of time.

A white Opel reached Wilson Square and turned into Krasińskiego Street. The theological college should be somewhere on the right. Somewhere by the church where Father Popiełuszko said his masses for the homeland during martial law. Heinz remembered that there was a club in one of the side streets. He saw several gigs there in the 80s. That's where he heard a Swiss band playing industrial rock. The musicians were a bit too much to handle and nobody wanted to listen to them back home. It was two and a half hours of torture in the company of a girl who had promised more than she delivered. Enough of it.

He found the seminary building without any problems. A clumsy grey block, interspersed here and there with little stained glass windows à la Wyspiański. Heinz wondered if those windows, an architect's whim, were supposed to make you feel that by entering this building you cut yourself off from the outside world. Even if this was the intention – Heinz thought of Rakowiecki and Leski and their designer clothing – the practice didn't seem to follow the theory.

A grey façade. Inconspicuous building. Pure discretion. Well, let's see.

It wasn't easy to push the solid, wooden door. The hinges squeaked loudly, but that didn't draw anybody's attention. Do they leave the door unlubricated on purpose, he wondered? To be able to hear every person entering or leaving the building? But there was nobody in a small glass box, the type used by janitors in schools and colleges from time immemorial. Emptiness. Deathly silence and emptiness. There was a stained glass window on the landing with what seemed like Saint George fighting the dragon. He climbed the stairs and found himself in a surprisingly wide corridor. Classrooms and teachers' rooms were on the left-hand side, while the opposite side was taken by large windows, which he didn't expect to see. The whole thing reminded him of one of those primary schools built in the spendthrift 1970s, when the socialist breadth mattered, when the minimalism of the previous decade was overcome, with its numerous schools commemorating the millennium of the Polish state, packing thousands of students into each of them. He went to the window. To his astonishment he saw an internal courtyard, green bushes, ivy on the grey wall and several young, straight birch trees climbing towards the sky. Nothing bad will happen to those trees here. The wind won't hurt them. It should be the same for the seminarists. But it wasn't so. In the northern corner he saw the Virgin Mary shrine, just like the one he remembered seeing in Ząbkowska Street. Strangely, there was only one bench on the patio, enough perhaps for three people.

Suddenly three silhouettes entered his field of vision. Instinct told him to take a step back. He didn't want to be noticed. A man was walking swiftly along a gravel path with a spring in his step, gesticulating animatedly. His bald head was supported by a massive neck, which made Heinz think of a wrestler, rugby player or security guard. There was a few days' worth of grey facial hair on the man's cheeks. His looks contrasted with the ruddy boys in cassocks who could barely keep up with him. One of them had a chequered handkerchief in his hand, which he was using to wipe the sweat from his neck and forehead. Every five to seven metres the older man stopped, waited for his companions and told them something. Heinz narrowed his eyes. The wrestler was wearing a black jacket and a dog collar. The boys seemed a bit too young to be priests.

He turned away from the window at the sound of approaching steps. A young dark-haired man in a cassock was standing in front of him.

'Praise be to Jesus Christ.'

Heinz didn't say anything.

'What brings you here?' the young man asked hesitantly.

'I have an appointment with the Father Chancellor,' Heinz whispered as if he was in a confessional.

The dark-haired man made a welcoming gesture and started walking. Heinz followed the swishing cassock. A few metres away from the Chancellor's office the young man turned around, silently pointed to the door and left. The office was located by the side stairs, next to a room, which was a source of wailing that made him think of a bad horror film. Heinz made sure the corridor was empty and then put his ear to the door. *Gallia est omnis divisa in partes tres...* How peculiar that they should read Julius Caesar in the theological college. He looked around again. There was a huge cross in the middle of the corridor, next to a portrait of John Paul II on the wall. He left his position by the door and approached the painting. The Pope's massive figure seemed ready to bust the frame encrusted with some gilt blisters. The Holy Father was patting a little girl on her head. He was shown against the backdrop of a town square and tops of the mountains covered in snow shining further away, with doves flying across the blue sky. *Thank God, quench not the Spirit* – Heinz remembered the motto of one of John Paul II's visits to Poland, also commemorated above the painting.

Just like in a primary school, like in the crowded school he went to. Yet there it was the socialist Ludwik Waryński who was portrayed in a painting of similar size, holding the *Proletaryat* paper in his enormous hand. A hand that would befit a heavyweight boxer.

He went back to the Chancellor's office door and was about to knock, but stopped himself. He would not knock or ask for anything. He came here to get information needed to track a criminal. He pushed the door handle and this time the door opened noiselessly. He went in. A religious song was playing on the radio. Disoriented, he stopped by a dresser with a dusty potted fern sitting on top of it. He waited. He saw the door leading to the adjoining room and heard some rustle. Instinctively he flattened himself against the side of the dresser.

'Go through it again,' said a low voice.

'Like I said before, yesterday and today Antek was the last one to leave after the mass.'

'It could have been a coincidence...'

'It was not a coincidence. A week ago, during the spiritual alms we were listing bad attributes of Matthew...'

'Of which he had plenty,' the bass echoed.

'Of which he had plenty, just like you said, Father,' Heinz heard a nervous whisper. 'Antek was the only one who did not mention any of the bad attributes...'

It went silent. Heinz thought that the interlocutors stood by the door between the little room and the office.

'There is something I'd like to ask you, Master...'

'Speak, my boy.'

'I'm struggling with Latin this term, perhaps you could...'

Heinz cleared his throat and came from behind the dresser.

The older man twitched and quickly sat down at the massive mahogany desk.

'Excuse me,' Heinz said. 'I have an appointment with the Father Chancellor.'

The man rotated his wrist and pointed at the door. The boy started towards it. He moved fast and almost soundlessly. Like a shadow. Or a rat. He looked like one too, with his sunken cheeks.

As if he was able to permeate the door, Heinz thought.

A solo on keyboard instruments played through a small speaker.

'This is Father Majda singing. Our Chancellor.' The man in his forties with coiffed thick, curly hair which made him look like Charles Aznavour, pointed to the radio, which clearly also incorporated a CD player. 'The album,' he announced proudly, 'is called *Musings on God and Fatherland*. Did you come to pick the ordered twenty copies?'

'Not exactly. I'm from the police.' He showed his ID. 'My name is Heinz. Spelt just like the ketchup.'

The dark-haired man gaped at Heinz, as if trying to decide how to react. Finally he clapped his hands.

'And my name is Adam Adamski. Friends always say that I am a man of two first names. Others say that I am a guy without a surname,' he laughed. 'Anyway, I am not the Chancellor.'

'So who are you, Father?'

'Some call me a spiritual master.' Adam Adamski looked intensely at Heinz. 'There are others who call me a spiritual father...'

'Excuse me, Father, but I don't really know your local hierarchy...' Heinz scratched his cheek.

'It's understandable, sir, you are a police officer. Well, I am...' He spread his hands, 'partly a psychologist, partly a guide. Like a compass helping in spiritual formation of our students and getting them through to priestly ordination. I simply talk with those young people during their six years in the seminary. I talk, talk and talk...'

'Then you are just like me.'

Heinz patted the hair on his temples.

The Spiritual Guide winced, as if stung by some vicious insect.

The crackling speaker was now playing another song à la Cliff Richard or some other 1960s singer. An exalted voice with too much vibrato sang *Without God dries out the tree of the Fatherland, so damned are those who to Jesus' scars are blind.*

'So you must know a lot about your students, Father...?' Heinz asked loudly, trying to drown out the Chancellor's singing.

'You could say I know everything about them...' Adamski went quiet and then laughed out loud. 'I'm joking, of course. To be honest the more I talk to them, the more convinced I am that I know them very, very little...'

He nodded and picked up the album cover from the desk. Heinz noticed a purple background and a man in vestments holding a microphone.

'Let's talk about Rakowiecki and Leski. What can you tell me about them, Father?'

Adamski looked at Heinz.

'I am deeply shaken...'

'And apart from that?'

'Everything I could tell I already told your colleagues... And anyway the Chancellor requested that all interviews take place in his presence.'

Heinz narrowed his eyes.

'This is not a formal questioning. Not yet.' He wanted Adamski to feel threatened. 'Please forget that my colleagues have already been here and tell me everything from the beginning.'

The Spiritual Father tightened his lips.

'What does it mean that you said everything you could,

Father?' Heinz could feel himself losing patience.

He was angry at himself. He came to the seminary to talk about the victims. But here his interlocutors would not lose their self-confidence. It was their territory. They all felt at home within these walls. He shouldn't be making it even easier for them. He shouldn't have addressed this guy as 'Father'. That was a mistake. A stupid mistake.

'It means that there are things I know from my students which I can't share with you. A spiritual father is bound by the seal of confession.'

'Even when we are dealing with a double murder committed by some sadist?'

'Even then.'

Heinz sighed and then leant forward abruptly.

'Sir, did you know that Rakowiecki and Leski were gay?'

Adamski twitched.

'I refuse to answer that question.'

'So you knew, Father. And you still tolerated their stay in the seminary?'

Heinz was pushing. He purposefully changed the way of addressing his interlocutor and called him 'Father' again. Let the priest feel guilty for not doing anything.

'I refuse to answer,' the man cowered.

'Father, you knew they were male whores, you knew they screwed around for money. And you still...'

'Listen to me!' Adamski shouted. 'I can't answer those questions. I am bound,' he stressed the word, 'by the seal of confession. However there is one thing I can tell you: they were both good candidates for the priesthood. Leski was interested in theology, a top student. And Rakowiecki was a proper go-getter, perhaps a bit too much so for a theological college, but he certainly had qualities, which – if channelled the right way – could turn into real charisma in the future. Do you understand what I'm saying?'

Heinz waited, curious to find out what else he was going to hear.

'I could also add that in the fifth term Leski started neglecting his studies, he became somewhat nervous. I talked to him about it...'

'And?'

Adamski looked Heinz straight in the eyes.

'I am bound by the seal of confession.'

'I would like to congratulate you on your discretion,' Heinz growled. 'To hell with all that confidentiality!'

Only now did he realise that somebody was listening in on their conversation.

'It would be better not to mention hell here,' the newcomer said quietly. 'After all we are in a seminary.'

Deep wrinkles around the eyes and liver spots on the backs of his hands attested to the fact that he was surely much older than Father Adamski. However, short hair and a tan made him look much younger. Heinz noticed the well-tailored black suit, impeccable white dog collar and polished, elegant shoes.

'I'm so glad you are here, Father Chancellor,' Adamski whispered.

Heinz looked at the man's face again and then at the picture on the cover of the album, still lying on the desk. There was no doubt it was the same man, although in the photograph he looked much younger.

He probably used a picture that was a few years old and had it Photoshopped too.

'I'm glad you are here too, Father Chancellor,' he made sure his voice sounded warm, even though it wasn't easy. 'My name is Heinz. We had an appointment.'

He looked at the speakers. Discreet, but good quality. Perfect for a smart chancellor of the seminary.

'And since we have met in person now, could we please turn that music off?'

THE BELL reverberated in the corridor.

'Before we talk, let me show you around,' the Chancellor said and buttoned his suit jacket. 'As the proverb goes, the master's eye makes the horse fat.'

The Chancellor swiped an invisible speck off his jacket. I look like a rag-and-bone man next to him, Heinz observed. The corridor filled with the seminarists. Some of them looked just like other boys their age walking the streets of the cities, others – Heinz figured these were students of later years – were wearing cassocks. He looked around for Diesels and Pumas, but didn't spot anybody wearing those brands.

Majda was dishing smiles left, right and centre and even nodded slightly a few times. Heinz looked at young men strolling down the corridor towards the patio. Something in this image struck him, gave him a vague feeling, some kind of inkling, but he couldn't form it into anything concrete or turn it into a hypothesis or a question.

They stopped by the crucifix and the enormous portrait of John Paul II.

'The bell announcing breaks between periods... It's just like school,' Heinz finally opened his mouth.

'My own idea.' The Chancellor nodded to an older man, most likely one of the teachers. 'I like it when everything in the seminary runs like clockwork. I feel like a clockmaker, so to speak, regulating the mechanism, cleaning the cogs... Do you understand?'

Heinz nodded.

'Speaking of which... Come here, boy.' The Chancellor beckoned one of the passing seminarists.

The boy stopped and went pale, then approached Father Majda who had a kind-hearted smile plastered on his face.

'Order of the day, quickly!' Majda ordered.

The student straightened up like a soldier and quickly recited:

'Five thirty – wake up call, six thirty – prayers and meditation, seven – mass, eight – breakfast, eight thirty – classes, 2 p.m. – Angelus, examination of conscience, two thirty – lunch...'

'Enough,' the Chancellor interrupted. 'It's Wednesday today. What's at 6 p.m.?'

'Vespers.'

'Seven fifteen, Tuesday?'

'Choir practice and vocal exercises.'

'Well done!' The priest smiled once more. 'Go now, *carissime*.'

Carissime. How cute.

The Chancellor turned to Heinz.

'I've introduced the bell because I'm a perfectionist. When I do something, I like it done thoroughly. I stick to this rule in the seminary and also while recording my albums.'

He nodded to the older man in a cassock.

'This is our Confessor.'

'I thought the Spiritual Father was a confessor...'

'These are two entirely different functions.' The Chancellor smiled. 'You know, we have specialisms here too. You have different people working in the traffic police and in homicide. Here...' he went silent and sent somebody another smile. This overabundance of insincere kindness was sickening. 'And about the bells... The way some people behave you might think that a watch hasn't been invented yet. For example Professor Rutger...'

Professor Rutger. His mobile number was written on a piece of paper found on one of the murdered men.

'I know biblical studies is the finest of subjects, but... you know... You can't run over and take the time allotted for other subjects.'

Heinz noticed a hint of derision in the Chancellor's voice. He nodded.

The bell rang and the corridor emptied right away. But then something broke the silence. Somebody was running up the stairs. A young boy.

He saw the Chancellor of the seminary and slowed down.

'Apologies for interrupting,' he panted. 'A car is parked in front of the building, an old white Opel. Its alarm went off. I think it has a flat tyre.'

'Oh, fuck!' Heinz barked and the Chancellor instinctively lifted his shoulders, as if he wanted to cover his ears.

Heinz rummaged nervously for the keys and the remote. As usual, he couldn't find them. He took out the hotel room keys, dozens of little pieces of paper, a train ticket and a used tissue, which he had been carrying in his jacket pockets since late autumn. He shoved all that junk onto the white pedestal by the cross.

'Perhaps I could help with the car...' the student suggested.

'Go back to your classroom,' the Chancellor said sharply. 'I'll get help.' He started towards his office.

Heinz finally found the keys and the alarm remote in his inside pocket. He ran downstairs. A while later the car stopped howling.

'Fuck, fuck, fuck!' Heinz yelled, staring hopelessly at the punctured tyre.

He kicked the rim of the wheel and opened the trunk. The spare wheel wasn't there. He swore again. A thought flashed through his head. It must be Freddie Kruger's doing. He must have taken the spare wheel out on purpose, followed him here and damaged the car.

I'm being paranoid, he thought.

He reached for his mobile, but couldn't find it. Of course, he left the phone on the pedestal by the cross.

'I'm losing it,' he whispered and rushed back upstairs.

He found the phone, the keys and all his rubbish where he left them. Only the train ticket from Katowice to Warsaw was missing. The ticket, which should have been handed over to the accountant of the Metropolitan Police a long time ago.

Somebody nicked a used ticket, but left the phone. Miracles do happen. Especially in the theological college, Heinz thought and dialled Karloff's number.

***

An exasperated man crumpled a packet of menthol Red & Whites in his hand and threw it between the trees. For the past hour he had been going back and forth between the two local landmarks: a board with a map of the vicinity accompanied by the regulations, consisting only of bans, and a roadsign forbidding unauthorised cars from entering the area. Those two spots were fifty metres away from each other. He couldn't have missed anything. Two birds were perched on a nearby tree, staring at him curiously. He narrowed his eyes to see them better, but he still couldn't say what sort of birds they were. In a different situation he might try to solve this ornithological mystery, but today his thoughts were preoccupied with something entirely different.

Perhaps he had chosen a wrong spot? After all they could have arranged to meet by the main road leading into the woods, where cars with giggling young couples stopped and men like him came, sometimes on their own, sometimes in groups, always with plastic bags. He has seen plastic bags from cheap supermarkets Lidl and Leader Price, sometimes from electronics chain Media Markt and occasionally even from bookstore EMPiK. Regardless of the brand name on the bag, its contents were always surprisingly similar. Plastic bags contained a bottle of vodka, usually small, half-a-litre, a slice of bread and a piece of cheap sausage, some hot dogs or liverwurst. By the first fork in the road young lovers seeking fulfilment in the bosom of nature chose a different direction than the amateurs of the firewater: the first ones went to the left, the second ones' choice was a little hill on the right, where you could spread your provisions.

Wind violently rustled the bag at his feet. He wasn't like those who came here for a drink. He pinned the bag down with his foot to prevent it from flying away. He could feel a ball of string and something hard under his foot. He had no doubt that it was a handle of a big knife.

He took his mobile out and looked at the screen. 75 minutes. He was tempted to call and check what was going on, but he stopped himself. Yes, he had a new top-up card, which he bought yesterday far away from where he lived, but he still didn't want to risk it. He would wait. He waited so much in his lifetime, he could take a bit more. He suddenly remembered that the bag contained more than just the string and the knife. There was something else, something very fragile by nature. He picked the bag up and looked inside. Two thin crossed wooden sticks did not break under the pressure of his foot.

He was lucky. Everything was all right. He smiled to himself. He smiled for the first time that day.

THE OFFICER accompanying Karloff had trouble unscrewing rusty bolts securing the damaged tyre in place.

Heinz sat in the Chancellor's office drinking strong coffee. He asked if it was OK to smoke there. He found a crumpled packet in his back pocket, lit a cigarette and inhaled greedily.

'Perhaps this will calm you down,' he heard.

Majda got up and a while later Heinz heard the familiar song from the rasping speaker. The cup twitched in his hand and several drops of the black liquid seeped through his trousers.

'Do you like it?' the Chancellor asked.

'I prefer blues. Robert Johnson, for example. People say that his music has some kind of devilish power.' He sent Majda a meaningful look. 'The guy sang about Satan, alcohol, and, excuse me, Father, about whores... He died in unexplained circumstances.'

'A very fitting hero for a police officer,' the priest concluded.

'And when it comes to your music...' Heinz hesitated. 'Interesting choice of colours for the cover,' he pointed.

'Purple. Colour of Advent. The album was selling like hot cakes in many parish bookstores and shops before Christmas. We designed a different cover for Easter. I'm rather busy, you know... Albums, habilitation... All profits from the sale of the albums are for our seminarists.' Majda smiled.

'For Rakowiecki and Leski as well?'

The smile faded on the Chancellor's face as if it was a cigarette butt put out in an ashtray.

'First and foremost for the likes of those two.'

'Meaning?'

The priest narrowed his eyes.

'Meaning that we help students from poor families. Rakowiecki was brought up by a single mother. A very religious woman. They could barely make ends meet. And Leski's relatives are...'

He waved his hand, trying to find the right expression.

'Degenerates?'

'Something like that. If not for the vicar from Serock, the boy would go down too. I will have you know that we are also helping the families with their sons' funerals.'

As if. Funeral mass for free, perhaps with organist's services thrown into the package.

Heinz got up.

'Two things puzzle me.' He approached the CD player and switched it off. 'You said "those two", Father. You didn't say "Karol RIP" or "Grzegorz RIP", you didn't say "our sons" or something along those line. You said "those two"... As if they were complete strangers... Do you bear a grudge against them, Father?'

Majda didn't answer right away. He looked at Heinz like an experienced waiter testing a new client.

'I feel sorry for those two boys. I really do. And I said "those two" because I only get to know the seminarists better in their fourth or fifth year. Apart from that,' he shrugged, 'it is not in my habit to fraternise with the seminarists, like some do...'

'Like who does?'

Majda was silent.

Somebody knocked on the door. Before the Chancellor had a chance to answer, the door opened and they saw a woman with a hairdo big enough for Dolly Parton. She approached Majda. The priest tried getting up, but he didn't have enough time. The woman grabbed his hand, kissed it and started shaking it nervously.

'I heard... I heard that...' Her voice was like the purring of some exotic animal. 'They accused him of attacking Jews again, of saying that Jews control all the world's money in their greedy mitts. But I...' the woman stuck out her ample bust, 'I listen carefully and when I was young I even sang at the church choir.' She lowered her voice. 'It wasn't him. It wasn't Father Director, God bless him...' She raised her hands. 'Different accent, different set-up of the larynx, I know what I'm talking about. It's a good copy, but still just a copy...'

Am I taking part in the next edition of *Pop Idol*, Heinz wondered?

'It wasn't him,' the woman repeated. 'It was...' she took a deep breath, 'an impersonator. Some impersonator pretends to be Father Director and...'

'Mrs Wasiakowa,' the Chancellor interrupted. 'I have left the laundry in the basket.' He pointed towards the room behind his office. 'Sometimes Sister's Servants can't cope with washing and cleaning,' he looked at Heinz and spread his hands apologetically. 'When that happens, we seek external help.'

'I know what I know,' the woman kept mumbling. 'It's an impersonator.'

She grabbed the laundry and left. Her rumblings died away in the corridor.

'The unfortunate ones, like Mrs Wasiakowa, can count on our help too. And the other thing? You mentioned two...'

'The second question is as follows,' Heinz touched his temples with his fingers. 'There are strict rules here. So how is it possible that two seminarists left unnoticed? And why didn't you inform the police straight away when they didn't come back?'

'That's simple,' the Chancellor shrugged. 'These are adults we are talking about. They know what'll happen if they break the rules. And why we didn't call the police? Because serving God is a question of conscience and not the attendance list. It's quite straightforward,' he pointed to the window. 'Many can't take it and choose a different lifestyle. They leave the college without informing us. It happens mostly during summer holidays, but during the academic year as well. Those boys are often ashamed of their own weakness... They don't even tell their families... So what do you expect of us?' the Chancellor asked. 'Are we supposed to track them down or tell you about it? You don't have enough work? So do you have any other questions, because I'm rather busy today...?'

'That swot we met in the corridor recited the timetable for the day, but...'

Heinz paused and stared at the Chancellor's hands drumming on the desk. Let me push him a little bit further, the profiler thought.

'But what?' the priest barked.

'But I haven't heard the most important thing. When is the seminarists' free time? When can they go out on the town?'

'Usually on Thursdays, between 4 p.m. and 7 p.m.'

'Rakowiecki and Leski didn't leave on Thursday. It happened...' Heinz paused again, 'on Wednesday. So?'

The Chancellor sighed.

'I said it is usually Thursdays. If they want to go out on any other day, they just have to leave a note in a special log-out book. And they must be accompanied by a socius...'

'A chaperone?' Heinz asked snidely.

'If the range of your references is that limited, then yes,' Majda answered. 'A student has a companion. These are the rules.'

'I'd like to see that log-out book.'

Majda spread his hands.

'Your colleagues have already taken it. Can I help you with anything else?'

Heinz got up.

'Thank you for your time. I'd like to talk to Father Professor Rutger. When will I be able to see him?'

'He sees students today between 7.30 p.m. and 9.30 p.m.,' Majda growled. 'Here. In my,' he stressed, 'office.'

Heinz was quite impressed that the Chancellor knew the other teachers' schedules by heart.

He said his goodbyes and was already by the door, but then turned around abruptly.

'What happened to Father Kowalski? He used to teach here...'

Majda narrowed his eyes, as if he was trying to remember the person in question.

'Kowalski... Yes, there was somebody by that name... He left a few years ago. I think he had other plans...'

You are lying. I know you are lying.

'One more question. What do numbers twenty-one and thirty-seven mean to you, Father?'

Majda jumped up from his chair.

'You must be joking,' he said softly. 'For the past two years those numbers have meant only one thing to the millions of Poles. How dare you...' he hissed through gritted teeth. Heinz didn't budge. 'Ask Rutger,' Majda sputtered. 'Father Professor is an expert in that area. He specialises in biblical studies, after all,' he laughed.

The sound of the slamming doors reverberated loudly in the corridor of the theological college, as if it was a hatch leading to a crypt. I'm suffocating here, Heinz thought. He felt like he was shut in a gigantic coffin. As if somebody cut the flow of the oxygen to his lungs and brain.

***

Another cigarette butt disappeared, pressed into the sand. For some reason he remembered himself as a little boy squashing earthworms on an uneven pavement covered with huge puddles with petrol and engine oil floating on their surfaces. Once his shoes got soaked through and he was given a good hiding. It didn't hurt much, but he was so scared, he wet himself. So he got even more hammered. Much harder. He felt a pain growing in his lower abdomen. This time it wasn't fear. This time the cause of the pain was rage. He could barely stop his body from trembling. This could attract somebody's attention and he didn't want that.

Today everything was under control. Nothing and nobody could thwart him. Even that unreliable bitch, who deserves to die. If it isn't her, it will be somebody else.

He checked his watch one last time. The time was perfect. Mothers with prams had finished their late morning walks amongst the greenery, dog owners hadn't come back from work yet. His night shift started at 6 p.m., so he had plenty of time. Enough to go back home, have a bath and get some rest. Perhaps he might come back here again, to have a look at the police cars and the tape separating the crime scene from curious onlookers. He might even see the stuffed black bag? No. He won't do that. Curiosity was the undoing of many and he didn't want to give himself away in such a stupid way. He found too much pleasure in what he had embarked on recently.

Yes. If not this one, then somebody else.

Enough of waiting. He walked several hundred metres amongst the trees and reached a wide, well-used footpath. As he remembered, there were several benches not far from where he was.

He didn't have to wait long. He heard snapping branches and saw a woman. At first he thought it was her. Similar figure, ample breasts, thick, dyed hair, almost identical hair-do, matching age. But this woman wore glasses, while the other always bragged about her good eyesight.

He approached her quickly.

'Excu-u-use me,' he stammered. 'Did you leave a bag here?' He pointed to the plastic bag in his left hand.

'No... It's not my bag. I never lose anything.'

She turned her head and then suddenly laughed. Eyes wide open and a guttural voice. Just like the other one. The only thing she was missing was lipstick smeared on her upper incisor.

'What are you la-a-aughing at?' he asked and put his right hand into the bag. He grabbed the cold handle and felt relief.

'WHAT BOOK?'

It was the third time Heinz heard the question asked by yet another surprised interlocutor. He could feel his rage rising.

Neither Karloff, nor Baryka, nor the Gothic rock diva in heavy, military boots – simply nobody from the threesome – had heard anything about the theological college logbook.

'What's your worry? I'm sure it will resurface at some point.' Karloff shrugged his shoulders. 'Perhaps Poremba put it somewhere? You know... the one with the smashed nose. He was helping us a bit at the beginning.'

Poremba. Ah, so that's what his name is.

He zeroed in on the logbook, even though he didn't really expect to find any revelations in it. Doubtless there was nothing on Rakowiecki and Leski and their last trip. He was pretty sure that their outing on Wednesday, 11th April, was not noted there. How often did they organise similar excursions? Were they the only ones to take part in them? Perhaps he might learn about somebody else who often left the gloomy walls of the seminary? Perhaps that other person might know where Rakowiecki and Leski went? Perhaps he might have seen them somewhere by chance? And perhaps all those questions didn't make any sense at all. Perhaps one should simply ask: how often did they go out? The organiser of those little trips certainly wasn't listed in any log-out or log-in book.

He decided to look for information in the 'piss.' PIIS, Police Integrated Information System, a tree of knowledge of good and evil. Especially evil. The most detailed and most comprehensive catalogue of sins and misdemeanours of this world. It had an advantage over other data collections: it also included operational information, which never gets presented to the prosecutor, not to mention the trial.

He typed in Rakowiecki's details. Nothing. He typed in Leski's. Same result. He stared into the screen monitor. He typed in Chancellor Majda's details and then Spiritual Father, Adam Adamski's. No information.

He thought of the meeting ahead of him. A few more hits on the keys. Jan Rutger. Result similar to earlier searches. However, there was something that bothered him about Rutger, as if a delicately struck guitar string produced an off-key tone. As the old proverb goes, the bells were ringing in some church, but which one? How appropriate.

He decided to check a different database. For a change. Crimes committed by followers of different religions within the last year. First came the case of the Christian Church of Preachers of Good News, established by gangsters. Guys from the town imported cars and electronics worth a dozen or so million złoty taking advantage of rebates available for religious organisations. Next on the list was a vicar from Lower Silesia. For years he had been doing it with his own sister who worked in his vicarage. In the end, after yet another drinking bout, he stabbed her with a pitchfork. He later said that he did it because he was jealous.

Love forgives everything, he remembered the line from an old song. A few notes in and the tune changed unexpectedly into Zeppelin's sullen blues. The picture on the screen went blurry. That was not the right time for recollections. He got up from the desk and took a deep breath. Enough of it.

The TV was on in one of the rooms. Channel TVN24 was replaying over and over again the scene with Michel Platini, himself slightly incredulous, taking a piece of paper out of a large envelope. It said: Poland and Ukraine.

***

The woman laughed and shook her head again.

'I really never lose anything. I didn't lose my granddaughter either. Oh, there she is!'

A five-year-old girl came from behind the thicket.

'I'm done, Granny.'

The girl looked at the unfamiliar man. She thought he was quite funny, with those freckles and the plastic bag.

'Good morning. Are you mushroom picking, sir?'

He hesitated. He didn't know what to say. Fortunately the woman helped him out. She laughed again.

'No, sweetie. It's not the right time for mushrooms. This gentleman thought that I had lost my bag.'

He heard the girl saying something to her grandmother who then replied. A moment later their voices faded round the corner.

His stomach ache got worse. He didn't know what to do. He squeezed his right hand on the handle as hard as he could. And then he saw her.

Her gait was unsteady. As if she had had too much to drink and lost her orientation. She probably wasn't on her own. Somebody would start looking for her in a moment. He looked around. He had a few minutes at best.

He made a decision.

'You lost your bag,' he said.

'What's in it?'

The woman grabbed the bag eagerly.

She looked inside and tilted her head to the side.

'What's with you, man? What the fuck?'

She wanted to say something else, but she didn't manage to do that.

White plastic clung to her stomach. The man moved his hand away, but, strangely, the bag stayed in place, as if glued. The white surface of the bag turned red.

Now, without any rush, he pulled the handle. The woman staggered and instinctively leant against a tree. The second thrust got her in the lung, the third one in the crotch. With the next, blood flowed from her mouth.

When he was done, he wiped the sweat off his forehead. With quick, practised moves he took the clothes off the bloodied body. A piece of ripped fabric stuck dry to the skin and he had to pull harder. He took her trousers off and smelt them. As expected, they reeked of urine. He folded them into a neat square.

That's it.

No. That's almost it.

He reached into his bag again.

20

AT 7.15 P.M. he parked in front of the theological college. He looked at the stained-glass windows in the façade. How did the death of two students influence the rest of the seminarists? How did it influence those young men who filled the corridor and the courtyard today? What did they think about their colleagues' death? Colleagues? He had a feeling that this was not the right term. He remembered watching seminarists during a break. Something struck him in this image, something seemed almost unnatural. He still couldn't say what it was though.

Everything else was pretty normal. No different from any school or military unit when something horrible happens. He recalled the case of a raped and strangled fourteen-year-old, which he investigated years ago. They hung the girl's photo at school, they lit a candle and laid flowers. But laughter and bustle on the corridor did not fade. As if nothing had happened. It shocked him at first. Only years later did he understand that in such situations people close their ranks to renounce death, drive it off with their ostentatious, almost inappropriate vitality. Like survivors on a desert island, making a fire and gathering around blazing flames to suppress fear.

The janitor still wasn't there. Heinz went up the stairs, accompanied by the hollow sound of footsteps. There was nobody in the corridor. The smell of cleaning products was mingling with the aroma of gravy. It must be after dinner. Digestive fluids in his stomach stirred. He realised that he only had breakfast today.

He looked around again. When he was certain that nobody could see him, he pressed his ear against the Chancellor's office door. He heard a quiet moan. There was no mistaking it. Somebody's voice swayed behind the door, went up, stayed suspended there and then went down.

Heinz slowly pushed the door handle and opened the door.

It must have taken him a few seconds before he noticed a man sitting cross-legged on the floor. The man with a shaved head had his hands on his knees. A black short-sleeved shirt could not disguise his bulging muscles.

This guy spends more time in the gym than in the confessional, Heinz thought.

The rasping speaker was producing some melodeclamation. Heinz couldn't place it anywhere, but these were certainly not Chancellor Majda's songs.

He heard a familiar sound of Buddhist bells.

'Eight and a half,' the man said suddenly and the music stopped at the same moment.

'I've seen it,' Heinz replied. 'Splendid film.'

'No.' The man opened his eyes. 'I didn't mean Fellini. Eight and a half,' he repeated. 'Do you remember that martial law time joke about militiamen? Why do militiamen smoke the "Eight and a half" brand of cigarettes? Cos they finished eight years of primary school and six months of militia training. Judging by your age, you should remember those times well enough.'

He stared intently at Heinz.

'How do you know I'm a police officer?' he asked, ignoring his remark.

'Walls have ears in this building.'

The Professor made a theatrical gesture, as if he was putting his ear to the door.

He got up. He was more or less the same height as Heinz. He brushed off his black shirt, went to the tape recorder and switched it off. Then he sat behind the desk and pointed a chair in front of it to Heinz.

'What you heard a moment ago is Buddhist monks'chanting. I've been practising that form of meditation for years now. Which, by the way, is not always well received... But Father de Mello faced way bigger problems. And from Cardinal Ratzinger himself...'

'Listen to me,' Heinz interrupted. 'I'm not interested in Father de Mello's problems or your knowledge of militiamen and Fellini...'

'Rutger...' the man suddenly cut in and rubbed his grey facial hair.

'What?'

'My name is Rutger. Just like Rutger Hauer. Do you remember the psychopath from *The Hitcher*?'

'I have a pretty good memory for psychopaths. Better than for Father de Mello. Listen, Father...' he leant over the table, sensing that Rutger wanted to interject again. He smelt an unexpected smell. 'We have two dead bodies.' He straightened his index and middle fingers. 'Two students of this theological college. And...' he looked Rutger straight in the eyes, 'this is not a film. This has happened for real.'

'What do you want from me then? And anyway, do you have a name?'

'Heinz. Just like the ketchup. I actually only have one question for you. We didn't find any ID, bus tickets, credit cards by Rakowiecki's and Leski's bodies. In other words, there was nothing to help with the identification. The investigation would probably stall if not for one small detail...'

'You are talking about that note with my telephone number? You called, I came and identified the boys. What else do you want from me?'

Rutger clenched his fists.

'Well,' Heinz said firmly, 'There is something I have been asking myself from the very beginning. And now, since coming here, that question has become my obsession...'

'I would be happy to help you deal with your obsessions.'

Rutger kind of winced, kind of smiled.

'Considering the distance between teachers and students of the seminary, considering the pseudo-military drill, how is it possible for a student to have your mobile phone number? Can you please explain that to me?'

Rutger didn't answer right away. He opened a leather briefcase and began stuffing it with notes and books. On the spine of the thickest one of them there were five words written in a simple font. In the upper line: *Jan Rutger*, and below: *Ezekiel – Unusual Prophet*. The priest noticed Heinz staring intently at the pile of books.

'Ezekiel. My favourite prophet. Some say he was a bit odd. Nowadays people like him become pop stars.'

Rutger... He had heard that name before. That thought struck him earlier, when he was browsing through the police database.

Two metal locks rattled and the Professor put his briefcase aside.

'Before I answer your question, let me tell you something.'

He took a deep breath and closed his eyes. Heinz thought that Rutger started speaking to himself, as if he himself suddenly turned into an inspired Old Testament prophet.

'You mentioned the pseudo-military drill? You have no idea what you are talking about. It was a real drill when I was the age of all those Rakowieckis and Leskis... I remember forming two neat rows to go to the morning mass at six thirty. Every day we had to walk past the Deputy Master of Novices' door and our legs would shake with fear...' Rutger swallowed nervously. 'Sometimes that door would open and he would point at one of us without a word. This meant a sentence. Expulsion from the seminary. That student had to pack his things and leave without saying goodbye, no questions asked! That's what it was like then. And I tell you,' the Professor opened his eyes, 'those were good times.'

There was a sound of a mechanical cuckoo in the distance. A cuckoo clock here?

Green eyes bored into Heinz. In fact they were staring back into the past, hunting for distant memories.

And suddenly Rutger's eyes cleared and sharpened. He was back in the present.

'And now let me cure you of your obsession. Rakowiecki and Leski did indeed have my telephone number. These were curious students. Curious to a point... We even organised extra classes after hours.'

'Was Rakowiecki taking part in those meetings as well. They say he was a bit of a skiver...'

'What skiver!' Rutger huffed. 'He simply didn't like dogmatic twaddle. Or at least that's how it was at the beginning. In time I noticed that he lost interest in our meetings. With Leski it was a different story though. This one wanted to study, for example, René Girard's anthropology, he wanted to know what's the mechanism of looking for a scapegoat in different religions. The cases of Job and Jesus fall into that category. We also spoke about neurotheology...'

'About what?'

Before Heinz heard the answer, there was a gentle knock on the door. The boy with hollow cheeks was standing in the doorway.

Rat. The same one, who was earlier confessing to the Spiritual Father. Confessing. As if. He was simply informing on his colleagues.

'Father Professor, I brought the dumplings that Mother ordered,' Rat said, totally unfettered by Heinz's presence. 'With bamboo shoots, sprouts, Chinese black mushroom and... we didn't forget to make them vegetarian. Meat is replaced by tofu.'

'Stomach ulcers and joint aches are keepsakes from the martial law time and cold prison cells,' Rutger said. 'And bad eyesight too, as I was whacked with a truncheon on my head. That's why I don't like policemen, but I have to like doctors, who listen to my body confessing its ills.' He sent Heinz a meaningful look. 'Fate made me try eating those strange things and I have been feeling better ever since.'

Rat disappeared behind the door. The locks rattled jangingly again and the dumplings disappeared in the vast bag.

'And on the subject of Rakowiecki and Leski...' Heinz shifted impatiently in his chair. The last thing he wanted was a lecture about Girard, neuro-something-something and recollections on braziers in the snow. 'I'm not interested in your phone. I'm looking for their mobiles and laptops...'

He saw astonishment in Rutger's eyes.

'Private mobile phones and laptops are forbidden. These are rare remainders of the old style when the seminarists had to renounce all material things, especially their right to privacy. At the college they have to make do with computers available for general use...'

'So you don't know anything about them?'

'I don't. Anyway I suspended my private study group a couple of months ago. Since then I haven't seen Rakowiecki and Leski.'

'Why so? After all Leski was such a smart student... And Rakowiecki was not bad either...'

Rutger went quiet. The cuckoo clock sounded again in the distance.

'They should be like an army.' The priest put his fingers on his eyelids, as if he was closing a dead person's eyes. 'They need to be like soldiers staying away from temptation...'

'But not all of them are strong. Father, you found something out... Am I right?'

'I'm tired.'

Rutger closed his eyes.

They are like an army. Like inert robots. Mechanisms wound up by somebody else's hand.

He recalled the image of seminarists cruising the corridors during break. Now he understood what struck him in this picture.

'I'd like you to help me understand something, please. I've seen the seminarists between classes. They were seemingly talking with each other, but... It looked somehow contrived, distanced... As if they were not colleagues but strangers...'

The Professor half moaned, half sighed.

'You really have no idea about our ways here... Firstly, they are not colleagues. You have no friends here. Not even acquaintances.'

Sounds like the police, Heinz thought.

'Secondly, we observe the rule of *tactus*. *Tactus* means touch in Latin. You touch another seminarist, you pat him friendly on the shoulder and...'

He waved his hand towards the window.

'You get expelled?'

'Exactly.'

'I'm afraid we will need to follow up this conversation.' Heinz got up. 'Perhaps not in those comfortable armchairs. By the way, Father Professor,' he turned towards the door, 'I think that combining Buddhism with alcohol is not a good idea. Is that why you take walks with students in the courtyard? So that they don't smell it and realise that you have been drinking since the morning? Anthony de Mello would be appalled.'

Rutger was motionless. The wind moved the shutters, but Heinz – not for the first time today – felt suffocated.

The corridor was silent. The light of flickering fluorescent lamps reflected in the blue floor. The sizzling sound made him think of a crazed insect entering a room through a window and instinctively moving towards the light.

Heinz started towards the stairs. When he passed John Paul II's portrait, he heard a noise coming from under the ceiling. The rasping sound resonated again. It was coming from behind an opening, leading, as he managed to establish earlier, to a short little corridor. The opening was reinforced with a solid, unplastered pillar, most likely built at a later time. That's where the source of the noise was. Somebody stood there and stepped on a loose floor tile.

Heinz made up his mind. He took three more steps in the same rhythm, reached the opening and suddenly jumped behind the pillar. He saw a petrified face with sunken cheeks, which flushed with blood as soon as Heinz started crushing the boy's Adam's apple with his forearm.

'How now? A rat?' he rasped straight into the boy's ear. 'Remember this?'

He pressed even harder with his forearm. The boy started wheezing.

'You are probably not that happy about it, but I am very glad that I met you,' Heinz said through clenched teeth. 'A person like you surely hears a lot and sees a lot, isn't that so? You inform the Spiritual Father on other students, you lick Rutger's boots by bringing him some disgusting dumplings… What do you know about Rakowiecki and Leski? Where are their mobile phones and laptops? Where do you hide them, for fuck's sake?'

He released the boy who slumped to his knees and grasped his neck with both hands.

Somebody cleared his throat quietly behind Heinz. He looked around.

'He won't tell you anything.' Rutger swayed his briefcase back and forth nervously. A black jacket was thrown across his other arm.

Heinz went closer to the Professor. He smelt badly digested alcohol again.

'Rat won't tell? Why so? You will see for yourself, Professor, that he will spill.'

He looked at the boy.

'*Silentium sacrum*,' Rutger said softly, raising his finger to his lips.

'What?'

'*Silentium sacrum*. The sacred silence is part of ancient rules respected in theological colleges. *Silentium sacrum* started a few minutes ago. That's when my shift ends.'

The Professor swung his briefcase again.

Rat jumped up, as if he was given a signal, passed Heinz and ran down the corridor.

'Let go,' Rutger whispered. 'You entered unchartered waters here. This,' he pointed to the corridor, 'is an entirely different world.'

He swung his bag one more time to say goodbye. Heinz watched the Professor's hunched back and for the first time thought that Rutger must be much older than he seemed.

Something was crushing him into the ground.

Heinz was at the landing when he heard a muffled moan. He stopped dead. Slowly, so as to not make any noise, he went back upstairs. He looked around the dimly lit corridor. No, he was not mistaken. The door by the stairs was not shut entirely and that was where the noise was coming from.

'*Ad maiorem Dei gloriam examen conscientiae*,'[1] somebody whispered.

'*Ad maiorem Dei gloriam flagellatio*,'[2] a different voice answered.

Through a gap in the door he saw a silhouette of the old Confessor. The one the Chancellor greeted in the corridor.

---

1 Examination of conscience for the greater glory of God.

2 Flagellation for the greater glory of God.

He heard a dry crack and then a moan. The younger voice said something in Latin.

A blow and another muffled groan.

How did Karloff phrase it? They would create a sensation on YouTube? Those two here for sure.

He ran downstairs, opened the door and shook his head as if emerging from underwater. He inhaled violently and felt pain, as if his lungs were about to burst.

21

BEFORE HE GOT BACK to the hotel, he went to Wiatraczna Roundabout and easily found the place mentioned by Karloff. Even though it was after nine o'clock, the oriental cuisine eatery was full. Drops of grease trickled majestically from the roasting meat onto the tray below, the air was filled with a mixed aroma of aubergine and beans. Heinz felt a sudden twitch in his stomach. Digestive juices kicked in. Instinctively he stuck his thumb behind his belt. His trousers were less tight than they were a week before. He always lost weight when he worked outside of Katowice. When he was in Silesia, his fridge was his faithful companion and he ate compulsively to deal with stress. So perhaps it was not so bad after all – he checked the belt of his trousers again – that he was away from home. And anyway, he didn't really have a home, just a flat.

There was a signboard over the counter with information that the place was open from 9 a.m. until 2 a.m. He ordered an XXL-sized kebab and sat at a table. Three swarthy men were sitting at the next table. They looked at Heinz with suspicion and said something in a language that he didn't understand.

A different world, he thought half an hour later, stretching on his uncomfortable bed that squeaked badly with his every move.

I have entered unchartered waters. Cross Road Blues, a well-known standard by Robert Johnson, was playing through his laptop speakers.

He remembered what he heard from one of his mentors, the officer involved in the investigation code-named 'Anna'. It was the most famous investigation in the times of the People's Republic of Poland, concluded with a death sentence for a murderer of women, Marchwicki the vampire. *Don't just think about what you've seen, think about what was missing*, Major Arnold Talar used to say. Not all the wisdom needed to be imported from Liverpool or Quantico.

A different world. What was missing? The theological college was devoid of any traces of Rakowiecki and Leski. As if they have never studied there. They were erased, just like data gets erased from a computer hard drive. Two students got killed. In normal circumstances their pictures with black ribbons would be displayed somewhere, there would be a candle surrounded by flowers or a wreath. Yet there was nothing. Not even a shadow of mourning. He went around the building, he did it on purpose, to check it out. Together with the Chancellor he went to see the room that not so long ago belonged to the two dead seminarists. The view of the widely opened windows shocked him. Heinz stood in the doorway, looking at the clean bed linen on the two perfectly made beds. He peeked into the emptied wardrobe and drawers, gaping like a void.

As if the room got disinfected, he thought. Death got relegated with starch and fresh air.

The world of the seminary followed its own rules. Like a land drifting along a current known only to itself. *Tactus*. The seminarists were afraid of even the slightest physical contact, because that could make them the talk of the town. But two of them, at least two of them, betrayed the military discipline, as Rutger would probably phrase it. The Spiritual Father uses the seal of confession as his excuse and at the same time informing on others thrives in the college. He recalled the sunken cheeks of Rat. One thing on the outside, another on the inside.

Everything that goes on there seems to be just smoke and mirrors. Worse even than low prices in hypermarkets and zero per cent interest rates.

I found myself in some strange land with peculiar connections. One thing linked all of those people, he thought. They all didn't want to say anything.

Robert Johnson started an intro to another blues. Heinz shook his head. Genius. Real genius. Wonder how Chancellor Majda must be feeling, the lame singer and perfectionist through and through, the divine clockmaker winding the gears of the complex mechanism who lost control over everything in the seminary. The egotist sending smiles left, right and centre, infectious with kindness.

Suddenly he had an idea. He switched his laptop on and typed in the Chancellor's name. First listing was a link to Wikipedia. 'Jan Majda – a priest, star of sacro-pop music, Chancellor of the theological college in the Warsaw diocese,' he read.

Every time Majda mentioned Rutger, his face twisted in anger. Heinz typed in the Professor's name. A leading biblical scholar specialising in... Among numerous listed disciplines Heinz knew only biblical studies. His attention was captured by a comment that the Professor was one of the more controversial thinkers within the Church. In the further part of the article the author mentioned Anthony de Mello, the contentious theologian Hans Küng and several other names that Heinz didn't know.

Heinz was intrigued by this powerfully built priest, an ostentatious lover of Buddhism. He used the Chancellor's room, despite the fact that Majda wasn't his biggest fan. Why? Heinz didn't know that. Perhaps there was a connection between them that went beyond banal rules of academic interrelations.

What's more, Rutger liked a drink and that was not something you could hide in a seminary.

And then there was this mysterious Confessor reciting formulas in a dead language and performing sadistic rituals. *Ad maiorem Dei gloriam...*

He was woken up by his own scream at 2 a.m. He dreamt that he was tied to a tree, staring into feverish eyes of the Inquisitor, who held a whip in his hand.

'*Ad maiorem Dei gloriam, ad maiorem Dei gloriam!*' the Inquisitor screamed and drops of blood set on a leather braid embellished with a line of small hooks cutting into Heinz's flesh.

'THAT DOESN'T MAKE SENSE,' he said to Karloff when they sat down in Banja Luka restaurant in Puławska Street several minutes after twelve o'clock.

It was April the 19th, 2007. The headlines of all the papers were informing in red, festive font that something exceptional had happened. Poland and Ukraine getting to host the European Championships in 2012 was discussed in all possible columns, from front pages to sports pages, traditionally at the very back. Every title ended with an exclamation mark, obligatory on that day.

A national orgasm with the assistance of football. Heinz was angered by Poles' gregarious love of football. A gigantic balloon filled with hopes of power and frustration.

He met Karloff at 9 a.m. in the Mostowski Palace.

Karloff had been working since the morning. You could even say that he had been working hard. He was circling a table cluttered with documents. There were two more people in the interrogation room. Two baldheads, each no more than twenty years old, who cowered on their chairs every time the interrogator approached them like a predator nearing its prey. The questioning started 90 minutes earlier. Heinz watched it for twenty minutes, exchanged a few words with Karloff and then left the room. He went downstairs. Two women in their thirties worked in the information point of the Metropolitan Police Headquarters. Their job was to get rid of madmen and other intruders. He asked the more attractive one about the nearest drugstore.

'Go to the Blue Skyscraper in Bankowy Square,' she replied without hesitation, as if she was regularly asked these kinds of questions by the police officers working at the Headquarters.

Heinz went to the shop and asked for a pink lipstick.

'What kind of lipstick are you looking for?' a salesgirl asked him in a bored voice.

'Well... a pink one, Viola,' he answered hesitantly.

The nametag on her cream blouse said 'Viola – assistant make-up artist'.

'But what kind of pink does the lady use?' the make-up artist was not giving up.

Two women looked towards Heinz. In the past you would have described them as 'Roaring Forties'.

By the way, I wonder how you call women that age nowadays, he thought. I should ask my son, if I ever meet him again. He spread his hands in a gesture of helplessness.

'Try to remember. What lipstick does your wife use? Is it matt or pearl? And if matt, is it textured or not? And what shade of pink? Is it dusty pink or something lighter? Perhaps you remember the brand or the catalogue number...'

Heinz thought of his shelf with cosmetics under the mirror above the sink, constantly splashed with bits of toothpaste. His son had a whole battery of cosmetics. Those belonging to Heinz would fit into his trouser pocket.

He was fed up with meticulous Viola.

'Any pink will do. As long as it's cheap,' he said. 'And anyway,' he hoped the nosy customers would hear that, 'it's not for my wife. Not for any woman. It's for my dog.'

He was certain that three pairs of scandalised eyes followed him towards the exit.

He went back to the Mostowski Palace. Karloff, red in the

face, with the sleeves of his white shirt rolled up and huge rings of sweat under his arms, looked like a character from a French police film.

Heinz opened the door to the interrogation room at exactly the same moment Karloff's fist whacked the table.

He looked the petrified baldies in the eyes. Gone was all their courage that they usually show off with when they are in a group. He sat at the table and started casually browsing through the files. Finally he found pictures of Rakowiecki and Leski. The shaved heads were giving him pleading looks. They were looking for help, like a drowning person desperately searching for a life buoy.

'So how did it go?' he asked in a gentle voice of a person delivering a weather forecast. Karloff was the bad policeman and he was about to get into the role of a good one. 'You took care of this one?' Heinz addressed the taller boy and showed him Rakowiecki's photo. 'Or perhaps the other one? How did it all go, eh?'

'Sir, we had nothing to do with this,' the baldhead said frenetically.

'Bullshit!' Karloff said through clenched teeth. 'You see for yourself?' he addressed Heinz. 'All he is dishing out is bullshit...'

'Sir, I've already told your colleague...'

'Shut up!' The scar on Karloff's face went purple. 'How do you know, you shaven-headed trash, that we are colleagues?'

It was time for Heinz to get involved.

'So you have nothing to do with it... Can you prove it?'

'We were not even in Warsaw at the time...' the shorter one said.

'The thing is nobody will confirm that,' Karloff barked. 'And your buddies' testimony will make an exceptionally shitty alibi.'

'So where were you?' Heinz asked.

They both started speaking, one over the other. He knew they had already answered that question. The fact that they had already presented their version of events made them feel more confident. It was all about putting them off guard.

'And what about this?' Heinz interrupted suddenly and put the lipstick in the middle of the table. It looked like a bullet.

The shaved heads shifted nervously in their chairs, Karloff was breathing heavily.

'What about this?' Heinz repeated. 'Pink triangles. Twenty-one, thirty-seven,' he said slowly, staring intently at the interrogated.

He was not a good policeman anymore. The role was over.

The baldies looked at each other in astonishment. Finally the taller one burst out.

'What the fuck?' he sent Heinz an angry look. 'Triangles? Numbers? What is it, Bolo?' he turned to his colleague. 'Some lucky number or something?' He lifted off the chair slightly.

He wanted to say something else, but he wasn't given a chance. Karloff's hand tightened on the boy's white t-shirt and made him sit back down. They heard the tearing of fabric.

'Don't get up without permission or I will treat it as an assault on a police officer. And those t-shirts of yours are crap,' Karloff hissed. 'Some Asian rubbish...'

***

'That doesn't make sense,' Heinz repeated.

Karloff was browsing through the menu and it seemed that he wasn't listening.

'Your fucking Bolo and that other geezer have nothing to do with it. You think they carry lipstick with them on an everyday basis? Perhaps an eye shadow as well?'

'Personally I don't think anything,' Karloff turned the page of the menu. 'There are times that I am of the same opinion as my boss. And he thinks...' He looked for a waiter. 'He thinks that the neo-fascist trail is OK. Osuch also mentioned pressure from above to conclude the case.'

'Then find the murderer,' Heinz said. 'Rakowiecki and Leski were killed by somebody well prepared. Those triangles and numbers... That was not an improvisation. Somebody planned it well. And those two lemons have fewer brain cells than hair. Bald-headed halfwits... You said it yourself.'

'I am supposed to meet somebody here,' Karloff answered. 'He will shed some light on the matter. You can decide for yourself what to do with it. But in my personal opinion we are treading water.'

What happened later would keep returning in Heinz's recollections like a nightmare. A boy in bike courier gear approached their table. They learned that he worked for a foundation monitoring neo-Nazi movements.

'It's rarely about morals,' he said, impaling a cube of feta cheese covered with olive oil on his fork. 'Attacks of neo-fascists of different shades, as well as nationalists, are motivated mainly by race or ideology. They fight with gays during events like Equality Parade.'

He wiped his hands into a paper napkin and opened his canvas bag.

'Here,' he waved with a wad of papers stapled together. 'This is an excerpt from our black book for the last few years. That's where we keep track of our pets' activities. We list attacks on black students, fights with anarchists at concerts... Oh, here we even have skinheads' attacks on models at a fashion show in Katowice. By the way...' he looked up from densely printed papers, 'a black guy in a white Vistula suit makes for an interesting view...'

'Like *The Jazz Singer*.' Karloff recalled the title from the furthest recesses of memory. He put his clenched fist to his mouth and puffed up his cheeks, as if he was playing a trumpet.

Bits of red pepper and green cucumber flew towards a couple discussing the details of their planned wedding. Before the bike courier joined them, Heinz heard a hysterical whisper of the future groom.

'No donations for hungry little bellies of Ethiopians or toys for an orphanage. Dosh, love, dosh.'

The man was just shaking his bride's hand. Remains of salad landed on it. The groom stood up abruptly to protest. He must have noticed a glint in Karloff's eyes, because he sat down as quickly as he got up and started whispering something to the girl, looking towards the men at the next table.

'They deserved it.'

Heinz turned back to the guy from the foundation, rustling papers.

'The last case with gays and seminarists was two years ago. In Silesia. A group of skinheads attacked guests at a New Year's Eve party in one of the clubs. They later explained that they thought the costumed people were gay. As luck would have it, there were students from a theological college among those attacked, so all hell broke loose.'

Karloff smacked his lips and rubbed his stomach.

'Fabulous grub. But my bowels tell me it's time to pay my debts to nature. It comes in one way, it leaves the other,' he laughed. He had brown scraps of *gurmanska pljeskavica* between his teeth.

The bike courier stared at the back of disappearing Karloff.

'And since we mentioned Silesia...' he said. 'There is this very rowdy group there. It's called the White Point. We think it's a clone of the Blood and Honour movement... Your name is Heinz, correct?'

Heinz nodded.

'There is this guy in the White Point...' The courier was studying his paperwork. 'His name is Krzysztof Heinz. This month he took part in a demonstration against the March of the Living in Kraków, as well as in a nationalist convention in Annaberg. That's in Silesia. Quite recent stuff...'

Heinz felt blood flowing to his face. He got up from the table abruptly. Groups of businessmen having lunch whirled around him. He felt dazed. As if somebody had delivered a strong punch to his chin. Or as if he had had too much to drink. As much as in the old times.

He couldn't remember what happened afterwards. He came to after Piotrków Trybunalski. He had a splitting headache, made even worse by the wheezing of the company Opel. He felt better when he saw a sign informing himthat he was only 50 kilometres from Katowice.

He stopped at a petrol station, refuelled and ordered something to eat. He was finishing a hot dog with a sickly thousand island sauce when a truck stopped by. There was a sign on the side of the trailer that said 'Domesticated animals'. When he turned the key in the ignition, he saw a different sign above the registration plate of the truck: 'Livestock for slaughterhouse.'

He thought of Rakowiecki and Leski.

And about the pink lipstick.

And then about his son.

23

'SO HOW are we going to do it?' Lambros Kastoriadis asked, shifting in his car seat. 'My way or your way?'

'Your way,' Heinz muttered.

For the last half an hour the white Opel was parked not far from the Rio bar in Giszowiec estate. The Zillman brothers, architectural visionaries who designed the estate, couldn't have predicted a blemish like this Latino-named dump. Rio had a bad reputation. Three years ago a dismembered body of one of the owners was found in a voluminous bar freezer. And it wasn't any better nowadays. The establishment was considered a hangout place of hooligan fans of GKS Katowice team, who regularly created uproar during the football season.

'Are you positive?' Kastoriadis wanted to make sure.

'Enough of it,' Heinz confirmed.

Lambros Kastoriadis shared the fate of many Greek families who came to Poland when the Second World War ended and a bloody civil war between royalists and communists started. He was the son of a famous sculptress and a political science professor, a subtle researcher of Karl Marx's thought. He spent his childhood and youth in Poland. Towards the end of the sixties, when he turned twenty, he moved to California. Unlike many of his peers, he didn't end up at the farm in Woodstock and didn't become part of the bouquet of Flower Children. He dropped his anchor in a *dojo* of a Japanese karate master.

When Kastoriadis returned to Poland, he already had a black belt and the fifth Dan, which gave him a very high position amongst the martial arts masters. He married a Polish woman and ran karate courses in Silesia. Heinz was one of his students. Until the meeting with the Inquisitor.

That was when they parted. Sensei Kastoriadis and Rudolf Heinz met again 18 months later, on the occasion of one of the cases that the profiler was investigating. It seemed that the karate master might have used his skills in an inappropriate way. Firstly, the murdered person was Kastoriadis's neighbour. Secondly, reliable witnesses confirmed that three days before the killing, the owner of the black belt had a fight with the victim. And thirdly – a small issue – stuck in the body of the dead guy was *shuriken*, a deadly metal star used by legendary Ninja warriors, as well as by contemporary masters of martial arts. It was thrown with incredible precision and strength and it lodged in the eye socket and smashed the skull of Tadeusz Hibner, a person not unfamiliar to the police. The threat of a life sentence for Sensei Kastoriadis was becoming more and more real and who knows how the whole case would have ended if not for Heinz, who found the murderer. And fourthly, a while later, when the whole thing went quiet and nobody was interested in Kastoriadis anymore, the body of a murdered teenage girl was found at the allotment belonging to Hibner. The girl was pregnant.

'You have saved me from the rope,' Kastoriadis used to say since then. 'A real Greek would not survive prison. I would probably hang myself.'

The sixty-year-old *karateka* shifted in the car seat and scratched his grizzly head.

It was 6 p.m. Three hours earlier the white Opel parked in front of the 'corn-on-the-cob' on the Estate of the 1000-Years

Anniversary. Heinz ran into the building and bumped into Rubber Ear. The old woman was taking her dog for a walk. Heinz struggled with the lock at first, but the door finally gave in.

On the doorstep of his own flat he collided with a frightened girl.

'So this is how you study for A-levels? Congratulations,' he said through clenched teeth. 'Where is he?'

And he ran into his son's room, not waiting for her answer.

He didn't recognise him at first.

The boy's right eye had a purple ring around it. The left one was all swollen. Both lips were unnaturally puffy.

'What's going on here?' Heinz looked at his son and then at the girl.

'Don't tell him anything! None of his business!' the boy lisped.

He had probably lost his front teeth.

Heinz grabbed the girl by the elbow and took her to the kitchen. He pushed her against the fridge still dotted with yellow post-its. A jar of pickles fell out of the fridge and smashed to pieces. Heinz was standing in the puddle and could feel the moisture seeping through his shoes.

Fifteen minutes later he knew what had happened.

Such a cliché. A group of skinheads from the White Point were to organise an 'action'. They were supposed to wait in front of a student hostel for 'asphalts' – black-skinned students – and then give them a good hiding. Heinz Junior hesitated and withdrew from the action. His colleagues thought him soft. And when you are soft, the boss, known as Beanpole, teaches you a lesson.

Heinz opened the wardrobe, almost pulling the door out in the process. His baseball bat, a keepsake from the United States, was back in place.

He chose '5 Dan' from his contact list and pressed the green button.

They parked thirty metres from the bar's metal door. Lambros Kastoriadis and Heinz approached a 6' 6", shaven-headed boy who was chewing gum, clearly bored.

'Excuse me,' Kastoriadis said, looking up. 'Could we please go in?'

The baldie looked at the two men and spat the gum out on the ground in front of their feet.

'Get lost, grandpas. Wrong place. And anyway,' he looked at Heinz. 'Halloween is not for another six months, so take that troll away!' He pointed at Kastoriadis who wasn't very tall. 'What did I tell you? Fuck off!'

The boy puffed out like a toad. He spread his arms to the sides, as if he was carrying bags with shopping from the supermarket.

Mistake, man, Heinz thought almost compassionately. Never increase the surface you can be hit on.

The baldie made a step forward and at the same time Kastoriadis's foot went into contact with his sternum. The skinhead's back smashed heavily into the wall behind him and he slumped down.

Heinz opened the door and smelt the mixture of cellar mustiness and fresh air. Sound molasses was seeping from the speakers. *I've renounced Jesus Christ, this old Jewish pig*, Heinz could barely understand the lyrics of the song.

'What's up, Rod?' somebody from downstairs yelled over the music. 'You were supposed to stay in front of the door, not in the door!'

Kastoriadis threw unconscious Rod's body down the stairs and went down himself. He was on the second to last step, when his way was blocked by a boy who could be Rod's brother. Kastoriadis did a slight move with his forearm and the top of his fist landed on the bald skull. *Uraken uchi*, Heinz thought with admiration. That was the master's trademark blow.

'Stand by the wall, fuckers!' Heinz yelled at the three other men and knocked beer cans off the table, as well as a wheezing tape recorder. 'Unless you want to look like Rod and the other one.' He kicked the lying man in the stomach with the tip of his shoe. A moan reverberated in the cellar.

'Good acoustics, don't you think?' Heinz turned to Kastoriadis. 'But it stinks in here,' he sniffed and winced. 'You should be paid extra for spending time in harmful conditions.' He looked at the three petrified faces. 'Which one is Beanpole?'

Two of them looked involuntarily at the third one, the muscular boy in a t-shirt with a tight fist and a laurel wreath.

'My name is Gajda, not Beanpole!' the boy shouted.

Heinz flinched and hissed, 'Well, man, then you are fucked.' He suddenly punched Beanpole in the stomach. The boy doubled and went down on his knees. 'And you don't even know why. Let me explain...' he crouched and grabbed the boy by the chin. 'The name Gajda makes me think of a defender of Odra Opole football team in the 60s. And I hate football. And especially the 1960s Odra Opole footballers. Secondly,' he kicked the tape recorder. 'You listen to some real shit and I like good music. That would be enough. But, Beanpole, there is one more reason, the most important one...'

He was holding Gajda by his jaw now, driving his thumb and index finger into his cheeks. With open mouth and goggling eyes Gajda looked like an enormous fish.

'My name is Heinz and you hammered my son. I should kill you, but I won't do that. Instead let me tell you what will happen if one hair falls off my boy's head.' He threw Beanpole against the wall. 'If something happens to him, I will have you arrested for forty-eight hours under any excuse and then my colleagues will do that again and again and again. It will go on. And the other guys in custody will find out about this guy who likes small children a bit too much, you get it?' Beanpole twitched. 'I wouldn't like to be in your shoes then, you stinker.

If I were you, I would start digging my grave straight away. Or I would fuck off to Ireland. Enough of it.'

Kastoriadis approached Heinz. He put a hand on his old student's shoulder.

'I'm not sure if you remember,' the Greek said, 'but, like Sensei Funakoshi used to say, karate starts and ends with pleasantries. I have to be pleasant, but you... You don't have to...'

Heinz didn't need to be told twice. He did a half-turn and attacked Beanpole's body with his elbow. He hit his stomach with all his might. The skinhead went down and started wheezing.

***

They drove back in silence. Heinz kept nervously changing the stations playing tired songs and finally decided to switch the radio off. When they stopped in front of Kastoriadis's house, the karate master said:

'It was not a good stroke. The elbow one. Too much strength, too little technique. You used to have a better *empi uchi*. You need to practise.'

Heinz didn't say anything. He watched Lambros Kastoriadis getting out of his car, nodded goodbye and drove towards the Estate of the 1000-Years Anniversary.

The next three days Heinz spent with his son. His injuries were less severe than it seemed at first. The most important thing was that the boy didn't have a concussion. His teeth were slightly damaged, but not broken. It was the swollen lips that gave him a lisp. Swelling and bruises on his face, as well as a small cut on his head were not too big a price to pay for his immense stupidity. What worried him the most was the fact that there wasn't that much time left before his A-levels.

He didn't feel like talking to anybody during those three days. Nobody but his son and his girlfriend. Heinz talked incessantly, as if he wanted to get through the many years' backlog. Perhaps even the whole lifetime of backlog. On day one his son lay in bed facing the wall, on day two he was nodding, on day three he started talking.

There were a few dozen unanswered calls on Heinz's mobile, mostly from Karloff, but also – to Heinz's surprise – from the police station in Katowice. He erased them all without listening. He did the same with text messages.

On day four the phone rang at 6 a.m. Karloff again. It was Monday. What could he want at that time of the day? Heinz decided to answer.

Without letting Karloff speak, he explained what happened.

When he finished, he heard an enraged whistle. His interlocutor was breathing heavily into the receiver.

'Now you listen to me, Heinz. I wasn't thrilled by your story. And it was not the first time either. I will tell you one thing. I have received a message for you.'

'For me?' Heinz thought he misheard him.

'For you,' Karloff panted. 'It went more or less like this. "If you are interested in Rakowiecki and Leski, then get in touch. John Paul II Avenue, store 65. Eurogarb." You are supposed to be there today, Heinz, today at twelve.'

'Fuck!' Heinz swore and ran into his son's room.

An hour later he was on his way to Warsaw.

THE FIRST SURPRISE was Karloff's face, full of rage, but also full of silent reproach.

A bit more and I will start thinking that he missed me, Heinz thought.

The second surprise was in John Paul II Avenue. 'Eurogarb' store was located next door to a sex-shop called 'Sado-Maso Eros-Psyche'. Beneath the label 'Eurogarb' somebody added in smaller print: 'Military Clothing'.

Sex-shop and militaria. Quite an appropriate place to talk about murdered seminarists who were fans of male fondling.

Behind the counter there was a man in his fifties in a green, military vest. His long, grey hair was plaited, falling on his nape. He was chewing a pen and staring into a crossword spread on the counter in front of him.

'Pine's brother... Pine's brother...' he mumbled to himself.

Karloff cleared his throat and the man looked up.

'How can I help you?' He looked sceptically at the policemen's attire. 'It's springtime, how about a cotton sweatshirt in forest camouflage "Woodland" or night camouflage "Night Camo"?'

He turned towards the hangers.

It's a mistake. A total mistake, Heinz thought. Somebody is having us on. But why?

Karloff cleared his throat again.

'We have a different business. My name is Karewicz. Metropolitan Police. And this is Commissioner Heinz...'

A curtain dividing the shop from the backroom quivered slightly. A tense voice came from behind it.

'It's OK, Johnson. This really is Commissioner Heinz. Please come to the backroom, we can talk here...'

The man called Johnson returned to his crossword and Karloff pushed the curtain to the side. Heinz saw a short, broad-shouldered, dark-haired man. He tried remembering if he had ever seen him before, but to no avail. But there was no doubt he knew the other guy. The one sitting in the armchair. The boy with sunken cheeks. Rat. The nosy informer from the theological college in Żoliborz. Heinz's eyes bored into the boy who remained unfazed.

'My name is Roszkowski,' the broad-shouldered man said. 'One of you have already met my colleague, Jurek Szymczak. In two years' time we will both graduate from the seminary...' he looked at Rat. 'And we will become priests. God willing...'

'Wait a minute,' Heinz interrupted. 'How did you find me? And why did you want to talk to me?'

Roszkowski stayed quiet. Rat got up and started talking. This time there was nothing cajoling in his voice, not even a shadow of sycophancy that made Heinz cringe in the seminary.

'You went to switch off the car alarm and you left some of your rubbish by the cross. Your business card, a train ticket... I have the ticket with me. There you go...'

He retrieved the printed card from his pocket. It was folded several times.

'As you have noticed, I like knowing what goes on around me,' Rat smiled.

No doubt about it, rat face.

'I was intrigued by the fact that a police officer from Katowice came to our seminary. And then I thought that perhaps somebody sent you because you are not from Warsaw.

As an outsider, you are not involved in local dealings...'

Karloff cleared his throat as a warning.

'I talked to my colleague here, he in turn talked to his uncle,' Rat nodded towards Johnson. 'We decided it's worth giving it a try. Uncle left a message for you and...'

'You are lucky that it was me who answered that call,' Karloff said looking at Heinz. 'Otherwise... You know for yourself... The message would get sucked into the big black hole.'

'Is there a side entrance to your seminary or do you always use that squeaky door?' Heinz wanted to know.

'There is another door,' Roszkowski answered. 'In theory it should be locked, but...' He looked at his colleague. 'We have our ways, we can open it.'

'Probably not just the two of you...' Heinz murmured. 'OK, so what did you want to tell me about Rakowiecki and Leski?'

Roszkowski and Rat looked at each other with astonishment.

'We left a message saying that we could tell you something interesting about seminarists...' Roszkowski explained.

'And you didn't mean Rakowiecki and Leski?'

'No.'

'Then who?' Heinz's patience was getting short.

'Those two.'

Rat reached into his pocket and pulled out a picture.

Heinz looked at it. Two faces on the right-hand side he recognised straight away. However, the two on the left-hand side he didn't know. In the middle there was a man with a shaved head. He was embracing the seminarists with his muscular arms clad in a black polo shirt. His eyes were half closed, as if he was meditating. There was a wry smile on his lips.

The conversation in the backroom of 'Eurogarb' shop lasted another hour. It was interrupted by a customer trying on a Surplus Woodie sweatshirt in forest camouflage 'Woodland' and Johnson's triumphant scream.

'Pine's brother. Spruce. Of course! It's spruce!'

AT 4 P.M. Heinz drove down to a bar in Wola. It was *the* bar in Wola, as Karloff stressed. He explained that a few years ago five gangsters were executed there.

'Man, that was a real slaughterhouse!' Even years later Karloff talked about it with some unhealthy excitement. 'And now, the place is so peaceful and quiet... There is nothing like a place with a bad legend as a location for a meeting like ours.'

Before the meeting Heinz managed to find time to go to Praga and change. His shirt was soaked with sweat already a few hours ago, before he even reached Warsaw. He ordered a kebab with aubergine in the eatery at Wiatraczna Roundabout. Better to eat something beforehand. Who knows if they serve any food in Wola. One thing he knew – he didn't have to worry about drinks. He managed to swallow three bites of food when his phone rang. He saw the number of the police station in Katowice. He swore under his breath, wiped his hands on the napkin, came out of the bar and answered the phone.

He was immediately connected to the Head of the Criminal Unit. He thought he would have to explain his sudden disappearance and unanswered calls, but there was another surprise waiting for him today.

'You were right, Hippie,' Krygier started. 'Remember the Aniołów Woods? It happened again. Around ten stabs with a knife. He butchered her and then... Do you know what he did?'

'Put a feather in her hand?'

'No, undressed her. Took off whatever was left of her clothing. And folded it carefully.'

'Did he rape her?'

'No. We are certain of it now.'

'When did it happen?'

'Wednesday afternoon. We have a description of a strange guy seen in the woods at that time. I will send you all the paperwork today. See what you can do with it. I'm worried... I'm worried that this is not the end.'

They talked about the seminarists' case as well and then Krygier ended the call.

Heinz lost his appetite. He went back to the table, took his barely touched kebab and threw it into the bin.

Two dark-skinned men behind the bar sent Heinz hostile looks and said something in an incomprehensible language. Heinz was sure they were talking about him. And that whatever they were saying was far from appreciative.

When he entered the bar in Wola, he felt an unpleasant sting.

It was clearly a follow-up of the Day of a Surprised Police Officer. Karloff sat at the table accompanied by somebody who kept bursting with uproarious laughter, exposing his yellow teeth.

'People of good will welcome the cinder man who rose from the ashes!' Chlaściak yelled.

So Karloff told him about the Inquisitor. Heinz clenched his fists and made a step forward. He felt somebody holding him back by his elbow. The female fan of Gothic rock stood behind him.

'Don't worry. He's always like that. That's his style,' she whispered. 'Take a seat. Everybody is here.'

They all ordered beers. Heinz told them about the meeting

in 'Eurogarb'. He took out the photograph he got from Rat
and made circles with his finger around Rakowiecki and
Leski. He pointed to Father Professor Jan Rutger, a prominent
scholar in biblical studies, a lover of Buddhism à la Anthony
de Mello, an admirer of strong liquors. He relayed the meeting
in the theological college. Chlaściak and Gothic Jolka made
detailed notes.

'And now for the most interesting part. The seminarists in
"Eurogarb" didn't want to talk about Rakowiecki and Leski.
They wanted to talk about those two...' Heinz pointed to two
faces on the left-hand side. 'The first one on the left is...' he
checked his notes, 'Andrzej Skarga. The other one is called
Rafał Kotlarczyk. They should now be in their third year. But
they aren't. Our interlocutors gave us an interesting description
of them. Skarga was, as they said, a talented layabout, a guy who
tried hard to build beneficial connections within the seminary.
He used to brag about his folks having a lot of dosh, running
a large funeral parlour or some other chain for the deceased.
The talk was that he could afford gifts for the teachers. Really
nice fellow. And then Kotlarczyk... That's a completely different
story. Considered a genius as early as in the first year. The guy
could speak four languages fluently. Professor Rutger's pet.
Even our informers talked about Kotlarczyk with a mixture of
envy and admiration. Supposedly such wunderkinds do appear
every now and then in the seminaries run by religious orders,
but not in the diocese ones. In the diocese ones – the guys said
it themselves – the level is generally lower and nobody studies
too hard. You simply want to become a priest. But, as you can
see, there are exceptions.'

'Nobody likes a swot,' Chlaściak interrupted.

'Sure,' Karloff said. 'But that's not a reason for swots to
disappear without a trace.'

'Both Skarga and Kotlarczyk have left the seminary
and nobody's heard from them ever since,' Heinz went on.

'Skarga didn't come back after summer holidays, Kotlarczyk reported back on the first day of October, but disappeared shortly afterwards. Do you understand? No letter, not a word. Simply nothing. In both cases. And now we have Rakowiecki and Leski...'

'Are you trying to tell us that those two separate cases are somehow connected?' Gothic Jolka asked. 'That some maniac is hunting the students of this theological college?'

Heinz shrugged his shoulders.

'There are several overlapping elements linking those four seminarists. Same college. Shared photograph. Professor Rutger and his extra classes for them...'

'For that layabout Skarga too?' Chlaściak wanted to know.

'Yes, for him as well. And there is something else. In a theological college everybody watches everybody. They spy on each other and inform on each other. *Big Brother,*' he looked at Jolka, 'pales in comparison. One of our interlocutors – I call him Rat – told us about a certain incident. It happened in June last year, in the evening. Rat was in the corridor and saw limping Kotlarczyk covered in blood.'

'Fuck me!' Chlaściak exposed his yellow teeth. 'The swot got wasted!'

'Not quite. Rat told me what he managed to eavesdrop when Kotlarczyk disappeared in his room which he shared with Skarga.'

'What did he hear?'

'Kotlarczyk said something like this: "I was almost run over by a car. You won't believe it, but I thought...".'

'What?' Chlaściak asked.

'That we don't know,' Karloff interrupted. 'Rat heard Skarga replying "That's impossible". Unfortunately he didn't hear what they were whispering about earlier.'

'It's always like that,' Heinz muttered. 'No help from anywhere.'

'The thing is, somebody ran Kotlarczyk over, by accident or not. We have no reason not to believe him. When going out, Kotlarczyk should be accompanied by somebody. They call that person a socius.'

'Do we know who that was?' Jolka asked.

'No. Rat saw Kotlarczyk coming back on his own. But perhaps a swot like him was allowed to go out without assistance? Perhaps he was trusted by everybody?'

Heinz directed those questions more at himself than at the others.

He looked closely at the three police officers. Even Chlaściak was listening to his story with unusual seriousness and concentration.

Heinz went on.

'Over summer, his roommate, Skarga, disappeared. Genius Kotlarczyk showed back at the seminary in October, but then suddenly, a week later, he left the college. And now two other seminarists from the same college got smothered... Four seminarists from the photograph are gone...'

'By the way it would be interesting to know if Professor Rutger has a car.' Chlaściak looked at Heinz.

'He does,' Jolka said. 'Rutger is a rather interesting figure...'

She was interrupted by a strange crunching sound. Heinz turned around and saw two men crushing beer glasses with their teeth. A stocky woman was sitting between them. The table in front of them was full of empty bottles of 'Dębowe' strong beer. Shards of glass pierced one of the contestants' lips. Blood was trickling down.

'Fascinating.' Gothic Jolka puckered her lips. 'So, just like you asked, Karloff, I used my contacts. I talked to Krzysztof Bednarz, known as Little Brandy.'

'Is that a guy from the town?' Heinz wanted to know.

'No, he's a journalist. Anyway a guy from the town or a journalist... Sometimes it doesn't make a difference,' Jolka concluded. 'I asked him about this and that, over a bottle of something stronger, of course. This Rutger geezer is very well known. A world-class expert in Old Testament. Biblical studies specialist, whose books are supposedly read in seminaries all over the world. An interesting guy, slightly at odds with the doctrine. For a long time it has been openly mentioned that Rutger wants to leave the priesthood... People say it's just a question of time. He already dresses... wait a minute, I need to find it in my notes... He dresses *in mufti*.'

'*In mufti*?' Heinz was astonished.

'Little Brandy explained that this term describes a priest not wearing a cassock, but civilian clothes, whose only sign of priesthood is his dog collar.'

'Oh, it's just like with us!' Chlaściak couldn't stop himself. 'I don't wear a uniform either, but I have my Glock under my arm. But that priest... What's wrong with this guy? Is there a woman in the picture?'

'I don't think so. They say Rutger is a disciplinarian. A man who would like the church to be like an army. Strictly controlled. Faultless. Free of sin. His meditation and Buddhism are both only means to that end. Meditation supposedly helps one to get closer to God. They say that Rutger is in conflict with the Chancellor of the college,' Jolka looked into her notes, 'Doctor Majda. Though that doesn't stop him from using the Chancellor's office. Or at least that's what my boozer said.'

Heinz confirmed that bit of information.

'What was the source of their conflict? That military discipline?' Chlaściak asked.

'Little Brandy didn't know that. But he told me that the seminary in Żoliborz became famous when the news spread that several seminarists lead very active social lives. Do you know what I'm talking about?'

All three of them nodded.

'People do say that Majda is a good organiser. And he is well-connected within the Church establishment.'

They heard some rumbling from the next table. The contestant with the bloodied mouth slumped to the floor and whacked his head badly. He kneeled and started swaying rhythmically back and forth. Blood trickled from between his fingers.

'You idiot!' the woman screamed. 'You are bleeding like a pig! How will I take you home now, eh? We need to walk past the police station in Żytnia Street!'

That was clearly a rhetorical question and it was not the first time the woman had to deal with a similar situation. In one quick movement she pulled her skirt up, took her knickers off and applied them to the bleeding temple.

'And now...' she chirped. 'Let's go, Rysieniek! Oh, come on...'

'Look,' Chlaściak shrieked pointing at white panties quickly soaking red. 'Our national colours! Patriotism of tomorrow!'

The woman winced and looked towards four police officers.

'What did you say, you webbed pimp?' she hissed at Chlaściak.

Patriotism of tomorrow and a webbed pimp. Explosive mixture. An eloquent police officer and a golden-tongued female hobo.

The other contestant sent Heinz a fish eye.

'Laura, let go,' he said. 'These are pigs. You can tell from a mile away.'

Rysieniek, a woman called Laura and the third one started towards the exit. Nobody even budged at Heinz's table. The three men looked back at the only woman left in the establishment.

'I asked Little Brandy if Rutger had any friends. And, attention please, there is somebody. His name is Stanisław Bator. A legend. Once a commando, then a missionary in Asia and now a martial arts instructor. Do you know how I found out about him?' Jolka didn't wait for anybody to answer. 'I asked

Little Brandy what numbers twenty-one and thirty-seven mean
to him.'

'And he told you about the Pope's death?' Karloff finished
his beer.

'No. The numbers made him think of a club run by
Bator. The club is called... Well, guess for yourselves?' Jolka
straightened her hand adorned with purple nail tips.

HEINZ DIVIDED THE TASKS before they left the bar. Chlaściak was supposed to comb through the seminary once more and find out as much as possible about the four seminarists who disappeared mysteriously or were murdered. There must be some papers left behind. People don't just disappear. Kotlarczyk's case seemed the biggest mystery. No inspired genius leaves the seminary of his own accord. Especially a week after the beginning of a new academic year. And surely not without talking to his mentor. To the Professor who took him under his wings and watched over him. And perhaps, Heinz thought, understood it a bit too literally.

They decided that Gothic Jolka would check the Police Integrated Information System for any entries on the new characters. Earlier it was only about Rakowiecki and Leski, so they were a bit lost. But now there were two other seminarists to investigate, as well as Stanisław Bator. The legend.

Heinz decided that he would drop by the theological college in the morning, together with Chlaściak. He didn't trust the skills of the yellow-toothed officer. The guy hadn't earned any brownie points today either. He wasn't curious why the two nosy seminarists, Roszkowski and Rat, had decided to talk to the police. The answer to that question wouldn't be easy, but that was a different story. Heinz recalled the embarrassed look on Roszkowski's face, when he asked him about it himself.

'You tell them,' Roszkowski turned to Rat.

The runt took the photograph.

'These are four colleagues of ours. And our teacher. And he...' Rat looked at Roszkowski. 'He took that picture. So you see for yourselves...'

'What?' Karloff couldn't stop himself. 'You think that everybody who has something to do with this photo dies?' The scar on his face lengthened. 'That it's like in that film about the videotape that kills? I forgot the title...'

'*The Ring*,' Heinz helped.

'Exactly, *The Ring*. Man, you need to see a doctor.' Karloff looked at Roszkowski. 'You both do. And one more thing...' he lowered his voice. 'We appreciate the info you gave us, but from now on stop playing scouts and running a private investigation. Understood?'

So Chlaściak didn't ask the most obvious question. On the other hand Gothic Jolka didn't ask it either, but somehow Heinz was willing to give more slack to the policewoman with the looks of a gloomy vocalist. They would go to the seminary together. He might notice something, he might find something odd. Or perhaps witness another flogging session.

A theological college in the morning and high society at midday. The high life. He decided that he and Karloff would pay businessman Jan Kunicki a visit. It was Tuesday when Kunicki – if he wasn't on the other side of the world on business – gave lunches for his friends. And that meant everybody Kunicki did business with. As Karloff pointed out, fourth grade police officers definitely didn't belong to that group.

Heinz went back to his hotel in Sierakowskiego Street. His room didn't arouse any negative associations anymore. Actually he felt there now like he felt in his own flat. So-so. He put the picture on the desk covered with cigarette butt pockmarks. He wanted a smoke, but Jolka and Chlaściak had smoked all his straw-like Chesterfields.

He went downstairs and bought a packet of Marlboros and a four-pack of warm 'Lech' beer. He switched the laptop on and started the Boston concert of Fleetwood Mac from the times when Peter Green was still sane and a proper guitar genius. He downed a beer in one gulp and focused on the photograph he was given in 'Eurogarb'.

Four seminarists trustingly looking into the camera next to a man with squinted eyes. The picture was most likely taken on the patio in the seminary. He noticed some details that he had missed earlier. Rakowiecki and Leski, two blond boys. Skarga and Kotlarczyk, both dark-haired, of similar, medium build, as their descriptions said. From the distance you could even mistake one for the other. The genius and the layabout on the left. And on the right – the leader and the one always staying in the shadows. Shared rooms. We know that two of them were gay. What about Skarga and Kotlarczyk? So far nothing. Let's see what Jolka manages to find.

He drank another beer and got slightly dizzy.

Black Magic Woman and *Oh Well*, Green's trademark tracks, ended drowned in the clapping of the audience.

And then there was Stanisław Bator. Heinz typed four words into the search engine: Stanisław Bator martial arts. The web page of the club '21:37' came up at the top of the list. In the note on Bator he didn't find anything he hadn't already heard in the bar in Wola, to the accompaniment of chewed glass. He looked through the gallery of club pictures. Photos of students of different ages during training. The full age spectrum. The fighters in pictures were performing blocks and kicks that Heinz knew so well. Some were better at it, some worse. He felt a sting of jealousy. He remembered Sensei Kastoriadis and his invitation to come and practice.

He promised himself he would try again when all of this was over.

One photo held Heinz's attention for longer. It showed Bator and a man with squinted eyes. A caption underneath said: *Sensei Bator and his spiritual master, Professor Rutger*.

Heinz read the information published on the club website. When going through posts written by the fighters training with Bator, he finally understood what was bothering him. Though the blues machine in Boston played faultlessly, he finally located the out-of-tune note that didn't want to go away.

He opened the third can and went back to the tag: *About us*. He read slowly, like a child who doesn't want to make a mistake: *The club has existed under this name since March 2005*.

But the Pope died in April of that year. So the name of the club had nothing to do with the death of the most dignified Pole of the 20th century, swiftly renamed JP2. As if he was some second-rate rapper. *The club has existed under this name since March 2005*, he reread. Which meant the name was not given to the club later. The numbers twenty-one and thirty-seven had nothing to do with the Pope's death. Unless Stanisław Bator had prophetic powers.

He opened the fourth beer. Lack of sleep, food, as well as stress took their toll. He was drunk. It wasn't easy to find the number of his friend from the band. The number of Doctor Ryszard Burdyna, a guitarist by calling and a cultural anthropologist by profession. Burdyna had a finger missing on his left hand, the one you use to express your cordiality to enemies, but that didn't stop him from playing neck-breaking passages on four bass strings.

'Christ, Hippie, you either had your teeth knocked out or you are completely wasted,' the bass player said, when Heinz tried explaining the reasons for his call.

'Christ... Yeah, Christ... Good one... Wasted too,' Heinz stammered.

It took him fifteen minutes to explain everything.

'If I understand you correctly,' Burdyna said, 'you have a sports club and numbers. And religion in the background. You are after those numbers. After what they mean. They could mean anything. Do you remember that time when football fans used to bring banners with quotes from the Bible to the matches?'

Heinz shook his head.

'Are you there, Hippie?' the bass player sounded alarmed. 'I'm sure it's some kind of a quote from the Bible. Seek and you shall find...'

He heard a burp.

That night Heinz had a nightmare. It was night-time and he was walking down the street. He heard an approaching car and the kind of screeching that you hear when a bumper hangs on one hinge. Heinz felt a shooting pain in his loins. The car hit him and he was thrown a few metres away. He landed by a crude chain-link fence. The driver of the car got out. His pockmarked face was hidden under the brim of a hat. The man cast a shadow in the light of a street lamp, which touched the defenceless Heinz. He heard a rustle of shoes and then it went quiet. 'I am sawdust, Heinz. I'm made of sawdust.' The rustling sound got louder. The man leant down, took his hat off and pushed it against Heinz's face. Heinz opened his mouth and felt a smothering lump of felt blocking his throat.

It was 3.30 a.m. when Rudolf Heinz suddenly stirred in the police hotel in Sierakowskiego Street. Fresh air was entering the room through the open window. Heinz understood that he was woken up by his own scream.

It was a good time to wake up. A moment longer and his bladder would have burst. He went to the bathroom, took a leak and looked in the mirror. For a good minute he kept staring into his puffed up face and swollen eyes. He looked as if he had just had a twelve-round boxing fight. He knew very well that no contraptions would help. Nor aspirin, or any modern booster, for example 'Blowfish', which police youngsters like Baryka stuffed themselves with to tackle hangovers.

There was only one cure. Heinz knew what to do and the very thought of it made his skin crawl. He jumped under the shower and flogged himself with ice-cold water. Still wet he ran back to the room and did twenty press-ups. Another portion of flogging and more press-ups. Flogging and press-ups. He repeated the rounds five times. After five times he felt as if he was dying.

He did the sixth round of press-ups and slumped onto the carpet.

He got up, brushed the cigarette ash and lumps of mud from his body. His head was now working at full speed. He was like the Deep Blue computer, which had won a chess match against Garry Kasparov ten years before.

He replayed a sequence of thought that went through his head before he had slumped into a drunken torpor. Before he had got totally wasted. Martial arts club. A picture of Bator and Rutger. He remembered his meeting with the famous expert in biblical studies in the theological college.

He knew what he had to look for.

He got dressed, ran downstairs and woke up the groggy receptionist.

'Is there a church somewhere near here?'

The receptionist looked at Heinz as if he was some mutant from *The X Files*.

'St Florian's,' he mumbled. 'But at this time of the day... At this time of the day it will probably be closed. My deceased wife, may she rest in peace, liked going to the morning mass...'

Heinz didn't want to listen to the recollections from the receptionist's married life. Indeed. Soaring, but noble pseudo-Gothic. Heinz remembered the image of red brick church towers. At that time of the day – the screen of his mobile phone showed 5 a.m. – even old ladies permanently tuned to the religious Radio Maryja don't go banging on vicarage doors.

Heinz couldn't wait though. He knew what he knew. He was like a predator holding its prey by its throat.

He couldn't be wrong. But how to verify his suspicions? He was wondering whom to call. He had no Bible at home and his son would probably not answer the phone that early anyway. Burdyna must be fast asleep. He always switches his mobile phone off at 10 p.m. and he had the landline disconnected recently. But... yes, of course... He should have thought of it earlier. He checked the screen. It was 5.20. Oh well. He decided to take a risk.

He dialled the number.

'What's up, Heinz?' he heard a raspy, but at the same time alert voice of the Head of the Criminal Unit, Krygier. The tension was mixed with hope. 'You have something on our shit in the Aniołów Woods?'

The boss expected a phone call about that case. A salvation phone call. Before the murderer strikes for the third time.

'I haven't received the paperwork about the last incident yet,' Heinz started. 'Boss, I am calling with something else. Do you have a Bible at hand? I desperately need to check something.'

It went quiet. Heinz could hear Krygier's hasty breathing.

'Are you off your fucking head, Hippie? What the fuck do you need a Bible for?' Krygier sighed heavily. 'I don't use a Bible, but, as you know, my old woman does.'

Heinz quickly explained what he was after.

'Give me a second, I will be right back.'

A few minutes later Heinz recalled the look on Krygier's face on that Sunday afternoon when his boss told him what he was earlier told by somebody else. He was ordered to send Heinz to investigate the case of the murdered seminarists. Krygier's distressed look was not only linked to the fact that his Sunday lunch was interrupted. The Head was equally worried about the fact that the order from CBI disturbed his wife's plans for the day. After Sunday lunch, anorectic, talkative Mrs Krygier usually disappeared in church for several hours to help the poor.

Heinz heard shuffling of slippers and then Krygier's voice.

'So, Hippie, which fragment do you want me to find for you?'

Ezekiel. My favourite prophet. Some say he was a bit odd, he recalled Rutger's words. He thought of the photograph of the biblical scholar and Stanisław Bator.

'Book of Ezekiel. Chapter twenty-one, verse thirty-seven.'

Krygier looked for the right fragment. Heinz was crushing a pen in his hand.

'It's not so easy to find...' Krygier murmured. 'OK, got it. Here's how it goes: *You will be fuel for the fire, your blood will flow through the land, you will be remembered no more; for I, Adonai, have spoken.*'

Heinz asked him to read it again and wrote down the whole fragment.

'By the way,' Krygier went on, 'chapter twenty-one is entitled *God's Sword*. And, you know what? When you a look at it closely, there are some pretty good bits here, perfect for us. For example verse fourteen: *A sword, a sword has been sharpened and polished.* And then it says that it was *sharpened in order to slaughter and slaughter, polished to flash like lightning.*'

'Is there any comment at the beginning of the book? Something about Ezekiel?'

'Let me check.' Krygier went quiet. 'Yes, there is. Listen: *Despite the fact that some critics call Ezekiel an unsound fantast, a delusionary dreamer or even an epileptic, the content of his book and its historical accuracy prove that he really did have a gift of heightened perception of reality.*'

Nowadays people like him become pop stars. That's what Rutger said.

'Are you telling me that the murder of the seminarists had something to do with Ezekiel?' Krygier asked. 'That somebody is fulfilling his prophecy?'

Heinz put a cigarette into his mouth. His hands were shaking. It was not easy to spark it with a lighter.

'I hope not. I hope that the murder has nothing to do with it.' He exhaled the smoke. 'I hope it's a false trail.'

He was sweating profusely. He went to take another shower. God's Sword. Stanisław Bator. A clergyman, a missionary and a commando in one, a person who gave his sports club the name alluding to the Book of Ezkiel. And his mentor and perhaps a friend in the background, Professor Rutger, a big fan of the prophet who, according to some critics, was an unsound fantasist and a dreamer.

He remembered that he left his clothes by the shower cabin. His muscles screamed of muscle fever. Beer is good for muscle fever, as well as vitamin B6. Only laziness stopped him from going to get more beer. And a thought that at that time of the day it would be as cruel as waking Krygier up to ask him to read verses from the Bible.

At 6.30 Heinz promised himself that he wouldn't have another beer until he caught that motherfucker who killed Rakowiecki and Leski.

Then he would toast to the health and good shape of the judge dealing with the bastard.

'FOR FUCK'S SAKE, don't tell me that there is no trace of them left.' Heinz heard Chlaściak's irritated voice.

The police officer was sitting in the Chancellor's office. The Spiritual Father, Adam Adamski, the man without a surname or the man with two first names, was sitting on the other side of the desk, busy browsing through document files.

'I would like to draw your attention to the fact that you are not at the police station, this is not your territory,' Adamski said softly, looking up at the man entering the room. 'Perhaps you could...' he looked at Heinz, 'explain to your colleague that...'

'All my colleague was trying to say,' Heinz cut in, 'was that you are not being very helpful in the investigation.'

Chlaściak nodded ever so slightly. It could have easily gone unnoticed.

He is quite good, Heinz thought. He knows how to talk to this guy. Perhaps he knows it better than I do.

'We are trying to establish who killed Rakowiecki and Leski. There were two other seminarists who might be linked to that case. Skarga and Kotlarczyk. They disappeared into thin air.'

'Not exactly,' Chlaściak interrupted. 'Kotlarczyk sent a letter.'

'You mean an e-mail?' Heinz asked.

'No.' Adamski put the folder down. 'He sent a hand-written letter. Addressed to me. Explaining his reasons for leaving. He decided to go abroad. Reading between the lines I think he got involved with somebody.'

Heinz approached the table and leant over Adamski.

'I would prefer,' he said quietly, 'to read that letter myself than to be told what was written between the lines.'

'It was a private letter. Sent to me. I've destroyed it. I couldn't have known....' he rubbed his forehead, 'that it would be needed. I mentioned the letter only because...' he sent Heinz an icy stare, 'in this particular case I am not bound by the seal of confession...'

'I've found addresses of Skarga's and Kotlarczyk's families,' Chlaściak said. 'At least this much...'

Heinz wasn't listening. He was staring at the covers of Majda's records, glistening in the sun.

'The Chancellor is not in?' he asked.

'Unfortunately not. He is busy finishing his book.'

'He is probably playing catch-up with Rutger.' Heinz went to the windowsill and started turning the albums in his hands. The morning sunlight flickered on the office ceiling. 'There is,' he added 'some kind of a quiet competition going on between them, am I right?'

Adamski stood up.

'There is no competition,' he said slowly, 'between them. Rutger is an outstanding expert in biblical studies. But it is the Father Chancellor who got this college back on its feet. It's thanks to him that the number of students in our seminary is much higher than the average in the country. It's his doing that we have generous benefactors...'

'Yeah, yeah, yeah.' Chlaściak exposed his yellow teeth for the first time. 'The thing is the seminarists here are like tides, they come and go...'

He wanted to add something else, but he was interrupted

as someone knocked on the door. Heinz saw an elderly man with grey hair. The Confessor. He held a packet in his hands.

'They brought it to me,' he said to Adamski, ignoring two strangers in the office. 'They were supposed to deliver it to the Chancellor's office. I think it's the red-and-white chasuble with the eagle from the banner of the 1st Brigade of the Polish Legions. And a Roman style chasuble at that! Beautiful work! It must be the second one in Poland.' The Confessor was thrilled. 'There is also the embroidered stole encrusted with rhinestones...'

'The Chancellor seems to like luxury,' Chlaściak commented.

The Confessor went quiet.

'Let me introduce those gentlemen,' Adamski said. 'Both are police officers...'

The Confessor was taken aback.

'In this case... In this case I better stop disturbing you. Ah,' he turned to Adamski. 'There was a request,' he pointed to the chasuble and the stole. 'We are to bear Kunex Polska in mind and mention the company whenever appropriate.'

'*Ad maiorem Dei gloriam flagellatio,*' Heinz said, when the grizzly priest was in the doorway.

The Confessor twitched and turned around.

'I am not sure if I remembered the words correctly. Latin is not my forte.' Heinz combed his hair with his hand. 'By the way,' he looked at the two men in cassocks, 'quite a show you put up here. *Ad maiorem Dei gloriam flagellatio,*' he repeated in a soft voice.

'You are not bad at all,' the Confessor said. 'Your Latin teacher should be quite proud.'

'What did you tell him?' Chlaściak asked when they were driving back to the Mostowski Palace.

Heinz didn't answer. He was thinking about the stole encrusted with rhinestones and generous benefactors that the seminary Chancellor liked to surround himself with.

28

'UNFORTUNATELY I can not let you in.'

A guard in a black uniform came out of the warden's box similar to those seen in front of embassies. He looked alternately at the two police officers and the IDs they were holding in their hands.

It was 4 p.m. The dust-covered Opel was parked on a bumpy, muddy road leading to a residence in Konstancin-Jeziorna. Two other wardens, also in black uniforms, equipped with pressure guns, were busy trying to remove black smudge, a mixture of rain, sand and mud, which coated the bumpy area around the hand-wrought iron gate and fence. There was nothing unusual about muddy footpaths leading to expensive palaces built in the vicinity of Warsaw by businessmen, singers and politicians. At least that was what Karloff said.

'Do you know why they call Konstancin-Jeziorna a health resort?' he asked Heinz when they were passing the Old Paper Mill, a local cluster of restaurants, entertainment and art establishments.

'Why?'

'Because here sick fortunes and dirty money quickly get better and regain their shine.'

An hour ago a typical spring hailstorm went over Konstancin. Heinz looked again at two young musclemen trying to dry the road and thought of the mythical Sisyphus and his futile efforts.

He turned his head. A huge, two-storey building was hidden behind a little hill. Heinz knew it from some colourful magazine. To get there, you had to first get onto the grounds and these were guarded not by some pensioner paid peanuts, but by a twenty-year-old gorilla, who probably spent half his life in the gym.

Heinz looked at the robust, hand-wrought iron fence and two columns crowned with statues of lions ready to pounce. A primitive metaphor for strength, power and ferocious capitalism. Heinz shook his head with distaste. He looked towards three cameras aimed at the spot where he and Karloff were standing, and then he looked into the guard's face, burnt with ultraviolet lamps.

'There is one thing I'd like to ask you,' Heinz turned to the bodyguard. 'Do you use standing cabins or beds?'

'I don't understand...' the gorilla growled.

'I mean sunbeds. You must be using them at least as often as the Deputy Prime Minister. So cabins or beds?'

The boy remained quiet.

'Mr Kunicki won't see you, man. You are not on the list,' he said eventually.

'Let me give you some advice.' Heinz and the warden stared at each other like two boxers during the official weighing before a fight. 'First, change the tone when you are talking to Mr Kunicki's guests. Even unannounced ones, like us. You will make your boss happy if you manage to learn that. Don't you think, Karloff?'

'Uhm,' Karloff confirmed.

'The second bit of advice is more important though.' Heinz moved his head and the boy instinctively took a step back. 'It's about how not to lose this job. I know that you are just the first link in the chain of security here,' he pointed to the area behind the fence. 'So please pass on the message to whomever needs to hear it: if we are not let in within the next five minutes, two TV channels and several nosy, aggressive hacks will be here half an hour from now.' Heinz paused and checked the effect. He could see his words getting through to the warden faster than he had expected. 'And when they arrive, I will tell them in front of the cameras that we were not allowed to talk to a rich and influential businessman, even though he might have information about two seminarists murdered by the Vistula river. And the viewers will see it all against the backdrop of those cheesy marble lions,' he pointed. 'Do you want to write it all down or have you managed to memorise it?'

The guard managed to memorise. He shut himself in his warden's box with a bang and talked to somebody on the intercom.

Ten minutes later the dusty Opel entered the residence grounds.

'You played it well.' Karloff nodded with approval. 'There is this guy I've been dealing with recently. One lame businessman. The guy didn't want to talk so I had to inspire him.'

'Knowing you,' Heinz turned gently to the left, 'you kidnapped the man and told him to dig a hole in the ground.'

'You don't know me at all. Guess what I did? I kidnapped his cat.'

Heinz burst out with laughter.

'His cat?'

'Norwegian Forest Cat. The guy was in love with the creature. I realised it was a Norwegian Forest Cat only when he told his people to plaster ads on the lamp posts and had them published in papers too.'

'So what did you do?'

'I called him and told him that his meowing friend was missing home very much.'

'You are not normal.' Heinz looked at Karloff.

'That's why they call me what they call me.'

They got to the end of the gravel road, which suddenly split into two. On the left-hand side they saw a square car park covered with red crushed brick. The parking lots were marked with lines of white chalk. Brick and chalk. Kunicki obviously felt the need to stress his widely known love for tennis. Why didn't he put statues of Sampras and Agassi on the columns instead of the lions? That would be more original. Three parking places were taken. There were no signs of the recent storm here. On the left-hand side there was a white Audi A6, in the middle a Mercedes-Benz E-Class and to the right a Nissan Navara. Heinz switched the indicator and wanted to park in an empty spot next to the pickup, but a warden blocked his way. A man in a pristinely tailored black suit firmly pointed in the opposite direction, towards an empty asphalted car park.

As if the Opel was leprous and the three posh motors could get contaminated.

They got out of the car. The man still didn't utter a single word and pointed to a pathway by the house, which could be an object of envy of an owner of a Brazilian latifundium.

First the guard in a black uniform of a pseudo-commando, now the gorilla in a suit, which must have cost more than a police officer's wages. A chain of evolution.

Heinz did his homework in the Mostowski Palace today. The rule was simple: the more dangerous the opponent, the more you needed to know about him. And Jan Kunicki was undoubtedly amongst the top players. Heinz spent three hours browsing through the material with the help of Gothic Jolka and Baryka. Admittedly most was rubbish of no importance, but several pieces of information captured his interest, so he wrote it all down on a piece of paper.

Right behind the hacienda another guard took over and led them to a table under an enormous sun parasol. A heavily built man in a herringbone jacket was sitting there in a rattan armchair. Both his chins, the natural one and the one resulting from obesity, were moving rhythmically, as if they were having intercourse. A big piece of rare steak was rapidly disappearing from the plate.

By the barbecue stood a petit man in pale trousers, which would be perfect for playing golf. His hair was unnaturally black. His polo shirt was the same colour. No accessories, no labels, no logos.

Full asceticism.

'Since you are already here,' the man sprayed some water over the briquettes, which started sizzling, 'make yourselves at home. We are having rare steaks and mushrooms, Viennese style.'

He turned away. The skin of the fifty-five-year-old seemed unnaturally stretched. There was not one wrinkle on his face and forehead. So this is how Jan Kunicki looks like live and unplugged. Without cameras and microphones, not absorbed in encouraging people to invest their money and get richer by using his banks.

'Let me warn you though,' the businessman lifted his hand armed with a fork. 'We serve mushroom Viennese style the proper way, with calf's brains. In half an hour or so a restaurant will deliver temaki sushi. Accompanied, as you would have it, by yellow daikon radish sprouts.'

'You won that pickup in a radio contest?' Heinz retorted.

Kunicki winced, as if somebody tore the fork out of his hand and pricked him with it. Two Chins stopped moving.

'What have you just said?' Kunicki hissed.

'Nissan Navara... Just like the one in your car park. There is this radio contest. I thought you won it...'

Kunicki started laughing.

'You are a comedian, right? But I haven't ordered a clown for today.'

So much plastic surgery and he could still laugh properly.

'But perhaps you ordered some boys. As you often do.'

The businessman was not laughing anymore. He turned towards the man at the table, busy eating another steak.

'Perhaps, funny man, you should meet Attorney Warszawski. He is my lawyer. From now on think twice before you say anything, because this man will stick dynamite into your arse and light the fuse. You won't even realise what is happening before you are far far away from here.' Kunicki pointed towards the cloudless sky. 'And now please leave my property. You are spoiling my afternoon. The food might go off in your presence.'

He laughed at his own joke and went back to the barbecue. A droplet of sweat trickled from his forehead into the scorching abyss and sizzled. The audience with Kunicki had clearly ended.

Heinz and Karloff didn't budge.

Two Chins stopped moving again. The lawyer wiped his fleshy lips into a napkin.

'I recognise you. We've met before.'

He looked at Heinz as if he was scanning an instruction manual of a foam extinguisher.

'Really? I don't recall.'

'It was in Kraków. In court. Some three years ago. I was defending this guy who you wanted to put behind bars for double murder. Your role was secondary, what was crucial was olfactory evidence. I ate you alive. The Rosenthal's effect. Do you remember?'

Now he remembered. He recalled the image of two sisters with cut throats. Earlier somebody tied the old women to chairs and gagged them. Attorney Warszawski was not wrong: Heinz's task was just to prove that the brutal murder had nothing to do with two similar ones in Lesser Poland. What Heinz said in court was that these were no serial killings, that it was not the work of the same maniac. It was possible that the defendant killed the sisters, but had nothing to do with the other murders.

The pivotal evidence in the case was indeed olfactory evidence, and it pointed to the suspect. But during the identification of the smells a very basic procedural mistake was made. A trainer of a dog used for identification knew the placement of containers with smells. Therefore the trainer could have suggested – through gestures or behaviour – which sample the dog should pick. Attorney Warszawski was relentless in taking advantage of that procedural mistake. Enough of it.

'I do remember.' Heinz shook off the memories. 'I remember that thanks to you one more motherfucker went unpunished. The Rosenthal's effect or the Clever Hans effect. I wasn't present at the court then, but I've heard that you argued that the trainer influenced the dog to please the animal and to get some brownie points.'

'I might have said something along those lines, yes,' the lawyer admitted.

'That's all very interesting, but how about you have that conversation elsewhere.' Kunicki didn't even try to hide his irritation. 'Then you can talk about Rosenthal and Clever Hans to your heart's content.'

'Before we meet elsewhere though...' Heinz wanted his voice to sound menacing. 'Let me ask you three quick questions, OK? Firstly,' he went on, not waiting for Kunicki's reaction. 'Do you own the company known as Kunex Polska?'

'I presume you already know that,' Kunicki barked. 'And anyway everybody would figure it out from the name. Even a policeman.'

'And is it true that your bodyguard is Andrzej Kruk, former wrestling champion of Poland?'

'In a moment you will find out for yourself,' Kunicki puffed. 'He is coming.'

A man who was a real mountain of muscle and sinew came out of a nearby building, most likely an outbuilding.

His biceps were ready to explode any moment.

'Come here, Andrzej,' Kunicki waved to the gorilla. 'These men are from the police and they want to ask you something.'

Kruk gave Heinz and Karloff a black look.

'These are called cauliflowers, correct?' Heinz pointed to the ex-wrestler's ears. 'Ears mangled during fights are called cauliflower ears, right?'

Kruk made a step forward.

'What's your problem, man?'

His voice sounded like the spinning of a washing machine.

'Just wanted to start a conversation, you know...' Heinz smiled. 'On a serious note,' his facial expression changed, 'is it true that a year ago you assaulted a journalist who wanted to write an article about the strange closeness between your boss and young boys?'

'Don't answer.' Warszawski lifted his finger in a warning gesture.

'That's all tabloid gossip!' Kunicki yelled. 'There was no article! And now get lost or I will report you.'

Heinz didn't doubt that he would report them anyway.

'One last thing.'

Heinz reached into the inside pocket of his jacket. Kruk spread his hands as a warning and Karloff took a step back to be able to reach for his weapon in case of trouble.

Heinz took out two photographs in a slow gesture.

'One last thing,' he repeated. 'I have a message for you from the theological college in Żoliborz.' He looked closely at Kunicki, checking his reaction to what was being said. 'The stole encrusted with rhinestones, as well as the chasuble for the Chancellor, were delivered safe and sound. You sponsor the seminary and in return the Chancellor supplies you with boys, is that right? Those two, for example.' He threw pictures of Rakowiecki and Leski on the table.

'Don't say anything, Jan,' the lawyer lifted a finger.

'You bastard,' Kunicki said through clenched teeth.

They heard footsteps on the gravel path. Another guest of Kunicki's was approaching. Heinz saw a white chiton and a pink shawl. Almodóvar's successor, film director Latoszek was smiling widely and spreading his hands, as if he wanted to hug the whole world. The smile disappeared the moment he recognised Heinz and Karloff.

Love Parade, you son of a bitch. Latoszek approached the table with hesitation. He saw the seminarists' photos and went pale.

'There is one more thing I'd like to know,' Heinz said slowly. 'How powerful does one have to be, and how influential, to make people...' he looked towards Latoszek, 'too scared to mention one's name loudly. They talk about one's predispositions, they talk about the seminarists, but the name is passed written down on a piece of paper.'

Kruk sighed and looked carefully at the director. It was not a look of friendly concern.

'What I'd like to know is this: are you influential enough to cover a murder?' Heinz finished and quickly grabbed the photographs from the table. 'Have a nice day,' he said to Latoszek.

He was certain that the director would not consider this day a success.

None of Kunicki's gorillas accompanied them to the car. When they got to the car park, they heard somebody clearing their throat quietly. They turned around. A slim, shapely blond woman in dark glasses stood in the side doors.

So that's what she looks like now, Heinz thought.

It was Paulina Rudek, one of the first Polish supermodels and a TV star from the time of the beginning of the new Poland. In the 1990s her wedding to the businessman Jan Kunicki was widely spoken and written about. They got married in a hot air balloon several thousand metres above ground. Kunicki wouldn't be himself if he hadn't placed names of all the companies that he owned at the time on the envelope of the balloon. He also sold pictures from the ceremony to one of the gossip magazines for a lot of money. And then Paulina Rudek disappeared. Heinz remembered being told once that the model dropped her career and stayed in the shadow of her husband who was busy making more money. Now he could see that despite the passage of time, the former star's beauty remained magnetic and could still attract looks of admiration or envy.

'My husband...' She cleared her throat again. 'Has he done something wrong?'

She hadn't introduced herself. She didn't have to. She was one of those people who don't have to introduce themselves to anybody in the country. But it seemed they didn't have to present themselves either. Their profession was written on their faces.

'Why do you think your husband might have done something?' Karloff instinctively pulled his trousers up and his stomach in.

'Does it have anything to do,' she ignored the question, 'with the murder of the seminarists?'

'Since you already know about it,' Heinz shrugged his shoulders, 'then I will give you an honest answer. We are investigating that possibility. And now, honesty for honesty. Please answer my colleague's question.'

Paulina Rudek walked towards the police officers as if she was dancing. No, she didn't walk. She glided across the concrete. Heinz could smell some exotic perfume. He saw a slim hand with a packet of cigarettes in front of his face. What a surprise, he thought. I would have bet everything that she didn't smoke. A healthy lifestyle, et cetera.

'I don't smoke menthol cigarettes. I prefer my own, if you don't mind.'

They looked like three high-school students who left the school building on a long break to fall into the clutches of addiction.

'A young lady from one of the colour tabloids called me. She asked about the seminarists. That's how I know.'

'And what did you tell her?'

Heinz inhaled deeply.

'I told her to give it a rest. And not to call my husband.'

'So he doesn't have anything to do with it?'

He looked down at his feet where he flicked the ash.

She was silent. And remained silent for longer than she should have.

'Let me put it this way: a year ago a journalist from a different tabloid was investigating a similar case. He wanted to know if my husband likes boys. And if he uses the services – so to speak – of seminarists from a friendly theological college. And then, one evening, that journalist was found unconscious in the street. With his nose and all ten fingers broken. So that he couldn't write. Next to him somebody placed a picture of his daughter leaving her school. Do you understand? He is a beast.'

'Who?' Karloff asked. 'Your husband or the journalist?'

'Kruk. His bodyguard. You must have met him.'

'And I understand that after this incident nobody investigated the subject any further, right?'

Heinz put out his cigarette.

'You understand correctly,' she said sarcastically.

'We'd better get going. It's best if we are not seen together. Best for you. And, by the way, how do you manage to cope with it all?'

She smiled.

'We have already been seen together, that's for sure. And that's very good. You are my insurance policy. And how do I cope?' She nervously reached for another cigarette. 'I don't. Next elections are in three years' time...' She was deep in thought, as if she was talking to herself. 'Politicians from different parties are trying to convince my husband to run. They say he would have a big chance. But I won't let him take that chance.' She took her glasses off. The pale complexion of the former model contrasted with a purple bruise under her right eye. 'I won't let him take that chance.' There was unconcealed rage in her voice. She put her glasses back on, turned around and glided back towards the side door.

Karloff opened his mouth for the first time when they drove past the borders of Warsaw.

'My source of information went up in smoke because of you.'

'Who? Latoszek? What a piece of junk.'

'Junk or no junk. That's not something you do, Heinz.'

'His own fault that he earned himself a high place on my wish list. My transfer list, if you please. I wanted to transfer him from the land of permanent smile to the reserve bench. Don't be mad, Karloff.'

He was tempted to recall the excerpt from the Book of Ezekiel, but he stopped himself. Guilty conscience can be deadly.

They got stuck in traffic near Służewiec Horse Race Track.

'What do you think about it all?' Heinz asked, trying to break the stretch of silence.

'You mean Kunicki and the rest? Bunch of motherfuckers. Him, his brief and his gorilla. In my opinion it was that wrestler who played with the boys. But why? Did they blackmail Kunicki? And what's that got to do with the other ones, Skarga and Kotlarczyk? Unless...'

'Unless what?'

'Unless it's her.'

'The delightful Paulina Rudek?'

'Maybe she doesn't want her husband's secrets to be revealed. Her reputation would be tarnished for the rest of her life. Or perhaps, assuming that she does want revenge after all, she struck some kind of a deal with Kruk?'

Heinz didn't say anything. He was thinking about the

blonde with a black eye, once an alfa female from the first pages of magazines and a pride and glory of posh parties. A woman of success who suddenly disappeared off the face of the earth. What did she get in return? Maybe she stays in the shadows because it isn't easy to show in public with black eyes and bruises all over your body? It was all difficult to comprehend.

'You know what?' Karloff suddenly perked up. 'Did you see that wrestler's back? I was standing behind him and I saw him scratching his back…'

'I don't really care about this idiot's skin problems.'

'Neither do I. But it's interesting. When he was scratching his back, his t-shirt rode up. And you know what? Kruk's back looks like he flogs himself. Or somebody does it for him. Seriously.'

Ad maiorem Dei gloriam flagellatio.

In the morning somebody delivered the chasuble and the stole from Kunicki. Who was the courier?

'Find out,' he looked at Karloff, 'what kind of car Kruk drives. Check if it wasn't seen in the vicinity of the Olympic Centre. And close to the theological college in Żoliborz. Check the pickup and the Mercedes as well. Here, I wrote down the numbers.'

He handed Karloff a piece of paper.

ANOTHER PARCEL from Katowice was waiting for him in the Mostowski Palace. He ripped the tightly glued envelope and took a folder out of it. The murderer from the Aniołów Woods was back. At the top of a sizeable stack of papers Heinz found the facial composite. This time his colleagues worked fast. He was looking at a slender face covered with freckles and sparse facial hair. Like a teenager. That was something to work on. The police artist did well. Let's hope the witnesses did well too. Heinz had seen composites that resembled the perpetrator as much as Britney Spears resembles Mike Tyson.

He picked up a bunch of photos and photocopies of handwritten notes from the crime scene. He looked closely at the face. Open mouth with a dry trickle of blood in the corner and bulging eyes, incredulous at what was happening. The woman was naked. Arms and legs spread limply. He looked for a close-up of the hand. No. Krygier did remember that detail correctly. This time the fingers were not clenched on a bird's feather. The notes said that there was nothing in the tightly closed fist and the stretched out fingers of the other hand looked like an enormous spider clinging to the green vegetation.

He looked closely at long shots of the crime scene. The body was laid down by a tree, just like the first woman. Coincidence?

Or did it mean something? He decided to make notes on the back cover of the folder. Next to the victim there was a small pile of clothes. The motherfucker ripped clothing off the woman, folded it and placed it on the ground next to her. He arranged a staging. Heinz looked at the long shot again: two leaning trees, the body and the victim's clothes. He checked the notes. *Clothes worn out and partially dirty*, it read.

Suddenly he saw a hand with purple nails in front of himself. The hand put down a plastic cup with coffee. Gothic Jolka was in her purple edition today. Her hoodie and cords were the same colour.

'You took my place,' she smiled.

'I'm sorry. I didn't know. Let me move.'

He scanned the desk. No family memorabilia, soft toys or artificial flowers which many female police officers use to mark their territory. A female student told him once, that in this predominantly male world women needed to make a point of what was theirs. Otherwise they didn't stand a chance. There must be some truth in this explanation, since he himself had just taken a seat without asking for permission.

'Stay. I'm happy to watch the famous profiler Rudolf Heinz at work.'

He expected to hear a tone of irony, but it wasn't there.

'So, what do you have there?'

Jolka got another chair, looked at the pictures and flinched.

'That's a case from back home. As my boss says: shit in the Aniołów Woods.'

'Aniołów Woods,' she repeated. 'Angel Woods. What a cool name. Cool place to die. Death amongst angels.'

I should have thought of it myself. Heinz nervously reached for coffee. And then he hesitated.

'Is it OK?' he pointed to the cup.

'Don't tell me you are timid.'

Jolka squinted her eyes.

Timidness. In parallel to the killing in Silesia, the murderer from the Woods did not rape his victims. Perhaps in the company of women he felt... He felt uneasy. In every respect. He felt uneasy even in the company of dead women. But on the other hand the killing itself was not enough, so he staged a show, even though by doing so he risked getting caught. The need to create a staging was stronger than fear. The first time it was a feather and this time? He had a feeling he had missed something important.

'Did he rape her?' Jolka asked.

'No.'

'Then he raped her clothes.'

'What do you mean?' Heinz reached for his pen.

'It was so important for him to fold her clothes. When he took them off, he completely forgot about her. Look,' she pointed to spread legs and arms. 'He lifted her arms to get the blouse off and just let the body fall into this position. He didn't touch it anymore.'

'How about you write that expertise?' he mumbled angrily.

'No, you will do that,' she patted him on his back. 'But perhaps you will find useful what I have just said. Anyway, I have something else to tell you...'

'What?' Heinz froze.

'It's about Skarga. One of the two seminarists gone in mysterious circumstances. I asked around. It seems that our devout student knew some nice guys dealing in juice and steroids. They say he was selling it for them. And one fine day he disappeared with their dosh. Boys from the town were furious.'

Juice, steroids and mafia. It's becoming interesting.

'So they got furious and went after him?'

'Well, no, would you believe it? The boy disappeared without a trace two years ago. And it seems that he managed to pull a biggie. He decided to hide in a seminary and wait it out.'

'It would be safer to go away...'

Heinz rubbed his unshaven cheek.

'For some reason he didn't do it,' Jolka went on. 'I know what I'll do though. I will go to the fucking Żoliborz with Chlaściak. We will go through Skarga's paperwork again. A vicar from somewhere must have given him a recommendation. You can't walk in straight from the street and join the seminary. You want to come with us? Let's have a proper raid.'

'No.' He finished his coffee. 'I have an appointment with one so-called interesting man. And anyway,' he pointed to the folder. 'I have this shit to deal with. But I would like to ask you a favour. Actually two.'

She nodded. He took it as an encouragement.

'Check Jan Kunicki. What he did on the 11th and 12th of April, where he was. And check if his gorilla, Kruk, was with him.'

'And the other favour?'

Heinz asked her to check what Kunicki and Kruk did on a different day.

Jolka stared at the dates she had just written down.

'You know, it might be tricky,' she said. 'Kunicki travels a lot. He flies a private jet. If it's in Poland, he lands at VIP airports and leaves unnoticed.'

'But if he went abroad, then it's a different story,' he retorted. 'And don't forget to check Kruk,' he added, lost in thought.

He was already thinking of something else. He was getting ready to leave and couldn't stop thinking that there was something he had missed.

30

THE CLUB was located in Siennicka Street, not far from the 'Eagle' sports centre, which, after years of downtime, was flourishing again. He didn't have to look for the entrance to the training hall. He could hear the karate adepts' shouts. By the entrance to the hall there was a wall display cabinet filled with pictures. Heinz went through the same photographs he had found on the Internet. He looked at Bator's smile and Rutger's squinted eyes. He also studied several pictures not available on the Internet photo gallery. There was one that held his attention for a bit longer. It showed two boys in a *zanshin* stance. One of them had a green belt and his opponent – a blue one. The latter, more advanced in the ins and outs of karate, seemed familiar to Heinz. He stared at the focused face shown in profile. Where did I meet him? He rubbed his forehead.

The cries reverberated at exactly the same moment he grabbed the doorknob. He hesitated. He stood there briefly, trying to decide what to do. Finally he let the door go, leant down and took off his shoes and socks. He brushed his feet. The code of behaviour is very important, Lambros Kastoriadis used to say. He opened the door and bowed. There was a dozen or so fighters there, the youngest one about eight and the oldest Heinz's age. They were moving in one line, performing front kicks. Nobody even noticed him.

Nobody but a man standing further away and closely watching the newcomer. Slim, with short hair. He adjusted his black belt and walked up to the door.

'Would you like to join the group?' he asked.

'Not exactly.' Heinz took out his police ID. 'We need to talk.'

'Please wait till the training ends, I can't talk now.' Stanisław Bator turned towards the students. 'The same the other way round!' he shouted.

'I can't wait,' Heinz lowered his voice. 'I have a few questions about your friend, Professor Rutger. I'm afraid he is in trouble. Big trouble.' The last words were whispered.

Bator waited for the *karatekas* to finish the exercise.

'And now *Heian Shodan* and *Heian Nidan*! Three times each! Every other step forward!'

The students went into complex sequences of blocks, blows and kicks, which had to be done in a particular order. Heinz watched Bator's students performing moves which are the basics of the discipline and felt a sting of envy. When it all ends, he will arrange to meet with Lambros.

'What is it about?'

Bator stared intensely at the police officer.

Heinz told him about two bodies found by the Vistula. He didn't mention the plastic bags, lipstick and numbers left on the dead men's heads. He told him about the piece of paper with the telephone number of the expert in biblical studies. He said that Rakowiecki and Leski used to have private classes with Rutger. And that they were dismissed when it came out that they were gay. Worse, having sex for money.

'He's done the right thing.' Bator looked at his students. 'If I was in his shoes, I would have kicked them out with a bang. They should have been expelled from the college.'

'You don't have much sympathy for the dead,' Heinz whispered.

'It's not about sympathy. You need to have an inner strength and discipline. That's why my people,' he pointed to the *karatekas*, 'do what they do. It's no accident that three of them are clergymen...'

My people. Strength and discipline. Suddenly the training hall seemed stuffy, even though the windows were wide open, allowing fresh, April air in.

'You want to create a Polish version of Shaolin Monastery?' he couldn't stop his irony.

Bator didn't even look at Heinz.

'It wouldn't be all that bad.' It seemed as if he was talking to himself. 'They should be Christ's soldiers. Commandos of the Church. And if they are too weak, they should be punished. Of course...' he finally looked at his interlocutor, 'not the way those two...'

Commandos of priests and seminarists. Heinz had a feeling he must have misheard it. He decided to change the subject.

'How did you meet Professor Rutger?'

'In Asia, strictly speaking in Cambodia.'

Heinz shifted. He remembered what Shaggy said about torture in Cambodia during the autopsy of Rakowiecki and Leski. About smothering people with plastic bags in Pol Pot's times.

'That surprised you?' Bator asked. 'After fifteen years of Pol Pot's rule, the revival of religion began in Cambodia. I went there in 1992 as a missionary and I even met the vicar apostolic of Phnom Penh, Bishop Yves-Georges-René Ramousse. You need to know that the French church and its missionary tradition play an important role in Cambodia even today.'

'And Rutger? What brought him there?'

'His fascination with Buddhism. You probably know about it...'

Heinz nodded.

Bator clapped his hands.

'No. Not like that!' He walked into the middle of the room. The *karatekas* went still. They were all staring into one point.

Only now did Heinz realise how powerful this slim man with the master belt was. 'Forget about your hands!' Bator raised his voice. 'Imagine that your arms are strings and your hands are stones. Karate is about transmitting the shock, the energy coming from below, almost from the ground.'

He showed the mat on the floor. He pointed to one of the students, who quickly approached and halted in front of him.

'Look. First you use your breath and your body. Hands come at the very end!'

He made a swift gesture and his fist stopped before it hit the chin of the frightened student. He is good, Heinz thought. He is really good. I'd like to see him fighting Kastoriadis.

'*Heian Nidan* and *Heian Sandan* now! Again, three times each,' he commanded and rejoined Heinz.

Now. Now was the right time.

'Those two boys were smothered,' he whispered into Bator's ear. 'They were tortured and smothered with plastic bags on their heads. You must know that method…'

This time he scored a bullseye, he knew it. Bator went still, but Heinz was sure that his blow hit the target.

'How do you know?' He sensed a change of tone in Bator's voice. 'Rutger told you?'

Heinz was silent. The *karateka* looked at him and understood that he made a mistake.

'Rutger didn't tell me anything. But since you started yourself…'

Bator was not looking at his students anymore. He was lost in thought, somewhere very far from the training hall.

'The early 1990s in Cambodia were still quite turbulent times. Khmer Rouge survivors remained active. They caught me. I was tortured…' His voice quivered again. 'I know what it is like when a bag tightens on your head.'

'Rutger saved you?'

Bator nodded.

'I have no idea how he did it. But he managed to get me out of there. Afterwards he told me that all he did was talk to them. Conversation triumphed over strength... It triumphed over fit muscle...'

'You were a commando, then a missionary... Why did you stop?'

Bator straightened, as if dropping the weight of horrible memories off his shoulders. He was a master amongst his students yet again.

'Why are you asking? Writing a piece on me?'

'You got it,' Heinz smiled. 'I work for *Sports Review* after hours.'

'Some other time.' He clapped his hands again. '*Heian Shodan* one more time! Can you do it?'

'*Oss!*' a chorus of voices replied.

'I'd like to ask you something too. You mentioned that Professor was in trouble. Are you... Is he a suspect?'

'In my opinion he had nothing to do with it.' Heinz tried to sound believable. 'But Professor tells us less than he knows. He doesn't want to help us. He could really be in deep trouble...'

Bator sent Heinz a look full of absolute determination.

'If anybody steps on Professor's toes...'

'Yes, I know.' Heinz raised his hand in a conciliatory gesture. 'You will break this person's leg in three places, fracture with dislocation. Or...' he paused, 'smother him with a plastic bag.'

He didn't wait for Bator's reaction. He opened the door of the training hall to leave and almost bumped into a breathless boy.

'What a coincidence,' he said to Roszkowski, student of the fourth year of the theological college.

It was him who took the infamous photo of Rutger and the four seminarists, two of whom were dead and the other two disappeared into thin air. It was Roszkowski's picture that got

Heinz's attention when he was checking photos displayed in the club.

Roszkowski sent Heinz an anxious look and entered the hall.

***

It was 8 p.m. when he got back to his hotel room. He was exhausted. He would have loved to go straight to bed, but he knew he couldn't. He switched the lamp on. The light was insufficient, but he still opened the folder sent from Katowice.

I should get glasses, at least for reading, he thought. He decided to choose music at random. He heard the drumming rain, sounds of bells and thunderclaps. And then a heavy guitar of Tony Iommi. The guy could never play sophisticated solos, his technique wasn't the best in the world, he wasn't very fast, but he was capable of giving Black Sabbath's music appropriate power. He could transmit the shock, the same thing Bator mentioned to his students.

During training sessions for future policemen and profilers Heinz himself often used his passions as reference points. Blues and karate.

He understood that a profiler's work could be compared to a *kata*. To *Heian Shodan*, *Heian Nidan* and those more advanced, like *Bassai Dai* or *Hangetsu*.

'What are *kata*?' he would explain the basic karate term while strolling around the lecture room. 'It's a form of combat with an imagined opponent who attacked you first. That's why all karate forms start not with an attack, but with a defence. With a block. Profiling an unknown perpetrator,' he would add, 'is somewhat similar. It also is a way of fighting against an opponent whom we first have to imagine. And look at that.' He would write three mysterious words on the blackboard. '*Zanshin* plays an important role in karate, it's a physical and psychological readiness for an attack. You too should always assume that the perpetrator of serial crimes will strike again. Say goodbye to optimism. To hope that what has happened will not happen again! And another term: *mikiru*, which means an ability to estimate what your opponent will do. That has to be the essence of your work. How to achieve it? In the end it's all about...' he would point to the third word, 'sensing the moment when your opponent has *kyo*, a moment of hesitation, of losing focus, of stupid inattention. Then he is yours. The truth is brutal,' he would pause. 'You won't avoid an attack. Unless you are clairvoyants. But when he strikes...' He would make a swift movement with his hand. 'Then... Then be ruthless.'

Another track started on the medley of Sabbath's songs. *The Wizard* had a passage played by Ozzy Osbourne on harmonica. One very bluesy track amongst hellish howling and Gothic motifs which always annoyed Heinz. What is a serial killer's signature? It's using the same pattern. A pattern, as he used to explain, is like the twelve bars of blues. AAAA BBAA CCAA, he would draw on the blackboard. It's such a simple pattern, yet there are infinite ways of performing it and limitless individual varieties. The same goes for criminals' signatures.

OK, Heinz... He wouldn't mind a beer now, but he remembered what he had promised himself. So he reached for a cigarette. OK, Heinz, he repeated in his mind. Let's see if you really are that good. What those theories and analogies of yours are worth.

For the next two hours he carefully checked the pictures from the Aniołów Woods and read the notes. Several elements linked both murders. Same crime scene. Same time of the day – a weekday afternoon. The murderer was probably unemployed or did shift work – sometimes in the morning, sometimes in the evening. Stabbing with the knife was a link too. And female victims. But the longer he looked through the paperwork, the more differences he saw, not similarities. The women looked different. Heinz shook his head. It wasn't even the fact that one was dark-haired and the other one wasn't. It was more about the first one being well taken care of and the second being some tramp. The first one was spruced up, wearing make-up, while the second one wore dirty clothes, had greasy hair and got drunk before she died. That didn't add up. Also the number of stabs differed. In the first case it was several dozen jabs and in the second only nine. What does that mean? Perhaps the murderer was in a rush the second time round? He was expecting somebody to come looking for the woman and he still had to take her clothes off, fold them neatly and leave the crime scene safely. Or the other way round: the first woman was the 'right' victim, while the second a 'substitute', selected at random. Why? Because the one he had chosen was missing. Perhaps they were supposed to meet and she didn't show up? Changed her mind, felt unwell or simply forgot? But he had already killed her in his mind, he imagined how it would be. Such a disappointment. An accidental victim didn't fulfil his needs. It only gave him a temporary release. And if that is the case then... Then he will kill again.

He thought of a beer again. He went to the sink and filled a glass with water.

There still remained the issue of the murderer's signature. The bird's feather. He would bet anything that the feather in the victim's hand was not there by accident. He remembered Mo Hayder's book called *Birdman,* which was his compulsory reading during one of his internships abroad. The serial killer from the book placed small birds in the chests of murdered women. But that was fiction. And Heinz was dealing with a real live stinking shit. A bird's feather and clothes folded neatly didn't go together. Something was not right. An element of the puzzle was missing.

He emptied the ashtray filled with butts. He went through the photos again. One of them held his attention longer than others. He squinted and yet again thought of getting glasses.

He switched the main light on, stood right by its source. The picture showed the long shot of the crime scene, but it was clearly badly framed. The leitmotifs of the picture were two trees, as if the snapshot was taken by a nature lover, not a police photographer. You had to look really hard to notice the body hidden behind a branch.

Heinz looked at the spread fingers of the woman's hand. He looked at the crown of the tree. Yes. He was sure. There was something white amongst the green leaves. But what was it? He had no idea.

He grabbed the phone and dialled Krygier's number. He explained why he was calling.

'Oh, Hippie... Is it really that important what's in that tree? I have two matches of the English League recorded and I wanted to watch them today.' The Head didn't even try to hide his irritation.

'Boss, I will be honest with you.' Heinz swallowed. 'I don't care about your matches. Especially that you have them recorded.'

The TV commentary went quiet. Krygier must have hit the stop button on his player.

'This fucker...' Heinz was speaking quickly, as if he was worried that his boss's patience might run out. 'He will do it again. The second woman became a victim by pure chance. That's why he only stabbed her nine times. He didn't care about her...'

He went quiet.

'Go on.'

He heard a new tone in Krygier's voice.

'I need to know what's in this photo. I need to make sure that I haven't missed anything.'

Krygier promised to call him back with news. Whatever it would be.

He put the phone down and felt relief. His back hurt from sitting at the desk. He lay down on the bed, which produced a familiar sound. He dozed off when the Sabbath were playing

Changes, a ballad underrated for so many years. He woke up when the phone rang.

He jumped up and answered without looking at the screen.

'You were asleep?'

He was surprised to hear Doctor Kornak's voice.

'No,' he lied.

'Two things. Our charge asked about you again. I wouldn't bother you with it if not for our last conversation. I've checked Beckett.'

'Beckett?' Heinz couldn't remember.

'*Krapp's Last Tape…*'

Now he remembered.

'It goes like this, Rudolf: *Perhaps my best years are gone. When there was a chance of happiness. But I wouldn't want them back. Not with the fire in me now.*'

Heinz's heart was ready to jump out of his chest.

'Here's what I did,' Kornak said calmly. 'I checked with the institution he is held in if they still use maximum security. Everything is the way it should be.'

Not with the fire in me now.

'Could we add something extra? Electroshocks, for example?' Heinz was trying to be funny.

'Forget about it. Anyway, he is insane.'

'That's what everybody thinks. You know very well that he is as healthy as you or I.'

Heinz was still thinking about the Inquisitor when the phone rang again.

'Aspirant Werner speaking,' he heard a bark in the receiver. 'I have a message for you. It took us a while, but we finally got there. There was a kite in the crown of the tree.'

'A kite?' Heinz couldn't understand.

'Yes. A child's toy.'

Heinz sat at the table and directed his vacant stare at the scattered pictures. He was not able to focus. He could still see the smiling face of the Inquisitor in front of his eyes. The bastard knew how to make his life hell. Even from behind the bars of a secure unit. Something will have to be done about it. But not right now.

He could barely stop himself from going to the hotel bar to get two cold four-packs of beer.

He put John Lee Hooker's old blues on. Familiar sounds of the acoustic guitar and the monotonous, simple rhythm struck by the black master's shoe should calm him down. Should, but didn't. Not this time. He remained sleepless for a long time.

It was dawn when he finally drifted into a light half-sleep, as if expecting a visit from an unannounced guest.

HE DRAGGED HIMSELF out of bed at nine. He went to the hotel restaurant and ordered eggs and sausages, a timeless set in any decent hotel. And that meant any hotel serving uncomplicated stodge, just like the food disappearing from Heinz's plate at the speed of light.

He was finishing his sausage when the phone rang. He looked at the number on the screen. It didn't look familiar. With his tongue he moved pieces of bacon stuck by the upper second molar and then answered the call.

He immediately sensed that something had happened.

'Come to the factory.' Gothic Jolka's voice was blank, devoid of its usual strength and vitality.

'What happened?'

'I have some interesting information for you. But there is more...' She hesitated. 'There is more, one of our colleagues is dead.'

Heinz remained silent. He waited to hear more.

'Poremba. The one with the broken nose. You drive his car...'

Freddie Kruger. It could have been worse, he thought.

'What happened?'

'That's the problem. He broke into the Prosecutor's flat. One big fish investigating corruption and politicians. You know, it's a fashionable thing nowadays. He shot him. And then he shot himself in the mouth.'

That was something Heinz didn't expect.

'I will be there soon,' he said. 'I'm sorry...' he mumbled.

Ten minutes later he was running down the stairs in his corduroy jacket, thinking that it is better to inherit an Opel than a stinky kipper.

However he decided to keep that piece of wisdom to himself.

***

News like this always spread fast. In the Mostowski Palace he saw sullen, unforgiving faces of silent police officers. Two of them, whom he knew by sight, sent him looks full of grievance and started whispering something between themselves.

As if he was the one responsible for everything.

After a short look around he found Gothic Jolka. Purple nails were propping her temples. She was gazing at the computer screen. Heinz saw five smiling people on the monitor. Karloff and Freddie were toasting with their beer bottles and Jolka was raising a glass of red wine.

'That was two years ago,' she said quietly, still staring at the screen. 'He was a completely different person then...'

'Do we know what happened?'

'Our boss has been called on the carpet. The guys from the Bureau of Internal Affairs are sniffing around. Shit's hit the fan.'

'Why did he kill that prosecutor?'

'The fucker destroyed Poremba.' Heinz saw swaying Karloff in the doorway. It was obvious that he already found time to pay tribute to his colleague. 'Little fucked-up four-eyed careerist...' he sighed. 'And you,' he pointed at Heinz in an accusatory gesture. 'You never liked him.'

And *vice versa*.

'Leave him alone, Karloff,' Jolka hissed and went towards

the door. 'Leave him alone. There is enough shit around us, we don't need more.'

'Goodbye.' Karloff bowed. 'We,' he pointed at Heinz again, 'need to talk.'

'Sure.'

'He will get over it,' Jolka murmured when Karloff disappeared behind the door. 'He and Poremba were inseparable for two years. Like Laurel and Hardy.' She sat at the desk and turned the computer off. 'Let's change the subject,' she said. 'I have some information for you. Should be interesting.'

'Tell me,' he encouraged her with a gesture of his hand.

'Let's look at Skarga first. I asked around. He was working for Beetle, our own Warsaw second league player dreaming of joining the top league. They came up with this rather good and safe way of making money...'

'Safe?'

'Very much so. As you know, the active ingredient in cannabis is THC or Delta-9-tetrahydrocannabinol. However, genetically modified cannabis has been recently introduced to the market. Its content of THC is really low. What it contains is an intermediate product, which turns into THC only when burnt.'

'So it's a person smoking it who is an offender, not a dealer?'

'Exactly.'

'Which means Skarga was a distributor of safe goods.'

She nodded and reached for a menthol Marlboro.

'Later Skarga also handled steroids for Beetle. Supposedly they had some shit from China which they were mixing with our flour.'

'Fusion cuisine,' he wanted to show off.

Jolka laughed.

'And then Skarga disappeared. With a lot of money. Beetle got the money back from Skarga's father, a guy who would drop dead if he had less than two and a half BAC. And we found Skarga in the theological college in Warsaw...'

'The darkest place is often under the candlestick,' he muttered.

'Oh, wow, is it a day of aphorisms today?' she commented. 'Let me anticipate your next question...' She reached for another cigarette with a shaky hand. 'Why did Skarga stay in Warsaw? Perhaps because of the bird he was seeing. She disappeared as well. She was about to graduate from a local university. Maybe that's why our romantic boy didn't want to leave. Skarga's family are funeral tycoons. They run some kind of a chain of establishments with cute Greek names like Hades, Charon, Styx or something like that. Here's the address where you can find his old man. He is always there from midday.'

Bar Seagull. A street in Góra Kalwaria. He put the note with the address in his pocket.

'Apart from that,' she went on, 'I talked to Kotlarczyk's mother. That's the swot who disappeared at the beginning of the academic year, in October. She said the boy had changed during the last year.'

'Meaning?'

'He became surly, which was unheard of earlier. He gave his mother some money, but didn't want to explain where he got it from. I also spoke with Rakowiecki's mother. Her son also gave her money. I don't know about Leski, because his parents never get sober. What's more, Kotlarczyk started slagging off the seminary professors.'

'Who exactly?'

'His mother couldn't remember the names. Kotlarczyk hasn't been in touch with her since October. The woman still has a mass said for her son every Sunday. She prays for the boy to get back on track. That's what she told me.'

'Do you have anything on Kunicki?'

'Not yet. But I will.'

Before he left the Headquarters, he called the seminary. A female voice informed him that Professor Rutger cancelled his classes. Heinz found the biblical studies specialist's mobile number. Rutger's mobile was switched off.

He stood there for a while, not sure what to do. Eventually he came to a decision.

***

Wow, eyes get sore here, he thought when he entered the bar in Góra Kalwaria. Leaving Warsaw he got stuck in a row of big trucks. In his exasperation, he tried to overtake several times, but every time he had to give up to avoid a head-on collision. Góra Kalwaria, located not far from Warsaw, was a land of greenhouses, a gardener's paradise, just like nearby Grójec. There was this girl in his year at university. He had a crush on her. She told him that Góra Kalwaria used to be one of the more important Hassidic centres in Poland. He recalled it now, crawling behind the row of trucks, even though he couldn't even remember the face of that girl. Enough of it.

Bar Seagull was decorated with bouquets of dried flowers, a horseshoe and harness hanging on the wall and woodcuts with characters in regional costume performing some kind of a folk dance. Ideal place for some agrarian, conservative party conference. As long as there are sunbeds nearby.

The only modern elements of the interior decoration were Kinghouse Poker machines. On the left-hand side there were three of them, another threesome stood by the window on the right, divided from the rest by a curtain. It wasn't the first time Heinz encountered this kind of a set-up. The shrewdness of Poles knew no limits. Especially when you could take advantage of a loop in tax law, different for owning three game machines in an establishment and different when you owned more. What to do? You simply say that you own three and the other three are owned by your brother, matchmaker, aunt or some other distant relative. And make a division between them.

The barmaid sent him a cautious look. He ordered two Okocim beers. As if he was waiting for somebody. He held car keys in his hand. Let them see he was a cool dude. He smiled to the gloomy barmaid and sat down so that he could watch a man staring into the yellowish, frothy liquid in a massive, one-litre tankard.

Old Skarga. The godfather of funeral parlours. Marlon Brando would pale in comparison. Skarga moved his grey moustache as if he had a runny nose. Broad, navy blue braces bulged on his shirt which was bursting at the seams.

Is this guy able to get up from the table on his own accord, when he is sober, or is he too heavy for that, Heinz wondered?

The door to the bar opened and a man in a black suit approached the fat guy.

'You have a delivery tomorrow,' Skarga said in a surprisingly sober voice. 'And in the afternoon you are going to pick up a customer from Kielce. But, please,' he raised his finger which was as fat as a sausage, 'this time don't try to save money. No sanitary inspections!'

'Boss, you know that last time it couldn't have been avoided. The pigs got involved.'

'And no stamps, remember!'

Skarga pulled his navy blue braces.

A conversation of two professionals. Heinz understood what they were talking about. He had a brush with this line of business once. A delivery. Bier barons, as funeral parlour owners were called, use this term for a situation when a coffin needs to be delivered to a church and then a local team takes over. Warsaw is over 60 kilometres from Kielce. Travelling that kind of a distance the coffin should be sealed in the presence of a person from sanitary inspection. No one really does it, but clearly the guy in the black suit must have had some problems recently.

The poker machine jingled and some five-złoty coins spilled out. The player reached into his bag, took out an empty tube

that used to contain effervescent vitamin C tablets and started
filling it with coins.

Old Skarga was alone at his table now. When Heinz
approached him, the porky looked up from his tankard and
winced.

'I paid everything,' he said, staring at an unknown man with
a few days' stubble. 'What else do you want?'

'I want you to tell me where your son is?'

Heinz pulled out his police ID.

Skarga looked around nervously. The man at the machine
went to the bar and ordered another beer.

'I have no idea where the boy is. They say he is in England.
Pati,' he called towards the bar. 'Come over here! This is my
daughter,' he stuck his stomach out with pride.

Pati, probably Patricia, joined them with certain hesitation.

'Tell him,' he said quickly. 'Tell him it's true. Andrzej ran
away. The fucker did a runner with the money that didn't
belong to him. It's all because of this snotty-nosed whore...'

'Dad!' Pati shouted.

Snotty-nosed whore. Probably the first woman the porky
knew who almost graduated from university.

'Doesn't matter.' Skarga waved his hand. 'The boy messed
it up for me big time. You know what it means to have a debt
like this?'

Heinz nodded.

'I paid those bastards off. To the last penny. With interest.
And I don't want to ever see that motherfucker son of mine.'

He took one sip of beer. That one sip would be enough for
Heinz's three.

'Did you know that he was in a theological college in
Warsaw?'

At first Skarga didn't understand him. He wiped beer froth
off his moustache with his hand, looked at his daughter and
burst out laughing.

'What?' His belly jiggled on the tabletop. 'What? My son? A priest?'

He laughed so hard that he made himself cry.

'There, on my table, there are two beers. Untouched. I'm glad I made you laugh. Have a nice evening,' Heinz said.

He got up, grabbed the girl by her elbow and took her back to the bar.

'You were not surprised when I mentioned the seminary. You didn't laugh... You know perfectly well that your brother is not in England, am I correct?' He was staring at the girl. 'You know where he is. I must... I must see him.'

Pati looked nervously at her father, who was wiping his tears with a chequered handkerchief.

32

IT WAS a total disaster. She didn't tell him anything at all. She kept looking nervously at her father and then tried dishing out some feeble story about a text message sent from England. Of course she had already deleted it. Her brother said it would be best not to stay in touch. Best for everybody involved. And what about his girlfriend? The girl broke up with him and took a year off from university. That was lousy. She was no snotty-nosed whore, but she handled it with no class.

Heinz sat in the car. He could see a white bungalow through the trees. A gate with peeling green paint stood ajar. Either the doorbell was broken or the owner had forgotten to shut it.

He spent three hours trying to call Professor Rutger. His mobile remained switched off. He called the police station and asked for his address. The Professor lived in Radość on the outskirts of Warsaw, not far from the Children's Hospital in Międzylesie. This time the man with squinted eyes will have to look him straight in the eye. Heinz killed the engine and approached the gate. He waited for a barking dog running towards him, but that didn't happen.

Heinz entered the yard and looked around. He saw a substantially sized garage secured with an enormous bar. He went to the door and rang the doorbell.

'Come on in!' a loud voice said.

Rutger was sitting at a massive desk. On his left-hand side there was a statue of Buddha. On the right – a bottle of Finlandia vodka. He saw Heinz and flinched.

'You probably expected Bator the karate master?'

Attack. Simply attack.

Rutger closed his eyes and tilted his head.

'I wasn't expecting you, that's true...'

He had difficulty speaking. Heinz was wondering how much he had managed to drink already.

'I've already talked to Sensei Bator. And regardless...' He opened his eyes and spread his hands. 'I like knowing who I am dealing with. So let me welcome the famous profiler, Commissioner Heinz from Katowice into my humble abode. You intrigued me. Then, in the college...'

Smart-arse. He gathered information. Clearly there was somebody he could ask for information. What mattered most now was not to allow him to take charge, Heinz thought. And not let him catch me off guard.

'Did you know Father Kowalski? He used to teach in your seminary...'

'I did.' Rutger drawled the vowels. 'His expulsion was my doing.'

'Why?'

'He liked boys too much.' Rutger went quiet. 'But I'm sure you didn't come here to talk about Kowalski?'

'No. That's not why I came,' he answered sharply. 'Nice house you have here... For a priest...'

That blow should take him by surprise.

Rutger looked around the room with bookshelves full of books, photocopies and notebooks.

'You have no idea how priests live. Our Confessor, the Chancellor, even his halberdier, Adamski, whose parents got him a house and a car right after his first mass... I have earned money for this...' he made a sweeping move with his hand, 'writing books and selling them abroad. You really don't know how rich priests live...'

'Since you mentioned your books... Chancellor Majda told me that you specialise in numbers,' Heinz said casually.

'The Chancellor says a lot of things.'

'For example six and nine. What do you associate them with?'

Rutger got up from his desk and went to one of the bookshelves. He took the Bible out and put it in front of Heinz.

'The First Epistle to the Corinthians. Towards the end of the volume,' he sneered. *'Don't you know,'* he recited, *'that unrighteous people will have no share in the Kingdom of God? Don't delude yourselves – people who engage in sex before marriage, who worship idols, who engage in sex after marriage with someone other than their spouse, who engage in active or passive homosexuality, who steal, who are greedy, who get drunk, who assail people with contemptuous language, who rob – none of them will share in the Kingdom of God.* Paul, chapter six, verse nine and ten.'

Rutger lifted the glass and quickly downed it.

'Apart from that, six and nine makes me think of good rock. Of Hendrix's song. I used to go to the festivals in Jarocin in the 1980s as a chaplain.'

Of course! Rutger. Heinz finally understood why the guy seemed familiar. They must have met at the festival amongst the crowds of people dancing pogo. In the happier times, in the happier circumstances.

'Professor,' he said more softly. 'Please, listen to me. Since you mentioned homosexuality... One of those boys had your telephone number on him. Your new telephone number...' He stared at Rutger, waiting for his reaction. 'But you say you kicked them out of your private class...'

The expert in biblical studies reached for the bottle. He was about to fill his glass, but then he looked up at his interlocutor.

'Will you have a drink? Apologies for not asking you earlier...'

He got up slowly, holding on to the work surface of the desk. He made a step forward and staggered. Heinz instinctively extended his hands to save him from falling down.

'Forget about it, Professor.' He made Rutger sit in the armchair. 'I won't have a drink with you...'

'No?' It seemed the Professor quickly regained his balance. 'But you like a drink, don't you? Whatever... I've heard enough about you. I wasn't wrong thinking that we were alike.'

Heinz was silent. Interesting. Is he really that drunk or is he acting?

'Psychologists call it a borderline personality type,' Rutger went on. 'Disposition for extreme reactions and emotions, depressive disorder...'

'Yeah, you forgot to mention the acute feeling of loneliness,' Heinz cut in. 'Soon you will tell me that we were meant for each other. Like Laurel and Hardy. Like Lennon and McCartney. Like... Sacco and Vanzetti,' he remembered the names of two Italian anarchists sentenced to death by electric chair in America before the war.

'Sacco and Vanzetti, my, my...' Now Rutger looked at his interlocutor with interest. 'What an erudite you are...'

'My friends call me the Lawnmower Man, Professor,' Heinz said through clenched teeth.

'There, in the corridor at the seminary, you showed your real face, didn't you?' Rutger raised his voice. 'The mask of a subtle police analyser, a profiler, hides your rage and hatred for the world.'

'And what about your frustration, rage and hatred?!' Heinz shouted. 'Hidden for years under the cassock?' He lost control and whacked his fist on the table. 'You vented it by murdering those boys, correct? What did you do on the 11th of April after 4 p.m.?' he asked quietly.

He was looking Rutger straight in the eyes. The Professor rocked in his chair back and forth. He reached for the bottle of vodka with a trembling hand. It was shaking very badly, as if it was holding a jackhammer, which got suddenly switched on. Clearly he still hadn't had enough to drink to stop the tremors. He grasped his wrist with his other hand. Heinz quickly grabbed the bottle from the table. Rutger looked at him with hatred.

'I will fill your glass,' Heinz said. 'What did you do on the 11th?'

Rutger tilted his head back and narrowed his eyes.

'On the 11th... I can't remember... How can I be sure? Perhaps I was drinking... Just like today... My problems, so to speak... have resurfaced.' He focused his eyes on Heinz's hand holding the bottle. 'It's not a secret that I went through treatment in Nałęczów. There is a special rehab centre for priests there. Do you know,' he looked around the room dazedly, 'that they trained dogs in Nałęczów so they pick up the smell of alcohol? Please fill my glass,' he pointed to it.

Heinz obeyed.

'And anyway, it's not as bad as it used to be. In the past I couldn't fill my glass, my hands were much more shaky than now. I used to pour vodka into a pot and then drain it into a plastic bottle that used to contain contact lens cleaner.'

He reached for his glass and took a long swig.

'You didn't tell me why students whom you expelled a few months earlier had your telephone number. You lied,' Heinz said softly, 'when you said that you didn't maintain the contact, right?'

'They called me and asked for a meeting. They said they had an important thing to discuss. I said no... Now I regret it.'

The Professor hung his head.

'And don't you regret polluting the mind of your friend, Sensei Bator, with all that bullshit about the sharpened God's Sword? With all that Ezekiel? Don't you regret suggesting chapter 21· and verse 37? Don't you regret that?' he repeated, shaking Rutger's body. 'Don't you regret that this God's Sword of yours harvested Rakowiecki and Leski?'

'They deserved to be punished,' Rutger whispered. 'Not this way, but God's Sword was rightly over their heads.'

'You were called up to identify the bodies. Zealous policemen probably told you about the plastic bags and about twenty-one thirty-seven. You must have figured out the meaning of the numbers right away...'

Heinz gritted his teeth and bared them, as if he was about to bite Rutger.

The biblical studies expert remained silent.

'And then you thought of Bator, of his obsession with reforming people... And you fainted theatrically. You are so sensitive, aren't you?'

Heinz could barely control himself.

'Enough,' Rutger moaned. 'You speak of God's Sword. There is surely God's Sword above my head too. Did you see today's news on the Internet?'

'You mean the police officer's suicide?' Heinz was puzzled.

Rutger shook his head.

'I mean myself. I sent a statement to the Polish Press Agency. I've written that I am leaving the priesthood. Do you understand? I'm already on the other side...' His chin again touched his chest. He lifted his head with the uppermost difficulty. 'There is this saying that a hedgehog doesn't know about a lot of things, but it knows the most important thing,' he slurred. 'Unfortunately I am a hedgehog, not a fox...'

A moment later Heinz heard soft snoring. Rutger had fallen asleep.

Heinz went to the desk and opened the drawers. He didn't know what he was looking for. In the bottom drawer he found a hip flask. He shook it. Empty. He went to the kitchen. The cupboards were filled with plastic bags and sachets with herbs. There were soya sprouts and bamboo shoots on a plastic tray in the fridge. He winced. He heard something and looked through the kitchen window. A car had just stopped in front of Rutger's house. The driver switched the engine off, but didn't get out. Perhaps he was trying to decide what to do, or perhaps he had noticed something. Heinz went to the door quietly. He recalled that the entrance to the house was not visible from the street through the old trees. He sneaked outside without a noise and in three jumps hid behind the corner of the house. He could see the gate lit by a street lamp. He heard the clinking of a lock being opened and then the sound of slamming car doors. In the light of the street lamp he saw the grizzly head of the seminary Confessor. The older man walked through the gate and towards the entrance to the house.

Heinz was tempted to eavesdrop on the conversation. But there would be no conversation. Rutger was fast asleep. And he won't be back amongst the living for a long while still. Heinz knew very well how it worked. He knew it all too well.

A minute later he was sitting in his Opel and turning the key in the ignition.

***

He ate an XXL kebab, went back to his hotel room and got on the Internet. He easily found a link entitled *A well-known theologian abandons the priesthood*. Below the three-sentence information there was a link to the full text of Professor Rutger's statement. Heinz read:

> *After long consideration I have decided to inform my superiors, friends and my loved ones that I am leaving the priesthood. I have arrived at this decision gradually. Without going into too much detail, let me recall three dramatic events, which shook me to the core. The first one was finding out that Crimen Sollicitationis decree – one of the most shameful documents in the history of the Church,*

approved by the Holy Office in 1962 – was in force up until the beginning of our 21ˢᵗ century by consent of consecutive popes, including John Paul II. Consequences of this decree have left marks on many spheres of life, for example on how theological colleges are run. The second issue was the personnel policy of our Holy Father, who – undoubtedly succumbing to pressure and whispers – decided to put people of dubious intellectual qualifications, and often also moral ones, at the helm of the Church in Poland. And the third reason was an experience of a personal nature: as many people know I have been an advocate for combining Christianity with other religions, especially with Buddhism. In recent years my attempts to make the Church more open have met numerous and growing obstacles. And then there is one more reason for my decision. I shall release that information within a week. I apologise to those who feel personally offended by my decision. And to all people of the Church I would like to repeat the words of my favourite prophet, Ezekiel. Let the Lord give you 'a new heart and put a new spirit inside you'[3] (Ez 36, 26).

Professor Jan Rutger

Heinz read the statement once more and then typed into the search engine: *Crimen Sollicitationis*. He saw links to the articles in different languages. He quickly browsed through several of them. All of them stressed that the decree published in the early 1960s dealt with – here the Holy Office was quoted – 'the foulest crimes': 'sexual aggression committed by priests' or 'sexual advances towards juveniles of both sexes or animals'. According to the document, all such cases were to remain

3 The Complete Jewish Bible was used here, as it has the same division into verses as the Polish translation of the Bible (Biblia Tysiąclecia), based mainly on the Hebrew Masoretic Text.

an internal Church secret. Violation incurred a penalty of excommunication.

He thought of the paedophile scandals in the Church in the United States and homosexual follies in a theological college somewhere in Austria. Perhaps Rutger really was fed up? Or perhaps he wanted to divert attention from what had happened here, in Warsaw? He thought about the visit of the Confessor from the Żoliborz seminary in Rutger's house. The same one who liked when confessing sins was accompanied by flogging. Is ex-wrestler Kruk, Kunicki's bodyguard, also his customer, Heinz wondered?

He read Rutger's statement again. Twenty-one thirty-seven. Perhaps, after all, it is not about the quote from the Bible, but about the Pope's death. About the end which – he looked at Ezekiel's words – purifies and gives a new spirit?

Enough. Enough for today. He could feel pain in his temples. He switched the phone off. He started the Fleetwood Mac medley. He fell asleep to the first bars of *Albatross*.

HE WOKE AT 4 A.M., convinced that he had solved the case. He jumped out of bed and ran to the desk. He spread the pictures from the Aniołów Woods with trembling hands. He remembered the thought he had a moment before falling asleep to the sounds of the rock classic by Peter Green and Co.

He turned his laptop on and started typing quickly.

The key is the signature. In case of the first murder it was a feather, a pigeon's feather, to be exact. In the second case it was a kite. It wasn't there by accident. What links those two elements is the metaphor of floating, flying, taking off, being in a different, better world. The murderer kills, but at the same time he is elsewhere. In a land of fantasies, ideas and memories.

He read the written paragraph and reached for a cigarette. What he just wrote was far from the standard language of police expertise, but Krygier was used to his style by now. He stopped objecting when it became apparent that Heinz's observations helped capture offenders.

Why memories? The feather again – we can assume that it was a feather of a young pigeon – and the kite. Attributes of childhood, of immaturity (just like collecting feathers used to be in the past, though not anymore). Both killings were accompanied by acts of aggression. There were two possible explanations for that. Firstly, the killer recalls some events from his childhood. They are – in his opinion – what makes him do what he does. Something from his childhood, an experience or an incident, makes him murder. Secondly, the regressive tendency is supposed to justify the killer's actions. He kills because he feels like a child. What he does is a form of a play for him, an innocent game.

The regression state can also be linked with a pile of carefully folded clothes of the second victim. The second victim should be recognised as incidental.

He typed out the notes about the differences between the victims and his final suggestion that the woman the killer had arranged to see and who was supposed to be victim number two, probably didn't show up.

The symbolism of folded clothes: pedantry, order, discipline. Punishment for refusing to stick to the rules. Psychology knows obsessive-compulsive personality – behavioural pattern dominated by perfectionism and need for constant control. The killer probably tried to single out his victims from amongst women he associated with that type of domination. Let's look at the first woman: even her body type – strong build, ample shapes, distinct, intense make-up – makes one think of that model. It seems likely that a woman with those features (or one the murderer associated with those features) played an important role in the killer's life.

It was time to reach conclusions. He took a deep breath. What he was about to write would not be easy for Krygier to swallow.

Where to look for the murderer? Let's go back to the feather, which – after American profilers – could be called the alpha factor. It is an attribute, part of a signature of a serial killer, which organises the world of his metaphors (feather, kite and in case of the third killing – which, let's hope, we will manage to prevent from happening – it could be a paper plane, an assembled plastic model aircraft, et cetera). The metaphor of the flight seems to be very important for the murderer and could be linked with his hobby (present or past).

I would suggest taking the facial composite to the Polish Homing Pigeon Association in Częstochowa. It is possible that the killer is,

*or perhaps was (he seems to be quite fickle and volatile), a member
of that organisation. He's a loner, a shy person, not very good
looking (the composite shows it). Somebody very different from you,
Inspector! Regards – Hippie.*

He sent the email to the address that only the closest
associates of Krygier knew. He was sure that, as soon as the
clock struck 9 a.m., the Head, together with the police forces
in Częstochowa, would get all their available people up and
running. He himself could only sit tight and wait, hoping that
what he had suggested was the right trail.

He decided to take a day off.

Krygier called at 9.30.

'Hippie, are you sure that I am better looking than him?'

'Absolutely, boss. Compared with him you are Mr Universe.'

'So I'm not a suspect?' Krygier wanted to make sure.

'That's exactly what I wrote.'

'OK, I know what to do. Thanks, Hippie.'

It was about midday when he decided to go to the zoo. The
zoological garden in springtime attracted a lot of winos, chavs and
chavettes, as chavs' girlfriends were called. His son explained the
meaning of that term during one of their very rare conversations.
He hoped that recent events would change something in their
relations. Suddenly he missed his nondescript flat in the 'corn-
on-the-cob'. He decided that if nothing happened here, he would
go to Katowice for a few days. It might be a good moment to
make an effort, since, after so many years, he seemed to have
established contact with his son, found a common language.
Quite unexpectedly they were on the same wavelength now.

The case of the seminarists had lost its momentum. And
there were dark clouds gathering above the investigating team.
The killing of the Prosecutor who headed spectacular, high-
ranking cases was widely commented in the papers and on the
Internet. Commentators usually wrote that the whole thing
was devastating and the fact that the murderer was a police

officer only proved how low the ethical standards were in the institutions, which should be examples for everybody. Nobody cared about Poremba.

More bullshit.

The zoo provided him with another proof of how the world had changed. The cages and runs were dotted with information about sponsors of the animals. He learnt that the penguins were fed by Zielona Budka ice cream maker and the black panther was financed by Polonia team football fans. The thought of football was repulsive to him. He felt sick at the very thought of the European Championships in five years' time. He might go away for the duration.

The afternoon was hot. He stopped by an empty elephant run. A moment later he had the company of three people: two chavs and a boy in a wheelchair, also wearing a tracksuit.

'They are cool, the elephants. Just so wrinkly...' A blond guy leant over the barrier.

'Yeah, they all fucked off. Probably at the sight of him.' The disabled guy pointed at Heinz with his head.

He didn't feel like a fight. Not today. He walked away to the accompaniment of three people's cackling.

He wasn't far from the exit when a purple balloon rolled under his feet. He picked it up and looked around for a child, but didn't spot the potential owner of the balloon. He read a warning printed on the balloon in fat font: *Careful! Danger of suffocation! Children under the age of 8 might choke or get strangled with a flat or burst balloon.*

He imagined the murderer in a felt hat, just like the one the sawdust man from his dream was wearing, holding a burst balloon against Rakowiecki's and Leski's faces. He looked up. The sun was blindingly bright. He looked at the nearest tree. Multicoloured dots whirled around the bough.

The nightmares would not go away until he solved the case, he knew that. The traces and trails were like those whirling dots, circling around him closer and closer. Rutger and his need for revival. Bator and his killing machine made of arms and legs of his students. Kunicki, the college's sponsor paid back in kind. And his gorilla, Kruk, with his back flogged with a whip. The Confessor, who knows everything about everybody. Canny Chancellor Majda, a sacro-pop star, worried about humiliation and scandals. And the Spiritual Father, looking up to him as if he was some rock idol. Boys from the town, for whom it wasn't enough to chase Skarga, so they also went after his colleagues. And the colleagues who might have been involved in something that Heinz had no idea of.

He knew that one spark would be enough to make it all clear. But for now he was still steeped in darkness.

He went back to the hotel and switched the phone on. He saw missed calls from the police station in Katowice and from Karloff. He dialled Katowice.

'We got him,' he heard Krygier's triumphant voice. 'We followed your trail. You were right.'

'What did you do with him?'

'Nothing yet. The guy disappeared. But there was plenty of evidence on the clothing. He didn't show up at work either. But don't worry. Now it's just a question of time.'

'I will be in Katowice tomorrow morning,' he paused.

'Oh? You hope we will find him by then?'

'See you tomorrow, boss.'

He disconnected the call. Krygier was not wrong. He was hoping to be there to look the motherfucker straight in the eyes.

Late that afternoon, Heinz called Karloff. Two hours later he parked his car in front of a block of flats at Białobrzeska Street.

He expected Karloff to open the door on unsteady legs. He was wrong. When they sat down, Karloff gave him an icy stare.

'I know it was you. You did it to him in Regeneration. I can even imagine why.'

'Did you invite me to share your suspicions with me?'

'Not at all.' Karloff lit a cigarette. 'I wanted to tell you about Poremba.'

He told him a story of a boy from an out-of-the-way Mazovian village and his rapid career. Two years ago Poremba coordinated the operation against Warsaw's fuel mafia. They arrested the gangsters and a month later the Prosecutor destroyed Poremba. As those in custody testified, he had supposedly provided protection to mafia bosses in exchange for bribes. They said he warned one of them about the looming searches. In the end Poremba spent nine months behind bars. 'His wife left him. Such a shame.'

'And then it came out that he was innocent,' Heinz figured out the punchline. 'What is it, Karloff? Is it some special day today?' He changed the subject. 'We are talking without any vodka or beer.'

Karloff ignored the hint.

'He came back to work. He was in therapy, a wreck of a person,' Karloff said. 'Sometimes he was aggressive. All in all, he fell into the F48 category.'

F48. According to the International Statistical Classification of Diseases and Related Health Problems, F48 meant 'nonpsychotic mental disorder, unspecified'. Heinz thought of an ad for a deodorant for women, one of the stupidest he had ever seen. *We are all pH five and a half.*

We are all F48 should be an advertising slogan for the police.

'And yesterday that idiot paid the Prosecutor a visit and shot him in the forehead. In front of his wife and children ready to go to school. And then you know what he did...'

Heinz couldn't believe his eyes. Karloff wiped a tear.

'It's better to be F48 than have a 9 mm lodged in your head. I know something about it. I was an F48 myself,' he tried to sound conciliatory.

'As long as you don't stick that 9 mm in your mouth. I will also let you know that right now nobody is interested in our seminarists. The Bureau of Internal Affairs is checking who maintained contact with Poremba. They press Osuch to conclude the case and put some baddies behind bars. Good propaganda. And now, leave me alone, Heinz.'

He decided not to wait for the lift and took the stairs. Skilfully dodging spit and cigarette butts, he reached the first floor. He saw two women banging on a door.

'You are Satan! Open the door, Satan! We know she is there!'

Another thud on the door.

'Problems?' Heinz approached the women who looked at him with gratitude.

'That Satan!' one of them hissed. 'He is not letting us in to see his mother. He imprisoned her. He is there! Listen for yourself!'

He put his ear to the door. He recognised Tony Iommi's heavy guitar. He heard riffs of *War Pigs*. The Sabbath's classics.

'Let's call the police!' one of the block activists yelled.

'I'm the police.'

They looked at Heinz incredulously.

'I am the police!' he roared and took his ID out. 'Leave right now!'

The women looked at the picture of ten years younger Heinz and cowered. The younger one of them turned around and started climbing the stairs. The other one ran down the corridor, every now and then looking back, as if she was afraid that the madman pretending to be a police officer might chase her.

He lit a cigarette when he got to the car. He was thinking of Karloff's words. He felt disheartened. You become too involved in your job and there is guaranteed trouble waiting for you. Let them deal with that shit themselves, he thought. They don't need me. OK, off to Katowice first thing in the morning.

He flinched when he saw Karloff running out of the building and instinctively lowered his head. He followed the

Ford Mondeo at a safe distance. They didn't go very far. Karloff stopped by the Soviet Military Cemetery. He got into one of the cars parked there. A few minutes later he came back to his car and left. When the driver of a white Seat turned the key in the ignition, Heinz did the same.

The Seat's driver stopped in front of a house in Komorowo.

He opened the gate and was about to drive in, when he spotted a man in a corduroy jacket holding the door open casually.

'Who are you?' he whispered with fear.

'Harry Potter, son,' the stranger said.

34

AFTER TWO HOURS of driving, the windscreen of the Opel was covered with red and black dots. The insects splashed against the glass, leaving their wings and abdomens on it. Wipers only made it worse. Heinz stopped at a petrol station, cleaned the windscreen and ate a hot dog. He was wiping his mouth with a napkin with 'Petrol only with us' written on it, when his phone started ringing. Police station in Katowice.

'We got Marciniak,' he heard the excited voice of Krzysztof Kobuz, the officer with whom he shared his room.

'Marciniak is our dude from the woods?'

'Oh, yeah, right, you couldn't have known that. Yup, that's him. Do you know the City of the Holy Tower well?'

The City of the Holy Tower. He remembered the song by the band called T-Love. Częstochowa never meant anything positive for him. Perhaps it was so because of the masses of pilgrims coming to the monastery.

'So-so,' he muttered.

'Then wait for me at the borders of the city. I'll meet you by McDrive. Where Cobra is usually stationed. You know where?'

Cobra. He hadn't heard about her for a while. She was a legendary queen of Częstochowa lot lizards, a woman with a blonde mane and huge sunglasses. She always worked in the same spot and was a convenient landmark for truck drivers who would direct each other via CB radios towards Cobra.

'If you hurry up, you might make it for the show,' Kobus added.

'What happened?'

'We found him in somebody else's flat. Probably his woman's. The motherfucker must have figured it out and barricaded himself inside. Briefly speaking, quite a mayhem.'

When he put the phone down, Heinz had two thoughts. First, that he had to make it. Second, that he wouldn't want to be the woman who happened to make acquaintance with this geezer from the Aniołów Woods.

***

'Did I make it?' he asked Kobuz, who was nervously wiping ketchup and mayonnaise from his mouth.

'Leave that piece of junk here and let's go,' Kobuz pointed at a police van. 'Anti-terrorist forces are getting fidgety to shoot him.'

No wonder, Heinz thought.

'I lived here up until 2002,' Kobuz decided to entertain Heinz with stories from the past. 'By the Relax cinema. I was there at the very last film show, before they closed it down. I remember it was in December.'

'Do you remember the film?'

'*Space Cowboys*. With Clint Eastwood. I was the only person who bought a ticket, so they cancelled the show. But I was the last one.'

Let's hope we get there quickly, Heinz sighed. Otherwise he will kill me with his stories without punchlines. The police car was speeding along Pokoju Avenue. They got to the estate of blocks of flats called Raków. He could see from the distance that it was where they were heading. The area was blocked off by police vans, an ambulance and a firetruck. There were three groups of onlookers. The first were elderly residents, the second chavs, the third all the rest. They were all staring into the same spot.

'Fourth floor. There,' Kobuz pointed.

Heinz saw Krygier, the Head of the Criminal Unit, nervously explaining something to some guy. Heinz had seen him before. It was the police negotiator. The man with an earpiece in his ear looked like an American football coach giving instructions to his players.

'It's deadlock,' Krygier said when Heinz joined them. 'The guy is threatening to kill her and our people are more and more pissed off.'

'She is already dead,' Heinz said softly.

'How do you know that?' the negotiator asked sharply. 'Are you some kind of a clairvoyant?'

'I'm no clairvoyant. All I'm saying is that he will kill her... Even if he hasn't done it yet. And you...' He looked coldly at the negotiator. 'You could do with a visit to a psychologist.'

The crowd of onlookers stirred. As if a rock star had appeared on the stage to start the concert after hours of keeping the audience waiting. The curtains in the window moved and somebody's head appeared briefly.

And then things happened very fast. The balcony door opened with impetus. A man jumped the railing, spread his hands and went down like a stone. The onlookers' screams drowned out the sound of the crash. A woman holding the hand of a small child slumped to the ground. The little boy started crying at the top of his voice.

It's always the same.

'Did you see his trousers?' Krygier was motionless.

'Covered in blood...'

'Fuck. You want to go see? Or perhaps upstairs?'

'No.'

Heinz looked at the fire fighters slowly getting ready to leave. They didn't even put a fireman's trampoline by the side of the building. The area was gradually getting empty. The show had ended. Only the most curious onlookers stayed at the scene.

An hour later Kobuz approached him. 'I have three pieces of information. All are bad. Which one do you want me to start with?'

'The worst one.'

'The woman upstairs is dead. He punctured her with a knife, just like the ones earlier. He must have gone completely crazy... You know what he did? He killed her and then put her into the box of the sofabed.'

'And the other news?'

'The motherfucker survived the fall.'

Heinz already knew what the third bit of information was.

'He probably damaged his spinal cord. He will be crippled for the rest of his life and the state will have to provide for him. The boss says that you predicted he would kill her. How did you know?'

'The feather, the kite, the jump from the window,' Heinz listed. 'I didn't expect this last bit though. I only thought of it here, when I looked up at the balcony.'

'The feather, the kite, the jump from the window? I don't understand...'

'Doesn't matter.' Heinz dismissed it. 'You really did bring bad news.' He looked up. The police team was still working on the balcony. 'Will you give me a lift to the McDrive?'

It was Friday afternoon on the 27th of April and pretty much everybody was thinking about the May long weekend. Heinz had no plans. He wasn't in a hurry to go back to Warsaw. He had an appointment in the Institute of Rheumatology on the 7th of May. There was nothing to speed up the seminarists' murder investigation. Lots of trails, but nothing tangible. He knew from experience that sooner or later there would be a spark that will light the fuse. He would rather it was sooner. As it was, he had a beerless weekend ahead of him. He decided to stay in

Katowice. Play the guitar and annoy his first floor neighbour. He didn't count on being able to organise a joint music session. The chances were, his colleagues from the band were packing their bags now to go to the coast or to the lakes in Mazury. He might have a training session with Lambros Kastoriadis. That would be something. Just like in the good old times.

Good old times. Heinz didn't have anything to do. There was only one thing to sort out.

He took his phone out and called Doctor Kornak.

LEAFY LIME TREES provided some very welcome shade.

Hot weather in the 'corn-on-the-cob' could be unbearable. And it was not even the beginning of May. Heinz and Kornak were walking along a wide alley, listening to the rhythmic crunch of the gravel. They met by the gate five minutes earlier. One took his police ID out, the other his pass and they were allowed into the grounds of the institution.

'You managed to organise it fast,' Heinz broke the silence.

'I told you that I was friends with the director. And anyway it's an easy weekend. Fewer visitors, less staff. Easier to do things...' he was looking for the right term, 'informally.'

It could be quite nice here. Quite nice if not for the faces of the catatonics, confabulations of patients with Korsakoff's syndrome broken by moments of apathy, moans and screams of those with bipolar disorder. Even the building, with its whitewashed walls and dark green roof tiles, could be friendly if not for the sturdy bars in the windows.

Heinz had a short-sleeved shirt on. He didn't have to hide his burn scars here. He wanted the Inquisitor to feel satisfied seeing the burnt flesh. Satisfaction lulls you. It puts you off guard. And that's exactly what he was hoping for. In case the Inquisitor did have something to say.

They sat down in the director's office.

'They will bring him in a moment.' Kornak wiped sweat off his forehead. 'They have a special visiting room here, with a plexiglass partition.'

'I thought...'

'No.' Kornak shook his head emphatically. 'The director doesn't want any trouble. He doesn't want you attacking him. Or,' he looked at Heinz, 'him attacking you. Visiting room with a plexiglass divider. That's the director's condition.'

He didn't tell me anything earlier, Heinz thought and looked angrily at Kornak.

'So?' the Doctor asked. 'Are you ready?'

He sat in a slightly rickety chair and waited.

He heard the door opening. A cleanly shaven, grizzly-haired man entered the room on the other side of the plexiglass. He had aged. Only the eyes remained the same. Grey eyes looked at Heinz and stopped dead. The net of wrinkles on the Inquisitor's face seemed to flicker. The man raised a hand in a welcoming gesture.

Heinz didn't move.

'What happened to your manners?' the Inquisitor smiled. 'Last time we met... The only time we met... I did let you go in first, I'm sure you remember...'

'We are not going to talk about manners, you bastard,' Heinz drawled out.

'Careful or we are not going to talk at all.' The eyes the colour of cold steel followed Heinz's every move.

'How is your reading list? Read anything new recently? Except for Beckett? What do you want from me?'

He smiled and tilted his head, like an animal watching some strange phenomenon. After a while Heinz understood that Urbaniak was feasting his eyes on scars covering his arm.

'Who did it to you?' he made a slight gesture with his head. 'It must have hurt badly.' Heinz was happy there was a plexiglass wall between them. People here knew what they were doing. 'We haven't finished our previous conversation,' the Inquisitor drawled the vowels. 'I'm glad to see you.'

'I didn't exactly have a burning desire to see you.'

'You didn't have a burning...' Urbaniak burst out in hysterical laughter. 'You didn't have a burning desire, that's a good one... Heinz, you have a sense of humour.'

His confidence was gone. For the first time during this conversation he felt like he was losing ground beneath his feet.

Suddenly the Inquisitor was serious.

'You haven't confessed then. I had this feeling... And I was right...' His voice turned into a whisper. 'In places like this one here,' he swept around with his hand, 'you meet different people. A year ago I met somebody who remembered you very well.' He was staring at Heinz. 'He remembered year 93 and a terrible accident near Bogusławice.'

Heinz twitched.

'That was your friend by profession. He was in the traffic police at the time...' The Inquisitor was lost in thought. 'You haven't confessed, Heinz. Neither then, nor later...'

'What are you trying to tell me?' Heinz's voice was breaking. 'What are you trying to tell me, you motherfucker?!' He lost control. 'I will get you one day and then you will see for yourself that death can be a salvation! I'll give you real hell, you fucking bastard. Do you hear me?'

He whacked his fist on the plexiglass.

The Inquisitor got up.

'You are threatening an insane person. That's not very nice.' He shook his head in disgust. 'Really not nice.'

Heinz was trembling. He could feel Doctor Kornak's hands on his shoulders. He and a male nurse moved him away from the plastic divider.

'Where are your gallows, Heinz? Think about it...' the Inquisitor said and left, taken out by another male nurse.

He kept replaying the conversation with the Inquisitor in

his head through the rest of Saturday and Sunday, as if it was
a recording. Sentence after sentence, sequence after sequence.
A sound. A pause. A sound. A pause. He shouldn't have let the
emotions take over. As a result he lost more than he gained. What
was it really that this fuck-up of a person wanted to tell him? No,
he was not a fuck-up. He knew exactly what he was doing, he
knew all along. He followed the rules he set up himself.

He called Kornak and apologised for his behaviour.

'I'd like to ask you one more favour.'

Kornak remained silent.

'Could you get me a list of all the patients of this hospital
from, let's say, the last two years?'

'I'll see what I can do,' the Doctor answered with some
hesitation. 'But don't be too hopeful. If... If it gets out what
you were shouting yesterday, there will be trouble.'

Everything changed on Monday, April the 30th.

Gothic Jolka called unexpectedly at 10am. They spent a few
minutes talking about the investigation, which had come to
a standstill. So far she had only managed to check Kunicki's
travels. Thankfully he travelled less than Brad Pitt and his bird.

'What did he do on the 11th and the 12th?'

'Kunicki and Kruk went to France. I have their check-out
confirmed. I even managed to get a picture from the congress
in Lille showing Kunicki shaking hands with some VIP.'

'What about the other date?'

'Worse. Our oligarch was in Poland. In Poznań and Wrocław.
His gorilla, Kruk, is more of a problem. We don't know if he
went with Kunicki. I told you,' he heard a tone of impatience
in her voice, 'he is a VIP and they get better treatment than
ministers. He has his own plane and it's nobody's business who
accompanies him.'

Not enough, he thought, but didn't say it out loud. We still
don't know enough.

'Don't worry,' Jolka said, as if she could read his mind.

'When this fucking weekend ends, I will work on the families of the seminarists again. Bit by bit we will get somewhere, we will stumble upon something. I'm sure we must have missed something.'

Heinz remained mostly silent. From time to time he cleared his throat or dropped a monosyllable to indicate that he was still there.

'So what are you doing now?'

'Nothing.'

'Oh, right. You are so damn warm and welcoming.'

'Yup. In wintertime you can use me as a hot water bottle to keep your kidneys warm.'

He was eating his lunch and thinking about the conversation with the Black Witch. *Erebus odora*. We must have missed something. We haven't spotted something in time. *Erebus odora*. *The Silence of the Lambs*. Bit by bit and…

He finally understood. He jumped up from the table and spilled broccoli soup. He tried calling Karloff, but to no avail. Chlaściak's mobile was switched off. After another two hours he managed to get through to Jolka.

'The expertise! Where is it?' he asked without any introductions.

'What expertise?' she didn't understand.

'One of those boys' shoes,' he was speaking fervently and incoherently. 'The murdered one… A white and red Puma. New shoe. There was something strange in the tread… A grain or something… I had asked to have it done ASAP.'

'Man, it's a long weekend. Wait till Monday next week.'

'Get those results. I need to know what it was. That's…' he hesitated. 'That's what you were talking about. That's what we missed… Get in touch with Karloff, he was the one who sent it to the lab, perhaps he knows something.'

'I don't think so.' She sounded doubtful. 'And it's not going to be that easy, Heinz. All of Poland is on holiday.'

He lost it. Recently everybody kept telling him that things were impossible.

'You want that fucking case concluded?' he erupted. 'Then find me those results!'

On Monday and Tuesday Heinz's phone remained silent. On Wednesday he shivered seeing Karloff's name on the screen.

'I got it for you, Heinz. Our boys from the laboratory passed the case on to the University of Life Sciences. That's why it took a while. You won't believe it when I tell you what was stuck to the shoe of this sanctimonious faggot. This time we got the motherfucker.'

Karloff's usual blasé tone was gone, replaced by excitement.

'What are you talking about?'

Karloff paused for effect.

'Let me read it to you. Listen carefully. First it's some Latin rubbish, but then only nitty-gritty. Listen.'

Heinz listened.

'Amaranth was already known to humans five thousand years ago. It was known by the Mayan people, it was a staple food for Inca and Aztec people, next to maize and beans. The grains were ground and made into a paste, tortilla and drinks. Young leaves and shoots were used as vegetable and seasoning.'

Heinz's stomach rumbled.

'Pay attention now. *Amaranth had magical purpose during religious rituals of Indians. Amaranth dough with added human blood was used for making figures of Gods that were then sacrificed. Also breads were baked from it to give strength to the warriors.*

Indians considered amaranth a holy plant and called it "immortal". Conquistadors banned the cultivation of this "devil plant". Those who grew it had their hands cut off. Amaranth has become a forbidden plant and a symbol of paganism. According to the legend, the first conquistadors, avenging the death of a monk close to the Pope, and baking ritual flat breads made of his blood mixed with amaranth, almost completely destroyed the plant. Nowadays amaranth is

cultivated in both Americas, in Africa and – listen carefully, Heinz
– *in South-East Asia: India, Nepal, in the Himalayas, China and Sri
Lanka. For more than ten years it has also been successfully grown
in Poland.* Do you understand?' Karloff asked.

Heinz didn't answer.

'And now for the best bit. Let me read some more. *Because of
its qualities, amaranth is part of a diet of special forces. Commandos...*'

'Bator,' Heinz said quietly.

'Yes, Bator. Our boys went to detain him for forty-eight
hours. And, besides everything else, are you aware of the fact
that you fucked up my long weekend?'

***

Amaranth. Devil plant.

Heinz browsed through the notes he took while listening
to Karloff. It all added up. The grain associated with sin stuck
to the shoe of a sinner. And it was a sinner who committed a
heavy crime. Twenty-one thirty-seven. God's Sword cutting the
hands off. Hands were also cut off for growing amaranth too.
Cut with a sword. In both cases.

Rakowiecki and Leski committed a crime against the holy
order and got punished. There is no place for people like them
among Christ's soldiers. He recalled Bator's words. Amaranth is
cultivated in Asia. Perhaps it was there, in Cambodia, that Bator
got to know this plant. Or perhaps he knew it before? He was a
commando at the time. Triangles painted in lipstick were a sign
of a sin committed by the seminarists, completed by two other
signs. By the numbers on the bags and the plant on the shoe.

He waited for a phone call from Karloff and his triumphant
voice telling him that the former commando, then a missionary
and now a karate master, had confessed to the double murder.
But the phone remained silent.

He looked at the notes and decided to go through them
again.

No, it didn't make sense. The amaranth grain was only on one shoe, but there were two murdered boys. They both had triangles and numbers, but there was only one grain. Apart from that it was something easy to miss or ignore. They almost missed it too, during the investigation. And a grain could easily fall out of the shoe tread and then it would all go pear-shaped. No staging. No message.

Wait a minute. What did Karloff say? Some Latin rubbish, then nitty-gritty? Perhaps he read out loud only parts of the expertise?

He dialled the number.

'No. We haven't got him yet,' Karloff said unasked. 'But I expect it to happen any minute...'

'The report,' Heinz interrupted. 'Do you have its electronic version?'

'Yes. Why? Want me to send it to you?'

'Send it. And let me know when you catch Bator.'

Fifteen minutes later he received an email. He was right. Karloff only read those fragments of the report that he found interesting.

He read the whole thing. Then he reread the chapter entitled 'Medical benefits'.

Amaranth grain – Heinz read – *contains important bioelements: iron, calcium, magnesium, phosphorus, potassium. Their content is several times higher than in other grains. Amaranth also contains vitamins A and E, as well as B and C. It is however gluten free. Doctors and dieticians recommend it as a tonic. Amaranth improves memory and the nervous system, hinders the development of stomach ulcers. It has five times more iron than spinach.*

He read the whole document once more.

Stomach ulcers and joint aches are keepsakes from the martial law time and cold prison cells. And bad eyesight too, as I was whacked with a truncheon on my head. That's why I don't like policemen, but I have to like doctors, who listen to my body confessing its ills.

Heinz remembered Rutger talking about his health problems in the seminary.

Asia and stomach ulcers.

Rutger's new telephone number in the pocket of one of the murdered seminarists. Kitchen cupboards full of herbs and grains.

Rutger must have spilled it on the floor and missed it. *Bad eyesight, as I was whacked with a truncheon on my head.* One of the boys stepped on a grain.

It was not true that Rakowiecki and Leski wanted to meet the Professor. They have met. Rutger saw them alive. And he was the last person to see them before they died.

He called Karloff again. He explained the reasons for his call.

There was silence on the other side of the phone line.

'You want me to leave Bator alone?' Karloff finally asked. 'I won't do that!'

'Fine, but start working on Rutger as well. He is lying. He saw those boys shortly before they died.'

'Perhaps they did it together? Soul and body, judge and executioner. What do you think?'

'Find them. And then we'll see.'

It was 2 a.m. when he got a message from Karloff. *Both are gone. Without a trace. I will alarm whoever I can. Prosecutor, judges, regional police commandants and Border Guards. I will show you! It's a fucking long weekend, but they won't get away. Fuck me!*

Heinz read the text and put his phone away. Karloff was truly determined. Which was not a good sign for those he was chasing.

36

SOME GOOD NEWS came on May the 3rd. Things started getting clearer. Bator allegedly went to a karate master course. Heinz called Lambros and told him about the mysterious disappearance, which unnerved forces all over Poland. Well, that must have been the case if Karloff kept his word and indeed interrupted several VIPs' May long weekend.

'He could be anywhere,' Kastoriadis said. 'Master courses are organised regularly all over the world. The guy could be in Paris or in Moldova or in Los Angeles. If you want, I could call two, three places and ask around...'

'No, that's not necessary,' Heinz answered.

Karloff called in the evening.

'Still nothing. But we managed to get in touch with Rutger's neighbours. They came back from their summerhouse. They say they saw somebody visiting the Professor. The two left together in Rutger's car. The other one was driving. It all happened on Tuesday, May the 1st.'

Rutger was drunk again, Heinz thought. He couldn't drive. Who did he travel with and where?

'Would they recognise him? Rutger's companion?'

'They say they didn't have a good look. They were tired after hours of driving. But I will press them harder.'

Next day in the morning Heinz met with his colleagues from

the band. It wasn't a full line-up, the second guitar player was missing. They had just started Cream's *Sunshine of Your Love* when Heinz's phone started vibrating in his pocket. His son? Too early. They stretched the rock classic to a monstrous size so that each of the three instrumentalists could let the steam off and play a solo.

Sweat was running down Heinz's face. He reached for the steamed up phone with his wet hand and listened to the voicemail message.

He stood paralysed.

'What's up, Hippie?' Burdyna took a swig of beer from a bottle. 'Something happened?'

'Something happened,' he answered softly.

Thirty seconds earlier he heard Karloff's upset voice on his voicemail. 'We found Rutger. And the car. In a marsh. He is dead, Heinz. But that's not all. Call me.'

Soon after that message he received a phone call from his son. He claimed that Polish language A-levels were trivially easy.

***

He got to Warsaw that same day. He drove through completely deserted little towns. It was as if a plague or some other disaster visited them. As if everybody died in this fucking hot weather.

He met with Karloff in the Mostowski Palace at 9 p.m. There was a lot of commotion in several rooms of the Headquarters. Heinz could see people leaning over documents and photographs. He had never seen them before.

'The car was spotted by some tourists today in the morning. In a marsh near Mińsk Mazowiecki. Really bad spot. Accidents happen there quite often. It's been hot for the last two weeks, so the water started drying up and suddenly the happy family saw the drowned Volkswagen.'

He started fanning himself with several sheets of paper picked up from a pile on the desk.

'See. Nine in the evening and it's still so fucking hot!'

'Mińsk Mazowiecki?' Heinz frowned. 'What was he doing there?'

Karloff sent him a triumphant smile.

'You know what? I asked myself the same question. I called the theological college to let the Chancellor know. He wasn't there. But I was informed that he went away for the long weekend. Guess where?'

Heinz nodded.

'We found His Holiness in his house in Mińsk. He told us he was supposed to meet with Rutger on 1st May in the evening.'

'Same day Rutger ventured out with his mysterious friend?'

'Exactly. So we have a supposed time of death. Tomorrow Shaggy will tell us more. He wasn't a happy bunny when we told him he was needed back in Warsaw to cut up some priest.'

'There, in the marsh...' Heinz looked up at somebody new entering the room. 'Did you find only one body?'

'We are looking for the second one. But it seems the other guy got off. How do I know that? Because when we found the car, Rutger was sitting behind the wheel.'

Heinz suddenly perked up and looked at the busy police officers around him.

'Why is everybody rushed off their feet? What's so pressing? Something happened?'

Karloff wiped the sweat off his forehead.

'In the message I left you, I mentioned that Rutger's death was not all.' He looked around to check if nobody was eavesdropping. 'We found something in Rutger's car... A trifle... A pink lipstick.'

**

He was listening to Robert Johnson with the lights off and the window open, lying naked on the bedsheet, which burned like hot coal. He replayed the conversation with Rutger for the umpteenth time. He tossed and turned on the squeaky bed. No. Something still wasn't right. A key element was still missing in this wobbly structure.

He fell asleep in the early hours of the morning. He slept until midday. Surprisingly nobody woke him up with an unexpected call. He took a cold shower and called Karloff.

'Autopsy results will be available around 3 p.m. The information about Rutger's death has already reached press and Internet though.'

He switched the computer on. *A well-known theologian dies in a car accident*, he read on one of the websites. He started reading the comments. There weren't many. Most of them consisted of stars in square brackets: grave candles of Bill Gates's era. He read two comments. *I liked his books. I don't believe in God, but the guy was OK.* He found the other comment more intriguing. *He has only just left the priesthood and now he dies in a car accident. Isn't that a sign from the Lord?* Internet is full of paranoid people with conspiracy theories.

But perhaps the author of that comment, signed as St. Thomas, was right? Perhaps Rutger indeed was struck by God's Sword?

At 5 p.m. he was in a stuffy room at the police station, reading the autopsy report. He couldn't focus. I'm reading, he thought, but I'm not comprehending. Only after he read the whole thing three times, could he finally tell what was bothering him.

He caught Karloff running up and down the corridor.

'Listen,' he started with hesitation. 'Is Shaggy really such a pro?'

'If it didn't hurt, I would cut my hand off.' Karloff patted his wrist. 'I would then take it to Shaggy and he would saw it back with his eyes closed.'

Heinz didn't feel like cutting anything off to test the guy. Especially – Karloff was right on that one – as it would indeed hurt. He sat at the desk and dialled the number. He introduced himself and reminded his interlocutor how they met.

'OK, OK, I remember,' Shaggy said with irritation. 'How can I help? I would like to enjoy the rest of the weekend, if possible.'

Heinz took a deep breath. He remembered his conversation with Rutger in the seminary.

Stomach ulcers and joint aches are keepsakes from the martial law time and cold prison cells. And bad eyesight too, as I was whacked with a truncheon on my head. He could also hear what the drunk Professor said later. *It's not as bad as it used to be anyway. In the past I couldn't fill my glass, my hands were much more shaky than now. I used to pour vodka into a pot and then drain it into a plastic bottle that used to contain contact lens cleaner.*

'Hello? Are you there?' he heard Shaggy's anxious voice.

'I'm sorry. I only have one question, actually. You omitted contact lenses in your autopsy report, right?'

Shaggy didn't answer straight away. Heinz had enough time to get an earful of music playing somewhere in the medical examiner's close vicinity. It was some cheesy tune, a mix of gospel and a pompous theme from *The Star Wars*.

'During an autopsy I always make a note if a dead person is wearing contact lenses. Similarly I always inform about all prosthetics. It sometimes helps with identification. Every decent medical examiner does that.'

'Then why did you forget to mention Rutger's lenses? You were in a hurry to go back to your weekend or what?'

'Figure it out for yourself.' There was undisguised resentment in the medical examiner's voice. 'I didn't mention it because the guy wasn't wearing any contact lenses. Simple as that. He wasn't.'

Heinz wanted to talk to Karloff, but he had already left. He asked one of the police officers where he could find the wreck of Rutger's car. He was given the address and went there straight away.

To his surprise the car was only slightly damaged.

'People are often astounded,' Heinz was told by a technician whom he asked about it. 'They think cars would look like the ones in action movies. People think it's enough to kick a windscreen and it breaks. As if it wasn't made of laminated safety glass.'

Heinz had a good look at the car.

'All of the windows were up? Like now?'

The technician confirmed.

'Can I have a look inside?'

'Just don't change any settings,' he was warned.

He looked at the dashboard. He slipped his head out of the car and straightened up. He was still missing the main element of this puzzle.

The next day he learnt that Stanisław Bator was found. However 'found' was not the right term in this case. Bator came back from abroad. He was in Spain. He shortened his stay on the master course when he read on the Internet that Jan Rutger had died in a car accident.

37

ENGLISH LANGUAGE A-LEVELS were even easier than the Polish ones. Heinz kept wondering when was the last time he heard such enthusiasm in his son's voice. Maybe when the boy was a kid. Maybe when they went to the cinema together on one of those rare occasions. As embarrassing as it was, he had to admit to himself that he wasn't used to talking to his son. He didn't know what to say. He didn't know how to behave. He felt at home in the world of witnesses, suspects and victims. But he was completely lost trying to have a conversation with his own boy.

Shortly after noon he drove to Spartańska Street. Cheap clothes still hung on the gate to the Institute of Rheumatology. Doctor Piotr Poraj hadn't changed either. He tried to cheer Heinz up, as usual.

'It's springtime! What am I talking about? We have a hot summer already!' He patted his sturdy thigh. 'Raynaud's symptoms appear mostly in cold temperatures. You still smoke?'

'Unfortunately.'

'Coffee?'

'Unfortunately.'

'Then perhaps you could at least change your job to something less stressful, Commissioner.'

He was the last patient that day. They went out to the car park together.

'You have to make up your mind, Commissioner.' Poraj looked at Heinz with his pale blue eyes and shook his hand. 'One of my patients likes to say that a fox knows a lot of things and a hedgehog knows of just one, but it's the most important one.'

'What did you say?'

Heinz didn't release Poraj's hand.

The Doctor repeated the sentence. He was scared. Scared by the changed face of the police officer.

'That's what my patient used to say, Father Rutger.'

***

It was getting dark when Heinz finished reading. A few hours ago, in the sunny car park, he immediately realised why Rutger's name seemed familiar when he had first met him. It wasn't Jarocin or music links. There, in the seminary, Heinz reacted not to the sound of the name, but to the first name and surname written down on the cover of a book.

Just like in a patient's medical card.

Stomach ulcers and joint aches are keepsakes from the martial law time and cold prison cells.

Joint aches. They went to the same doctor, but they had never met here. However, Heinz must have memorised the Professor's name after seeing it during one of his appointments, written down in the medical card, one of many brought from the front desk and left on the rheumatologist's desk.

He let Poraj's hand from his steely grasp and told him about Rutger's death.

'Shocking. This is shocking.' That was all the Doctor was able to say. 'I didn't know... I didn't know he was dead. Although, to be fair, he hasn't been in a very good shape recently.'

'How recently?'

'I can't remember exactly. He brought some papers he wanted me to keep. Said it was his insurance policy.'

Heinz felt all of his muscles tensing.

I don't like policemen, but I have to like doctors, who listen to my body confessing its ills.

'He left something with you?'

'Yes. And I...' Poraj was clearly uneasy. 'And I, not knowing about his death, sent the papers this morning to the theological college. I'm going away for three months, so I didn't want to keep those papers. My house is getting renovated. I didn't want anything to get lost.'

'You sent it?!' Heinz shouted.

'I left it at the front desk to be sent by recorded delivery. Usually they go to the post office at 1 p.m. Or a little bit before. Recently I wanted to send...'

Heinz was not listening anymore. He yanked his phone out of his pocket and looked at the screen. It was 12.50. He ran towards the main entrance to the Institute of Rheumatology.

He read through photocopies with parts marked in green and red. He sighed deeply.

He knew why the two seminarists had died.

He knew everything. Almost everything.

It was the evening of 7th May. His first instinct was to jump into the car. He reached for his car keys, but changed his mind. No. He would go tomorrow. He will be there when they open the establishment.

***

The next day he drove to Góra Kalwaria. The monstrous chubby, *capo di tutti capi* of undertakers and memorial stonemasons, was sitting at his table with his head hung down.

Heinz went to the bar. This time he didn't order beers. He took a photo out and showed it to the barmaid. The girl looked at the four young boys and a man in the middle. They talked in quiet voices for a few minutes. At some point the girl reached for a handkerchief and wiped her eyes. Finally she came from behind the bar and went to the table where her father was sitting.

'Dad. Help him. Please,' she said.

Old Skarga looked at Heinz. This time his eyes were not hazy with alcohol and his breath was free from drunken miasma.

'What do you expect of me?' he asked, examining Heinz with a surprising alertness.

38

SEVERAL TRUCKS drove by in a row and stirred up the dirt on the side of the road. He could feel dust and sand particles penetrating his skin and lungs. He filled the jar with water and put the flowers in. He got an impression that the cross was slightly tilted to the right. Perhaps it was so because of the winds that accompanied spring storms. Or perhaps the cross was not tilted at all and he just believed it was.

He believed in lots of things. He believed that the Inquisitor wanted to tell him something important. And the truth was that the ruthless murderer, pronounced insane at the time of the offence, simply wanted to have some fun at his expense. Kornak hasn't called back. And he probably won't. Heinz wondered if he should call and apologise for his behaviour again. But, to be honest, what was he supposed to apologise for? Anyway, best to let things take their course.

Just like he let things take their course in the early summer of 1986, when he went to Warsaw Remont club to see *The Song Remains the Same*, film footage of Led Zeppelin's concerts in New York. At the beginning of a complicated blues in a minor scale, which he knew by heart, he saw a dark-haired girl staring intensely at one of several screens hanging above their heads. The girl was standing right by the speaker, indifferent to the fact that John 'Bonzo' Bonham's percussion was bombarding her guts. When *Since I've Been Loving You* ended he saw that the girl was crying. He made up his mind. He approached her with a handkerchief. And that was how he met his wife.

'From now on we will be like Lennon and McCartney,' Heinz muttered. He had had quite a lot to drink already.

'Like Bonnie and Clyde,' she answered.

'Like...' he was thinking. 'Like Page and Plant,' he pointed to the screen.

'Like Sacco and Vanzetti. Do you know why I was crying?' The dark-haired girl looked at Heinz. 'Because I thought they were screening a different concert tonight. I thought I would see The Police. I was crying with rage.'

He learnt that the girl was from Silesia and came to Warsaw to study. Soon he also learnt who Sacco and Vanzetti were. Two Italians with melodious names and fucked-up lives.

Let the things take their course. Heinz got up and straightened. He reached into his trouser pocket for the car keys. Instead of them he found a wad of paper. It was a written note from Osuch to the Head of CBI to close the case due to the death of the main suspect. He didn't doubt what the Central Bureau of Investigation would do. Happily consent.

He finally found the keys and got into the car. He was about to press play on his CD player when he heard his phone ringing. Private number. He sighed and answered.

'He will see you. Today would be best,' the voice said.

He didn't have to ask who was calling. He knew.

'LET'S START with the evening when Kotlarczyk burst into your room and told you that somebody was trying to run him over. He was bruised, had scratches on his face. That's what he looked like, more or less.'

Heinz spoke slowly. He wanted to get every word through to the boy. They were alone in the backroom. This time it wasn't the girl who served customers behind the bar, but a 6' 6" tall muscleman. He was clumsy, but nobody seemed to mind.

It was 15th May. People have a right to have a drink at 9 p.m.

'You understood right away what was going on. You and Kotlarczyk looked alike. Same hair colour, same physique. Easy to make a mistake in the darkness. You realised that somebody was hunting you, not him. Who could want something from a theological college top student? You, on the other hand... That's a different story. Shady acquaintances, dodgy dealings and that scam you pulled on the boys from the town. You hid in the seminary. I still can't understand why. You had money, why didn't you just leave?'

'My girlfriend couldn't go,' the boy answered. 'She was pregnant, she wanted to complete the year at university. And doctors wanted to keep an eye on her. I read once about a guy who went to a theological college to hide from the mafia. I talked to the vicar, compensated him appropriately for his support and keeping his mouth shut...' He smiled. 'Actually it was quite amusing. You had quite a lot of freedom in the seminary. If you had dosh...'

'But it wasn't so amusing for the others. You realised that somebody wanted to harm you and decided to disappear before the end of the academic year. You asked your father for help. He paid off your debts, but you were still scared, so you stayed hidden...'

'I wanted everything to go quiet,' he explained.

'A new academic year started and then, as soon as it started, your friend, Kotlarczyk, vanished. We still don't know what happened to him.'

'I had no idea,' Skarga said quietly.

'You also didn't know that somebody smothered two other seminarists. They died in terrible agony. Believe you me. This whole case is not about you.'

'Then about what?'

There were raised voices in the bar and then a clinking sound of coins pouring out of a poker machine.

'I told you how they were killed. I don't think it was the guys from the town who did it. Because that would mean you had some kind of a deal with Rakowiecki and Leski, which was not the case. That would mean you were all dealing juice or steroids. But there was another possibility. Rakowiecki and Leski were male whores. Leski joined this business later than Rakowiecki. Rutger found out about it a few months ago and kicked the boys out of his special class.'

'That was the only sensible class,' Skarga muttered. 'Wait a minute,' he reached for the beer. 'So was that Rutger who killed them?'

'No. And it wasn't Stanisław Bator either, Rutger's friend. A former commando and a missionary. Even more obsessed than the Professor with the idea of the Church as an immaculate army.'

'Rutger told us about him. He is...' Skarga bit his lips, 'some lunatic.'

'Anyhow, it wasn't him. And not Rutger either. I won't waste time explaining why. Rakowiecki and Leski were male whores, right? Perhaps they started blackmailing somebody? And they got it wrong. For example there is this businessman who used to use their services and in return provided financial support to the seminary. Your Chancellor, that lame singer, informed the diocese about increasing income and everybody was happy. The thing is, the blackmail scenario doesn't make sense either.'

'Why?'

'There were pink triangles on the plastic bags that Rakowiecki and Leski had on their heads which suggests without any doubt that they were killed for being homosexuals. Why would a businessman using the boys' services leave a trace leading to himself? And in any case that businessman had methods at his disposal to persuade two youngsters against blackmailing. He could use the services of his bodyguard, former wrestler, who could break their arms and legs. That would do the job.'

'A wrestler,' Skarga whispered. 'I remember one. He used to come to the seminary.'

'The guy seems to know pain. Delivered to others and to himself.' Heinz remembered the flogging scene. 'Whatever. This businessman torments his wife. Perhaps it was her who struck a deal with the wrestler and decided to frame her husband for a double murder? No, that's not it either. She didn't have to go as far as killing somebody to destroy her darling. I presume she has gathered a big enough dossier on him and is just waiting for the right moment.'

'So if nobody could kill, who killed then?' Skarga asked impatiently.

Heinz didn't answer. He opened his briefcase and took out a bunch of papers stapled together. He passed them on to his interlocutor. Skarga thumbed the papers. First slowly and then faster and faster.

'What's that? I don't understand...'

'These are photocopies of articles written by Chancellor Majda. And fragments of his books. The second folder contains works that the Chancellor plagiarised. Written by seminarists from different parts of Poland and beyond. Your friend Kotlarczyk gathered the material. He probably shared it with one of the guys from Rutger's private class. My bet is it was Leski. Do you understand? He gathered evidence that Majda's texts are all one big piracy. Kotlarczyk went missing, Leski is dead, Rakowiecki is dead,' Heinz counted on his fingers. 'And now,' he moved his face close to Skarga's face, 'let's go back to that moment in the evening when bloodied Kotlarczyk burst into your shared room. He told you that he had recognised the car trying to run him over. He couldn't believe it himself, but he told you everything, didn't he?'

Skarga slowly nodded.

40

A MAN as grey as a dove left a pale wood confessional. Above the shriving pew – Heinz remembered that term from a very distant past – there was a woodcut depicting the ninth Station of the Cross. The journey to Golgotha is almost over. Christ falls the third and last time.

He knelt down and looked through the grill at the face resting on the hand. He noticed that the confessional had a plaque affixed to it, which said 'Confess your sins to Father Chancellor Majda'.

'What's up, son?' he heard the familiar voice. 'Praised be Jesus Christ and then: "The last time I confessed my sins was…", et cetera, et cetera.'

'I came to confess… Confess for you, Father. For "Thou shall not kill" and "Thou shall not steal"…'

The priest flinched. He peeked through the grill.

An eye of a screw. An eye full of contempt. As if he was staring at a convict through a Judas hole.

'Several mistakes…' Heinz whispered. 'You made several mistakes, Father… The lipstick in Rutger's car was unnecessary. A needless gadget. A sin of exaggeration or whatever you call it,' he whispered fervently. 'Would a subtle analyst like Rutger really leave crime evidence in his car? And since we are talking about the car… Two more mistakes… The windows of the car that went into the marsh didn't shatter. Contrary to common opinions car windows are quite strong and can take a lot. Even a fall into the water. All the windows in the car were shut. And it was a very muggy evening, when you and Rutger took off from his house. Even at night. The storm was approaching. I have checked that. And the windows stayed shut. You made a mistake, Father. You put the air conditioning on. It was set on 18 degrees. If Rutger drove the car, he would never have done it, not with a rheumatic condition. But that's really nothing in comparison to your cardinal mistake...' He paused, as if he was listening to the singing of the faithful during the mass. 'Rutger was blind. Blind as a bat. It was a token of the martial law times and militia truncheons. He didn't use glasses. He always wore contact lenses. I've checked that too. And suddenly we find him in the driving seat. A man as blind as a bat drives a car not wearing his contact lenses. Isn't that strange?' He heard heavy breathing. 'Here's how it went. You picked him up and you were supposed to go to Mińsk Mazowiecki together. Rutger was drunk. Favourable circumstances. You drove, Rutger was asleep. You got to the marsh, you moved him to the driver's seat and pushed the car into the water. I don't know if it was an improvisation inspired by the fact that wasted Rutger was asleep or it was preplanned. But the result was so-so. Because drunken Rutger, assuming that he wouldn't be driving, didn't put his contact lenses in... Or he couldn't... The earlier bit came out so-so as well...'

He felt somebody patting him on the back.

'Excuse me, are you going to be confessing much longer?' An annoyed elderly lady leant towards Heinz.

He pierced her with his eyes.

'It's going to be long. And it's only mortal sins that I'm confessing.'

He turned back towards the grill.

'There was another mistake you made earlier. The triangles painted in lipstick. The numbers, supposedly associated with the time of death of the Pope, and also, in a less obvious way, with prophet Ezekiel. The chain of associations should suggest a crusade run by some religious maniac... A madman or a doctrinaire... And then the plastic bags... Rutger must have mentioned the torturing methods used in Cambodia. Indeed. Our suspicions focused on him and his friend from Asian times, Stanisław Bator. The man running a karate club called "21.37". I'm sure that if I hadn't figured it out myself, you would suggest it to me sooner or later, Father.'

'What was my mistake?' the priest opened his mouth for the first time.

'God's Sword. God's Sword has been sharpened and polished. That's what Ezekiel says. Religious killers make sure to keep the message clear. Word for word. They worry that the meaning might be misunderstood, which would make their elaborate work go to waste. They want to send a clear message. Without relying on perspicacity of dumb police officers. Rakowiecki and Leski,' he paused, 'should have been gutted with a knife. With God's Sword. The numbers should be cut out on their bodies. Smothering with a plastic bag is not mentioned in the Bible... *Modus operandi* doesn't match the suggested meaning. Doesn't match the message. The whole circus with triangles and numbers... It was not done by a religious maniac. These are just my,' Heinz raised his voice slightly, 'little private teachings. After all this is a place where...' he patted the plaque on the confessional, 'Father Chancellor himself listens to confessions.'

'Why did they die? I'm just curious.' There was derision in the priest's voice.

'Because of this.' Heinz got up, stood by the door to the confessional and passed on several sheets of paper. 'Because of this,' he repeated. They were not divided by the grill anymore. He was staring the priest straight in the face. 'First you tried killing Kotlarczyk who discovered the whole thing. I was curious how the killer found out about the plagiarism. And then I understood. Who knows most about the seminarists? About their problems? After all it's common knowledge that in a theological college you do not trust your colleagues, because they might be informers. Important issues can't be discussed with just any teacher. But there is somebody in the seminary who can guarantee more than confession. He can guarantee an honest conversation, but also full discretion. You are that person.' Heinz pointed at the Confessor. 'A spiritual father is that person.'

He heard Adam Adamski shifting in the confessional, as if he suddenly felt uncomfortable.

'Kotlarczyk, in his naivety, said a few words too many. He assumed that the nice man with two first names or without a surname would observe the seal of confession. You probably promised him to take care of it, to sort it all out... Empty words. So Kotlarczyk trusted the inconspicuous Spiritual Father. What the students didn't know was that their Master was so devoted to his preceptor that he would do anything for him. You are like Chancellor Majda's shadow, Father. When he was climbing up, he dragged you with him. The Chancellor knew that he had your absolute loyalty. Eventually you became the Spiritual Father. That was some achievement in the hierarchy of the theological college. Even now... You must be very proud that you are allowed to use the confessional reserved for the Chancellor.'

'You are crazy,' Adamski whispered.

'I was suspicious of you. One thing especially bothered me. No, it wasn't your alibi. In the world of a theological college nobody really has an alibi. There is no family, you see friends less often than laymen... I simply couldn't understand your reasons for killing the seminarists. Rutger and Bator with their strictness and mission written on their faces were in the circle of suspicion. They would have eradicated the plague of homosexuality. Businessman Kunicki could have been worried about blackmail. So he had a motive too. One could think of several other possible combinations. But you, Father?' Heinz paused. 'And then I found those notes.' He shook a bunch of papers.

'You are crazy,' Adamski repeated.

'I'm not crazy. Kotlarczyk had proof that Majda plagiarised texts for his habilitation and that's why you killed him. But Kotlarczyk shared it with somebody. With whom? He probably told Leski the swot. He would have understood the value of the gathered material. Skarga was on the margins, because he went missing in June. And Leski might have mentioned something during an honest conversation with you, Father. Leski was involved in sex for money, but he wanted to get out of it. He decided to use information about Majda to negotiate his position in the seminary and graduate easily... He might have even come to you with the proposition.'

'And supposedly what happened then?'

'Leski didn't quite trust you. And he was right, it seems... He decided to insure himself. He begged for a meeting with Rutger and gave him the information on Majda. He died on the same day. Together with Rakowiecki. They went to see Rutger in their evening gear, their elegant, faggot attire, so they probably planned to see somebody later. You were supposed to take them there. My guess is it wasn't the first time. You were supposed to deliver them to some businessman. Leski might have thought he was doing it for the last time. But Adam Adamski gave the boys some kind of a date-rape drug and put them through hell. By the fickle finger of fate, one of the seminarists had Rutger's telephone number on them. The Professor looked through the papers and realised how big a bomb it was. He had been thinking for a long while about leaving the priesthood. What he read in the materials brought by Leski tipped the scales. He was sick and tired of all that shit. He released a statement for the press. There are two mysterious sentences in it. *There is one more reason for my decision. I shall release that information within a week.* I have to admit that at first I ignored this part. But now I know that the Professor meant the plagiarism. Rutger wanted to make Majda resign from his position as the Chancellor. He threatened to make everything public otherwise. This is the meaning of those two sentences. And that's why Rutger had to die too. Enough of it.'

'You have no evidence.'

'I have photocopies which prove that Majda plagiarised academic texts. I also spoke to your neighbours, you bastard.' Heinz drawled with disdain. 'They say that you made a bonfire in your garden last year in autumn. They remembered it because you've never done it before. You always had some boy from the college to do it for you. And here, such a surprise... Adam Adamski busy as a bee. You chose your moment carefully, the neighbours were supposed to be away for a few days. But they surprised you, Father. They forgot something and had to come back. And they remembered that day. Do you know why, Father? Because it stank like hell. Not at all like leaves that you burn in the autumn. I will personally dig your whole plot and find Kotlarczyk's body. Even if you used burnt lime, I will find traces. Do you understand, motherfucker? And I will make sure that the Chancellor is treated as your accomplice in those killings.' Heinz leant heavily on the confessional, as if he was about to slump down. 'You have only one choice. You will confess to the killings and tell us where you burnt Kotlarczyk. You will also tell us about businessman Kunicki renting seminarists and paying big money for that. If you do that, I might leave Majda alone. I might... But that will only happen when you sign your testimony.' He took two steps backwards. 'You have time until tomorrow morning,' he said loudly.

He left the church and looked towards the Volvo parked

nearby. He nodded. He was sure the driver of the Volvo noticed that gesture. He reached for his car keys. Again he found the crumpled piece of paper saying that the murderer of the students of the seminary had died. He jerked it out of the pocket and angrily chucked it in the bin.

41

ADAM ADAMSKI packed his hand luggage. First thing in the morning he went to the bank and withdrew money from his account. Together with what he had stashed away at home it should be enough for a long while. He kept the money in his office. Just in case. In case of trouble. Trouble began when this nosy police officer with grey facial hair joined the case.

He had to act fast. The most important thing was to leave Warsaw. Then get on a plane. Which, if Heinz kept his promise, would be more and more difficult with every passing hour.

Adamski liked planning. He thought of Rakowiecki and Leski. They were an easy catch. The date-rape drug worked spotlessly. The only mistake he made was pushing them a bit too much. Leski didn't say anything about giving the papers to Rutger. Well, tough, it's done.

He recalled tightening the bag on Leski's head for the last time. Mistake. The boy died too quickly. And before he died he shitted his pants. Several minutes later, Rakowiecki was dead too.

Adamski could remember the veins swelling for the last time on the boy's wrists, when he tightened the bag on his head and whispered into his ear:

'What was it your guru used to say? His favourite proverb? A fox knows a lot of things. And a hedgehog knows of just one, but it's the most important one. I thought your friend would spill the guts. But he didn't want to. So you tell me. Tell me everything you know. Who else?'

Rakowiecki's head dropped. It was the end.

Adam Adamski pushed the net curtain in the kitchen to the side. A sleepy May morning in a one-horse town near Piaseczno. His nosy neighbours left for work, to oversee unreliable employees in their company. He opened the door and took his black wheelie suitcase down the stairs. He would come back for the other suitcase in a moment and then lock the door.

He looked towards the garden and the fence dividing his plot from his neighbours and realised he was wrong. The red sports car was still in the driveway. They haven't left for work yet. Which meant...

'Are you going away, Father?' he heard a polite voice behind his back.

He turned around.

At first he didn't recognise the face in front of him. And when he did, he wanted to scream.

He didn't manage to do so.

A massive blow crushed his Adam's apple. Adamski slumped to the ground. He was wheezing, as if trying to beg for mercy.

***

'That theological college is cursed.' Karloff nervously ripped the label from the 'Żywiec' beer. 'You know, they found Adamski, the Spiritual Father, dead in his home near Piaseczno. His flat had been looted. Murder and robbery.'

Heinz took a long swig from his tankard.

'You know what intrigues me?' Karloff sent him a crooked smile. 'The priest's Adam's apple was crushed. And then somebody sat him in an armchair and...' he sighed heavily, 'shoved a ski pole into his right eye.'

'The season is over,' Heinz muttered. 'Keeping dangerous skiing equipment at home can be dangerous.'

'It made me think of this karate master of yours who once threw a metal star into somebody's eye. And now Adamski with a stick in his eye socket... Striking similarities. Tell me,' he grabbed Heinz's hand. 'Did you talk to Bator? Did you tell him about Adamski? Did you want the priest killed? I talked to Jolka. She agrees with me...'

'Jolka? Haven't seen her for a while...'

'She was on holiday. Don't change the subject. So how did it go?'

'I asked you to comb his garden... looking for Kotlarczyk's body.' Heinz looked up. 'Do you remember our meeting after Poremba's death at yours?' he asked suddenly.

'Yeah, I do. Why?'

He sensed tension in Karloff's voice.

'You ran out then. I followed you. You went to the Soviet Military Cemetery. And later I spoke with the guy you buy from...' he paused.

'I have a deal with him,' Karloff panted. 'None of your business! I had to have a sniff,' he added, looking around nervously. 'Sometimes I have to, otherwise I would go mad!'

Heinz knew that he and Karloff had just struck a different deal. The deal was that none of them would ask any more uncomfortable questions.

'Believe me,' Heinz wanted his voice to sound conciliatory. 'Adam Adamski was a real son of a bitch.'

'I still don't understand why you think he was the killer.'

'Rosenthal's effect,' Heinz was deep in thought.

'What?'

'Don't you remember? It was mentioned at Kunicki's. Without Majda, Adamski felt like a nobody. And rightfully so. He was a nobody. He killed to save the Chancellor from disgrace and humiliation. And to save face. His own. But first and foremost he wanted to please. Like a dog wanting to please its trainer. Or a slave his master... He simply decided that it needed to be done, whatever the price.'

'But not at that price!' Karloff shrugged his shoulders. 'Man, give me a break!'

Karloff got up.

'Let me tell you something.' Heinz leant towards his interlocutor when he returned from the toilet. 'Konrad once said that justice needs to be rendered to the visible universe. Do you know that saying? So I...'

'Konrad?' Karloff cut in. 'Konrad Osuch? I didn't know you are on first name terms now!'

Heinz sighed heavily and finished his beer. He was allowed to have a drink now. Finally. And he wasn't drinking to the judge's good form.

He left the bar, which had got full within the last hour. It was Friday afternoon, the beginning of another weekend. Heinz didn't have anything else to do in Warsaw. He went to his car. He decided to drop it off at the Headquarters today. He took an advertising card of an escort agency from behind the wiper. The girl in the picture had a red and white scarf. Her breasts were hidden behind two footballs. 'All football fans are welcome,' he read. 'It's time to start getting ready. We will make sure you are in good shape.'

A few more years and he would have to get out of this country.

42

HEINZ'S FISTS were tightly clenched.

'Attack!' Kastoriadis shouted.

Making a move means exposing yourself. Showing your *kyo*. Hesitating and losing control over what you are doing. Did he have to wait for the murderer's move? Did Rutger have to die, so that he could get on the right track? Did the Professor have to remain a suspect until he was too much of a suspect?

Probably.

The investigation of the murder of the two seminarists was officially closed. The murderer of Father Adamski remained on the loose. Chancellor Majda resigned from running the theological college in Żoliborz. The audit in the seminary exposed numerous irregularities, which one paper described as 'scandalous'. On Papal Nuncio's request, the seminary was closed down.

Other than that everything went back to normal. It was so-so again. His son got a place at university. They had an argument a week ago and Heinz was told that he had never been much of a father. They haven't spoken since. Maybe it had to be like that.

Heinz felt Kastoriadis's fist ramming into his ribs. He moaned and winced in pain.

'Where are you, Hippie? Not here, that's for sure. Not in the *dojo*!' Lambros yelled.

'You are right. A fox knows a lot of things, but a hedgehog knows of the most important one...'

'What did you say?'

'Nothing. That's just something one wise man used to say.' He recalled the man with squinted eyes. 'I seem to be a fox, not a hedgehog...'

'I don't care who you are,' Kastoriadis said. 'As long as you attack properly! Focus on what you are doing! Go on!'

Heinz straightened up, clenched his fists and went forward.

acknowledgements

I WOULD LIKE TO THANK those who enriched this novel with their knowledge and experience. I have received invaluable and unfailing help from Doctor Jakub Trnka from the Institute of Forensic Medicine at the Medical Academy in Wrocław, a man of colossal knowledge and also literary sensitivity. I would like to thank Commissioner Krzysztof Tkaczyk for numerous consultations. I also owe thanks to Inspector Tomasz Bednarek, Head of the Crime Laboratory of the Metropolitan Police, for Rosenthal's effect and several other clarifications. I am grateful to Rafał for stories from the crypt or an introduction to the world of funerary parlours.

I thank the first readers of the typescript: Gosia and Marek Krajewski, as well as Wojciech Burszta for his insightful reading and comments. Of course all shortfalls of the book remain the responsibility of the author.

I was introduced to the world of martial arts, which plays such an important role in the book, by colleagues from the Traditional Karate Federation of Poland, and especially Sensei Szczepan Thomas. *Oss!*

The theological college in the vicinity of Wilson Square is my own invention. However numerous stories from the seminary life come from a few well-informed people. Respecting their wishes I do not mention their names, but I am grateful for their help.

I dedicate *21:37* to my wife, Ania. I hope this was not the worst idea I have ever had.

Mariusz Czubaj, July 2008

about the author

MARIUSZ CZUBAJ is a cultural anthropologist and a bestselling author in Poland. His first crime novel featuring profiler Rudolf Heinz, *21:37* (*21:37*, 2008), won the High Calibre Award for the Best Polish Crime Novel in 2009. He has co-authored two crime novels with Marek Krajewski: *Aleja samobójców* (*The Avenue of Suicides*, 2008) and *Róże cmentarne* (*Graveyard Roses*, 2009). In 2011 he published the second book on Rudolf Heinz, *Kołysanka dla mordercy* (*Lullaby for a Murderer*), and the third, *Zanim znowu zabiję* (*Before I Kill Again*), was released in 2012.

21:37 is Czubaj's first novel to be translated into English.

about the translator

ANNA HYDE studied Art History in Warsaw, Film Studies in Kraków and Arts Policy and Management in London. She has been translating from English to Polish since 1998 (mostly children's and young people's fiction) and from Polish to English since 2008 (fiction, art exhibition catalogues, film subtitles). Apart from translating, she has worked in museums and a radio station, run magazines, written on art, film and theatre and published some poetry.

also available from stork press

Madame Mephisto by A. M. Bakalar
ISBN Paperback: 978-0-9571326-0-3
ISBN eBook: 978-0-9571326-1-0

The Finno-Ugrian Vampire by Noémi Szécsi
Translator: Peter Sherwood
ISBN Paperback: 978-0-9571326-6-5
ISBN eBook: 978-0-9571326-7-2

Freshta by Petra Procházková
Translator: Julia Sherwood
ISBN Paperback: 978-0-9571326-4-1
ISBN eBook: 978-0-9571326-5-8

Illegal Liaisons by Grażyna Plebanek
Translator: Danusia Stok
ISBN Paperback: 978-0-9571326-2-7
ISBN eBook: 978-0-9571326-3-4

Mother Departs by Tadeusz Różewicz
Translator: Barbara Bogoczek
Editor: Tony Howard
ISBN Hardback 978-0-9573912-0-8
ISBN Paperback 978-0-9573912-1-5
ISBN eBook 978-0-9573912-2-2